The Queen of Nothing

BY HOLLY BLACK

The Folk of the Air

The Cruel Prince

The Wicked King

The Queen of Nothing

How the King of Elfhame Learned to Hate Stories

The Stolen Heir

The Stolen Heir

Other

The Darkest Part of the Forest

The Coldest Girl in Coldtown

PRAISE FOR

THE FOLK OF THE AIR SERIES

"Lush, dangerous, a dark jewel of a book."
—Leigh Bardugo, #1 *New York Times* bestselling author of *Six of Crows* and *Crooked Kingdom*

"The experience of reading a novel like this is something like being surrounded by magic." —*The New York Times Book Review*

"Holly Black is the Faerie Queen."
—Victoria Aveyard, #1 bestselling author of the Red Queen series

"Mordant, intoxicating, ruthlessly twisty."
—Kelly Link, author of *Get in Trouble*

"All that glitters is deadly in Holly Black's Faerie world. Readers will be positively entranced." —Megan Whalen Turner, *New York Times* bestselling author of the Queen's Thief series

"An epic saga of palace intrigue and deception."
—*Entertainment Weekly*

★ **"Intense and entertaining storytelling at its finest."**
—*BookPage*, starred review

The Queen of Nothing

HOLLY BLACK

LB

LITTLE, BROWN AND COMPANY
NEW YORK BOSTON

This book is a work of fiction. Names, characters, places, and incidents are the product of the author's imagination or are used fictitiously. Any resemblance to actual events, locales, or persons, living or dead, is coincidental.

Copyright © 2019 by Holly Black
Illustrations by Kathleen Jennings
Excerpt from *The Stolen Heir* copyright © 2023 by Holly Black

Cover art copyright © 2019 by Sean Freeman. Cover design by Karina Granda.
Cover copyright © 2019 by Hachette Book Group, Inc.

Hachette Book Group supports the right to free expression and the value of copyright. The purpose of copyright is to encourage writers and artists to produce the creative works that enrich our culture.

The scanning, uploading, and distribution of this book without permission is a theft of the author's intellectual property. If you would like permission to use material from the book (other than for review purposes), please contact permissions@hbgusa.com. Thank you for your support of the author's rights.

Little, Brown and Company
Hachette Book Group
1290 Avenue of the Americas, New York, NY 10104
Visit us at LBYR.com

Originally published in hardcover and ebook by Little, Brown and Company in November 2019
First Trade Paperback Edition: November 2020

Little, Brown and Company is a division of Hachette Book Group, Inc.
The Little, Brown name and logo are trademarks of Hachette Book Group, Inc.

The publisher is not responsible for websites (or their content) that are not owned by the publisher.

"Elfin Song" by Edmund Clarence Stedman, first published in 1860
"A Fairy Tale" by Philip James Bailey, first published in 1855

The Library of Congress has cataloged the hardcover edition as follows:
Names: Black, Holly, author. | Jennings, Kathleen, illustrator.
Title: The queen of nothing / Holly Black ; illustrations by Kathleen Jennings.
Description: First edition. | New York ; Boston : Little, Brown and Company, 2019. | Series: [The Folk of the Air ; 3] | Summary: "As the exiled Queen of Faerie, Jude must travel back to Elfhame to help her twin sister, Taryn, and uncover how to break a dark curse threatening the whole Faerie world."— Provided by publisher.
Identifiers: LCCN 2019021819| ISBN 9780316310420 (hardcover) | ISBN 9780316310406 (ebk.) | ISBN 9780316310390 (library edition ebk.)
Subjects: | CYAC: Kings, queens, rulers, etc.— Fiction. | Courts and courtiers— Fiction. | Fairies—Fiction. | Sisters—Fiction. | Twins—Fiction. | Blessing and cursing—Fiction. | Fantasy.
Classification: LCC PZ7.B52878 Que 2019 | DDC [Fic]— dc23
LC record available at https://lccn.loc.gov/2019021819

ISBNs: 978-0-316-31037-6 (pbk), 978-0-316-31040-6 (ebook)

Printed in Indiana, USA

LSC-C

Printing 15, 2026

For Leigh Bardugo,
who never lets me get away with anything

Crooked Forest
Palace of Elfhame
Milkwood
INSMIRE
Lake of Masks
Madoc's Stronghold

Map of the Shifting Isles of
ELFHAME
Locke's Estate
INSMOOR
Tower of Forgetting
INSEAR
INSWEAL
Hollow Hall

Book One

And the Elfin-King has sworn to wed
A daughter of Earth, whose child shall be,
By cross and water hallowéd,
From the fairies' doom forever free.
What if there be a fated day !
It is far away ! it is far away !

—Edmund Clarence Stedman,
"Elfin Song"

PROLOGUE

The Royal Astrologer, Baphen, squinted at the star chart and tried not to flinch when it seemed sure the youngest prince of Elfhame was about to be dropped on his royal head.

A week after Prince Cardan's birth and he was finally being presented to the High King. The previous five heirs had been seen immediately, still squalling in ruddy newness, but Lady Asha had barred the High King from visiting before she felt herself suitably restored from childbed.

The baby was thin and wizened, silent, staring at Eldred with black eyes. He lashed his little whiplike tail with such force that his swaddle threatened to come apart. Lady Asha seemed unsure how to cradle him. Indeed, she held him as though she hoped someone might take the burden from her very soon.

"Tell us of his future," the High King prompted. Only a few Folk were gathered to witness the presentation of the new prince—the mortal Val Moren, who was both Court Poet and Seneschal, and two members of the Living Council: Randalin, the Minister of Keys, and Baphen. In the empty hall, the High King's words echoed.

Baphen hesitated, but he could do nothing save answer. Eldred had been favored with five children before Prince Cardan, shocking fecundity among the Folk, with their thin blood and few births. The stars had spoken of each little prince's and princess's fated accomplishments in poetry and song, in politics, in virtue, and even in vice. But this time what he'd seen in the stars had been entirely different. "Prince Cardan will be your last born child," the Royal Astrologer said. "He will be the destruction of the crown and the ruination of the throne."

Lady Asha sucked in a sharp breath. For the first time, she drew the child protectively closer. He squirmed in her arms. "I wonder who has influenced your interpretation of the signs. Perhaps Princess Elowyn had a hand in it. Or Prince Dain."

Maybe it would be better if she dropped him, Baphen thought unkindly.

High King Eldred ran a hand over his chin. "Can nothing be done to stop this?"

It was a mixed blessing to have the stars supply Baphen with so many riddles and so few answers. He often wished he saw things more clearly, but not this time. He bowed his head so he had an excuse not to meet the High King's gaze. "Only out of his spilled blood can a great ruler rise, but not before what I have told you comes to pass."

Eldred turned to Lady Asha and her child, the harbinger of ill luck. The baby was as silent as a stone, not crying or cooing, tail still lashing.

"Take the boy away," the High King said. "Rear him as you see fit."

Lady Asha did not flinch. "I will rear him as befits his station. He is a prince, after all, and your son."

There was a brittleness in her tone, and Baphen was uncomfortably reminded that some prophecies are fulfilled by the very actions meant to prevent them.

For a moment, everyone stood silent. Then Eldred nodded to Val Moren, who left the dais and returned holding a slim wooden box with a pattern of roots traced over the lid.

"A gift," said the High King, "in recognition of your contribution to the Greenbriar line."

Val Moren opened the box, revealing an exquisite necklace of heavy emeralds. Eldred lifted them and placed them over Lady Asha's head. He touched her cheek with the back of one hand.

"Your generosity is great, my lord," she said, somewhat mollified. The baby clutched a stone in his little fist, staring up at his father with fathomless eyes.

"Go now and rest," said Eldred, his voice softer. This time, she yielded.

Lady Asha departed with her head high, her grip on the child tighter. Baphen felt a shiver of some premonition that had nothing to do with stars.

High King Eldred did not visit Lady Asha again, nor did he call her to him. Perhaps he ought to have put his dissatisfaction aside and cultivated his son. But looking upon Prince Cardan was like looking into an uncertain future, and so he avoided it.

Lady Asha, as the mother of a prince, found herself much in demand with the Court, if not the High King. Given to whimsy and frivolity, she wished to return to the merry life of a courtier. She couldn't attend balls with an infant in tow, so she found a cat whose kittens were stillborn to act as his wet nurse.

That arrangement lasted until Prince Cardan was able to crawl. By then, the cat was heavy with a new litter and he'd begun to pull at her tail. She fled to the stables, abandoning him, too.

And so he grew up in the palace, cherished by no one and checked by no one. Who would dare stop a prince from stealing food from the grand tables and eating beneath them, devouring what he'd taken in savage bites? His sisters and brothers only laughed, playing with him as they would with a puppy.

He wore clothes only occasionally, donning garlands of flowers instead and throwing stones when the guard tried to come near him. None but his mother exerted any hold over him, and she seldom tried to curb his excesses. Just the opposite.

"You're a prince," she told him firmly when he would shy away from a conflict or fail to make a demand. "Everything is yours. You have only to take it." And sometimes: "I want that. Get it for me."

It is said that faerie children are not like mortal children. They need little in the way of love. They need not be tucked in at night, but may sleep just as happily in a cold corner of a ballroom, curled up in a tablecloth. They need not be fed; they are just as happy lapping up dew and skimming bread and cream from the kitchens. They need not be comforted, since they seldom weep.

But if faerie children need little love, faerie princes require some counsel.

Without it, when Cardan's elder brother suggested shooting a walnut off the head of a mortal, Cardan had not the wisdom to demur. His habits were impulsive; his manner, imperious.

"Keen marksmanship so impresses our father," Prince Dain said with a small, teasing smile. "But perhaps it is too difficult. Better not to make the attempt than to fail."

For Cardan, who could not attract his father's good notice and desperately wanted it, the prospect was tempting. He didn't ask himself who the mortal was or how he had come to be at the Court. Cardan certainly never suspected that the man was beloved of Val Moren and that the seneschal would go mad with grief if the man died.

Leaving Dain free to assume a more prominent position at the High King's right hand.

"Too difficult? Better not to make the attempt? Those are the words of a coward," Cardan said, full of childish bravado. In truth, his brother intimidated him, but that only made him more scornful.

Prince Dain smiled. "Let us exchange arrows at least. Then if you miss, you can say that it was *my* arrow that went awry."

Prince Cardan ought to have been suspicious of this kindness, but he'd had little enough of the real thing to tell true from false.

Instead, he notched Dain's arrow and pulled back the bowstring, aiming for the walnut. A sinking feeling came over him. He might not shoot true. He might hurt the man. But on the heels of that, angry glee sparked at the idea of doing something so horrifying that his father could no longer ignore him. If he could not get the High King's attention for something good, then perhaps he could get it for something really, really bad.

Cardan's hand wobbled.

The mortal's liquid eyes watched him in frozen fear. Enchanted, of course. No one would stand like that willingly. That was what decided him.

Cardan forced a laugh as he relaxed the bowstring, letting the arrow fall out of the notch. "I simply will not shoot under these conditions," he said, feeling ridiculous at having backed down. "The wind is coming from the north and mussing my hair. It's getting all in my eyes."

But Prince Dain raised his bow and loosed the arrow Cardan had exchanged with him. It struck the mortal through the throat. He dropped with almost no sound, eyes still open, now staring at nothing.

It happened so fast that Cardan didn't cry out, didn't react. He just stared at his brother, slow, terrible understanding crashing over him.

"Ah," said Prince Dain with a satisfied smile. "A shame. It seems *your* arrow went awry. Perhaps you can complain to our father about that hair in your eyes."

After, though he protested, no one would hear Prince Cardan's side. Dain saw to that. He told the story of the youngest prince's recklessness, his arrogance, his arrow. The High King would not even allow Cardan an audience.

Despite Val Moren's pleas for execution, Cardan was punished for the mortal's death in the way that princes are punished. The High King had Lady Asha locked away in the Tower of Forgetting in Cardan's stead—something Eldred was relieved to have a reason to do, since he found her both tiresome and troublesome. Care of Prince Cardan was given over to Balekin, the eldest of the siblings, the cruelest, and the only one willing to take him.

And so was Prince Cardan's reputation made. He had little to do but further it.

CHAPTER 1

I, Jude Duarte, High Queen of Elfhame in exile, spend most mornings dozing in front of daytime television, watching cooking competitions and cartoons and reruns of a show where people have to complete a gauntlet by stabbing boxes and bottles and cutting through a whole fish. In the afternoons, if he lets me, I train my brother, Oak. Nights, I run errands for the local faeries.

I keep my head down, as I probably should have done in the first place. And if I curse Cardan, then I have to curse myself, too, for being the fool who walked right into the trap he set for me.

As a child, I imagined returning to the mortal world. Taryn and Vivi and I would rehash what it was like there, recalling the scents of fresh-cut grass and gasoline, reminiscing over playing tag through neighborhood backyards and bobbing in the bleachy chlorine of summer pools. I dreamed of iced tea, reconstituted from powder, and orange juice Popsicles. I longed for mundane things: the smell of hot asphalt, the swag of wires between streetlights, the jingles of commercials.

Now, stuck in the mortal world for good, I miss Faerieland with a raw intensity. It's magic I long for, magic I miss. Maybe I even miss being afraid. I feel as though I am dreaming away my days, restless, never fully awake.

I drum my fingers on the painted wood of a picnic table. It's early autumn, already cool in Maine. Late-afternoon sun dapples the grass outside the apartment complex as I watch Oak play with other children in the strip of woods between here and the highway. They are kids from the building, some younger and some older than his eight years, all dropped off by the same yellow school bus. They play a totally disorganized game of war, chasing one another with sticks. They hit as children do, aiming for the weapon instead of the opponent, screaming with laughter when a stick breaks. I can't help noticing they are learning all the wrong lessons about swordsmanship.

Still, I watch. And so I notice when Oak uses glamour.

He does it unconsciously, I think. He's sneaking toward the other kids, but then there's a stretch with no easy cover. He keeps on toward them, and even though he's in plain sight, they don't seem to notice.

Closer and closer, with the kids still not looking his way. And when he jumps at them, stick swinging, they shriek with wholly authentic surprise.

He was invisible. He was using glamour. And I, geased against being deceived by it, didn't notice until it was done. The other children just think he was clever or lucky. Only I know how careless it was.

I wait until the children head to their apartments. They peel off, one by one, until only my brother remains. I don't need magic, even with leaves underfoot, to steal up on him. With a swift motion, I wrap my arm around Oak's neck, pressing it against his throat hard enough to give him a good scare. He bucks back, nearly hitting me in the chin with his horns. Not bad. He attempts to break my hold, but it's half-hearted. He can tell it's me, and I don't frighten him.

I tighten my hold. If I press my arm against his throat long enough, he'll black out.

He tries to speak, and then he must start to feel the effects of not getting enough air. He forgets all his training and goes wild, lashing out, scratching my arms and kicking against my legs. Making me feel awful. I wanted him to be a little afraid, scared enough to fight back, not *terrified*.

I let go, and he stumbles away, panting, eyes wet with tears. "What was that for?" he wants to know. He's glaring at me accusingly.

"To remind you that fighting isn't a game," I say, feeling as though I am speaking with Madoc's voice instead of my own. I don't want Oak to grow up as I did, angry and afraid. But I want him to *survive*, and Madoc did teach me how to do that.

How am I supposed to figure out how to give him the right stuff when all I know is my own messed-up childhood? Maybe the parts of it I value are the wrong parts. "What are you going to do against an opponent who wants to actually hurt you?"

"I don't care," Oak says. "I don't care about that stuff. I don't want to be king. I *never* want to be king."

For a moment, I just stare at him. I want to believe he's lying, but, of course, he can't lie.

"We don't always have a choice in our fate," I say.

"*You* rule if you care so much!" he says. "I won't do it. Never."

I have to grind my teeth together to keep from screaming. "I can't, as you know, because I'm in exile," I remind him.

He stamps a hoofed foot. "So am I! And the only reason I'm in the human world is because Dad wants the stupid crown and you want it and everyone wants it. Well, I don't. It's cursed."

"All power is cursed," I say. "The most terrible among us will do anything to get it, and those who'd wield power best don't want it thrust upon them. But that doesn't mean they can avoid their responsibilities forever."

"You can't make me be High King," he says, and wheeling away from me, breaks into a run in the direction of the apartment building.

I sit down on the cold ground, knowing that I screwed up the conversation completely. Knowing that Madoc trained Taryn and me better than I am training Oak. Knowing that I was arrogant and foolish to think I could control Cardan.

Knowing that in the great game of princes and queens, I have been swept off the board.

Inside the apartment, Oak's door is shut firmly against me. Vivienne, my faerie sister, stands at the kitchen counter, grinning into her phone.

When she notices me, she grabs my hands and spins me around and around until I'm dizzy.

"Heather loves me again," she says, wild laughter in her voice.

Heather was Vivi's human girlfriend. She'd put up with Vivi's evasions about her past. She even put up with Oak's coming to live with them in this apartment. But when she found out that Vivi wasn't human *and* that Vivi had used magic on her, she dumped her and moved out. I hate to say this, because I want my sister to be happy—and Heather did make her happy—but it was a richly deserved dumping.

I pull away to blink at her in confusion. "What?"

Vivi waves her phone at me. "She texted me. She wants to come back. Everything is going to be like it was before."

Leaves don't grow back onto a vine, cracked walnuts don't fit back into their shells, and girlfriends who've been enchanted don't just wake up and decide to let things slide with their terrifying exes.

"Let me see that," I say, reaching for Vivi's phone. She allows me to take it.

I scroll back through the texts, most of them coming from Vivi and full of apologies, ill-considered promises, and increasingly desperate pleas. On Heather's end, there was a lot of silence and a few messages that read "I need more time to think."

Then this:

> I want to forget Faerie. I want to forget that you and Oak aren't human. I don't want to feel like this anymore. If I asked you to make me forget, would you?

I stare at the words for a long moment, drawing in a breath.

I can see why Vivi has read the message the way she has, but I think she's read it wrong. If I'd written that, the last thing I would want was for Vivi to agree. I'd want her to help me see that even if Vivi and Oak weren't human, they still loved me. I would want Vivi to insist that pretending away Faerie wouldn't help. I would want Vivi to tell me that she'd made a mistake and that she'd never ever make that mistake again, no matter what.

If I'd sent that text, it would be a test.

I hand the phone back to Vivi. "What are you going to tell her?"

"That I'll do whatever she wants," my sister says, an extravagant vow for a mortal and a downright terrifying vow from someone who would be bound to that promise.

"Maybe she doesn't know what she wants," I say. I am disloyal no matter what I do. Vivi is my sister, but Heather is human. I owe them both something.

And right now, Vivi isn't interested in supposing anything but that all will be well. She gives me a big, relaxed smile and picks up an apple from the fruit bowl, tossing it in the air. "What's wrong with Oak? He stomped in here and slammed his door. Is he going to be this dramatic when he's a teenager?"

"He doesn't want to be High King," I tell her.

"Oh. That." Vivi glances toward his bedroom. "I thought it was something important."

CHAPTER 2

Tonight, it's a relief to head to work.

Faeries in the mortal world have a different set of needs than those in Elfhame. The solitary fey, surviving at the edges of Faerie, do not concern themselves with revels and courtly machinations.

And it turns out they have plenty of odd jobs for someone like me, a mortal who knows their ways and isn't worried about getting into the occasional fight. I met Bryern a week after I left Elfhame. He turned up outside the apartment complex, a black-furred, goat-headed, and goat-hooved faerie with bowler hat in hand, saying he was an old friend of the Roach.

"I understand you're in a unique position," he said, looking at me with those strange golden goat eyes, their black pupils a horizontal rectangle. "Presumed dead, is that correct? No Social Security number. No mortal schooling."

"And looking for work," I told him, figuring out where this was going. "Off the books."

"You cannot get any further off the books than with me," he assured me, placing one clawed hand over his heart. "Allow me to introduce myself. Bryern. A phooka, if you hadn't already guessed."

He didn't ask for oaths of loyalty or any promises whatsoever. I could work as much as I wanted, and the pay was commensurate with my daring.

Tonight, I meet him by the water. I glide up on the secondhand bike I acquired. The back tire deflates quickly, but I got it cheap. It works pretty well to get me around. Bryern is dressed with typical fussiness: His hat has a band decorated with a few brightly colored duck feathers, and he's paired that with a tweed jacket. As I come closer, he withdraws a watch from one pocket and peers at it with an exaggerated frown.

"Oh, am I late?" I ask. "Sorry. I'm used to telling time by the slant of moonlight."

He gives me an annoyed look. "Just because you've lived in the High Court, you need not put on airs. You're no one special now."

I am the High Queen of Elfhame. The thought comes to me unbidden, and I bite the inside of my cheek to keep myself from saying those ridiculous words. He's right: I am no one special now.

"What's the job?" I ask instead, as blandly as I can.

"One of the Folk in Old Port has been eating locals. I have a contract for someone willing to extract a promise from her to cease."

I find it hard to believe that he cares what happens to humans—or cares enough to pay for me to do something about it. "Local *mortals*?"

He shakes his head. "No. No. Us Folk." Then he seems to remember to whom he's speaking and looks a little flustered. I try not to take his slip as a compliment.

Killing and *eating* the Folk? Nothing about that signals an easy job. "Who's hiring?"

He gives a nervous laugh. "No one who wants their name associated with the deed. But they're willing to remunerate you for making it happen."

One of the reasons Bryern likes hiring me is that I can get close to the Folk. They don't expect a mortal to be the one to pickpocket them or to stick a knife in their side. They don't expect a mortal to be unaffected by glamour or to know their customs or to see through their terrible bargains.

Another reason is, I need the money enough that I'm willing to take jobs like this—ones that I know right from the start are going to suck.

"Address?" I ask, and he slips me a folded paper.

I open it and glance down. "This better pay well."

"Five hundred American dollars," he says, as though this is an extravagant sum.

Our rent is twelve hundred a month, not to mention groceries and utilities. With Heather gone, my half is about eight hundred. And I'd like to get a new tire for my bike. Five hundred isn't nearly enough, not for something like this.

"Fifteen hundred," I counter, raising my eyebrows. "In cash, verifiable by iron. Half up front, and if I don't come back, you pay Vivienne the other half as a gift to my bereaved family."

Bryern presses his lips together, but I know he's got the money. He just doesn't want to pay me enough that I can get choosy about jobs.

"A thousand," he compromises, reaching into a pocket inside his tweed jacket and withdrawing a stack of bills banded by a silver clip. "And look, I have half on me right now. You can take it."

"Fine," I agree. It's a decent paycheck for what could be a single night's work if I'm lucky.

He hands over the cash with a sniff. "Let me know when you've completed the task."

There's an iron fob on my key chain. I run it ostentatiously over the edges of the money to make sure it's real. It never hurts to remind Bryern that I'm careful.

"Plus fifty bucks for expenses," I say on impulse.

He frowns. After a moment, he reaches into a different part of his jacket and hands over the extra cash. "Just take care of this," he says. The lack of quibbling is a bad sign. Maybe I should have asked more questions before I agreed to this job. I definitely should have negotiated harder.

Too late now.

I get back on my bike and, with a farewell wave to Bryern, kick off toward downtown. Once upon a time, I imagined myself as a knight astride a steed, glorying in contests of skill and honor. Too bad my talents turned out to lie in another direction entirely.

I suppose I am a skilled enough murderer of Folk, but what I really excel at is getting under their skin. Hopefully that will serve me well in persuading a cannibal faerie to do what I want.

Before I go to confront her, I decide to ask around.

First, I see a hob named Magpie, who lives in a tree in Deering Oaks Park. He says he's heard she's a redcap, which isn't great news, but at least since I grew up with one, I am well informed about their nature.

Redcaps crave violence and blood and murder—in fact, they get a little twitchy when there's none to be had for stretches of time. And if they're traditionalists, they have a cap they dip in the blood of their vanquished enemies, supposedly to grant them some stolen vitality of the slain.

I ask for a name, but Magpie doesn't know. He sends me to Ladhar, a clurichaun who slinks around the back of bars, sucking froth from the tops of beers when no one is looking and swindling mortals in games of chance.

"You didn't know?" Ladhar says, lowering his voice. *"Grima Mog."*

I almost accuse him of lying, despite knowing better. Then I have a brief, intense fantasy of tracking down Bryern and making him choke on every dollar he gave me. "What the hell is *she* doing *here*?"

Grima Mog is the fearsome general of the Court of Teeth in the North. The same Court that the Roach and the Bomb escaped from. When I was little, Madoc read to me at bedtime from the memoirs of her battle strategies. Just thinking about facing her, I break out in a cold sweat.

I can't fight her. And I don't think I have a good chance of tricking her, either.

"Given the boot, I hear," Ladhar says. "Maybe she ate someone Lady Nore liked."

I don't have to do this job, I remind myself. I am no longer part of Dain's Court of Shadows. I am no longer trying to rule from behind High King Cardan's throne. I don't need to take big risks.

But I am curious.

Combine that with an abundance of wounded pride and you find yourself on the front steps of Grima Mog's warehouse around dawn. I know better than to go empty-handed. I've got raw meat from a butcher shop chilling in a Styrofoam cooler, a few sloppily made honey sandwiches wrapped in foil, and a bottle of decent sour beer.

Inside, I wander down a hall until I come to the door to what appears to be an apartment. I knock three times and hope that if nothing else, maybe the smell of the food will cover up the smell of my fear.

The door opens, and a woman in a housecoat peers out. She's bent over, leaning on a polished cane of black wood. "What do you want, deary?"

Seeing through her glamour as I do, I note the green tint to her skin and her overlarge teeth. Like my foster father: Madoc. The guy who killed my parents. The guy who read me her battle strategies. Madoc, once the Grand General of the High Court. Now enemy of the throne and not real happy with me, either.

Hopefully he and High King Cardan will ruin each other's lives.

"I brought you some gifts," I say, holding up the cooler. "Can I come in? I want to make a bargain."

She frowns a little.

"You can't keep eating random Folk without someone being sent to try to persuade you to stop," I say.

"Perhaps I will eat *you*, pretty child," she counters, brightening. But she steps back to allow me into her lair. I guess she can't make a meal of me in the hall.

The apartment is loft-style, with high ceilings and brick walls. Nice. Floors polished and glossed up. Big windows letting in light and a decent view of the town. It's furnished with old things. The tufting on a few of the pieces is torn, and there are marks that could have come from a stray cut of a knife.

The whole place smells like blood. A coppery, metal smell, overlaid with a slightly cloying sweetness. I put my gifts on a heavy wooden table.

"For you," I say. "In the hopes you'll overlook my rudeness in calling on you uninvited."

She sniffs at the meat, turns a honey sandwich over in her hand, and pops off the cap on the beer with her fist. Taking a long draught, she looks me over.

"Someone instructed you in the niceties. I wonder why they bothered, little goat. You're obviously the sacrifice sent in the hopes my appetite can be sated with mortal flesh." She smiles, showing her teeth. It's possible she dropped her glamour in that moment, although, since I saw through it already, I can't tell.

I blink at her. She blinks back, clearly waiting for a reaction.

By not screaming and running for the door, I have annoyed her. I can tell. I think she was looking forward to chasing me when I ran.

"You're Grima Mog," I say. "Leader of armies. Destroyer of your enemies. Is this really how you want to spend your retirement?"

"Retirement?" She echoes the word as though I have dealt her the deadliest insult. "Though I have been cast down, I will find another army to lead. An army bigger than the first."

Sometimes I tell myself something a lot like that. Hearing it aloud, from someone else's mouth, is jarring. But it gives me an idea. "Well, the local Folk would prefer not to get eaten while you're planning your next move. Obviously, being human, I'd rather you didn't eat mortals—I doubt they'd give you what you're looking for anyway."

She waits for me to go on.

"A challenge," I say, thinking of everything I know about redcaps.

"That's what you crave, right? A good fight. I bet the Folk you killed weren't all that special. A waste of your talents."

"Who sent you?" she asks finally. Reevaluating. Trying to figure out my angle.

"What did you do to piss her off?" I ask. "Your queen? It must have been something big to get kicked out of the Court of Teeth."

"*Who sent you?*" she roars. I guess I hit a nerve. My best skill.

I try not to smile, but I've missed the rush of power that comes with playing a game like this, of strategy and cunning. I hate to admit it, but I've missed risking my neck. There's no room for regrets when you're busy trying to win. Or at least not to die. "I told you. The local Folk who don't want to get eaten."

"Why *you*?" she asks. "Why would they send a slip of a girl to try to convince me of anything?"

Scanning the room, I take note of a round box on top of the refrigerator. An old-fashioned hatbox. My gaze snags on it. "Probably because it would be no loss to them if I failed."

At that, Grima Mog laughs, taking another sip of the sour beer. "A fatalist. So how will you persuade me?"

I walk to the table and pick up the food, looking for an excuse to get close to that hatbox. "First, by putting away your groceries."

Grima Mog looks amused. "I suppose an old lady like myself could use a young thing doing a few errands around the house. But be careful. You might find more than you bargained for in my larder, little goat."

I open the door of the fridge. The remains of the Folk she's killed greet me. She's collected arms and heads, preserved somehow, baked and broiled and put away just like leftovers after a big holiday dinner. My stomach turns.

A wicked smile crawls across her face. "I assume you hoped to challenge me to a duel? Intended to brag about how you'd put up a good fight? Now you see what it means to lose to Grima Mog."

I take a deep breath. Then with a hop, I knock the hatbox off the top of the fridge and into my arms.

"Don't touch that!" she shouts, pushing to her feet as I rip off the lid.

And there it is: the cap. Lacquered with blood, layers and layers of it.

She's halfway across the floor to me, teeth bared. I pull out a lighter from my pocket and flick the flame to life with my thumb. She halts abruptly at the sight of the fire.

"I know you've spent long, long years building the patina of this cap," I say, willing my hand not to shake, willing the flame not to go out. "Probably there's blood on here from your first kill, and your last. Without it, there will be no reminder of your past conquests, no trophies, nothing. Now I need you to make a deal with me. Vow that there will be no more murders. Not the Folk, not humans, for so long as you reside in the mortal world."

"And if I don't, you'll burn my treasure?" Grima Mog finishes for me. "There's no honor in that."

"I guess I *could* offer to fight you," I say. "But I'd probably lose. This way, I win."

Grima Mog points the tip of her black cane toward me. "You're Madoc's human child, aren't you? And our new High King's seneschal in exile. Tossed out like me."

I nod, discomfited at being recognized.

"What did *you* do?" she asks, a satisfied little smile on her face. "It must have been something big."

"I was a fool," I say, because I might as well admit it. "I gave up the bird in my hand for two in the bush."

She gives a big, booming laugh. "Well, aren't we a pair, redcap's daughter? But murder is in my bones and blood. I don't plan on giving up killing. If I am to be stuck in the mortal world, then I intend to have some fun."

I bring the flame closer to the hat. The bottom of it begins to blacken, and a terrible stench fills the air.

"Stop!" she shouts, giving me a look of raw hatred. "Enough. Let me make *you* an offer, little goat. We spar. If you lose, my cap is returned to me, unburnt. I continue to hunt as I have. And you give me your littlest finger."

"To eat?" I ask, taking the flame away from the hat.

"If I like," she returns. "Or to wear like a brooch. What do you care what I do with it? The point is that it will be mine."

"And why would I agree to that?"

"Because if you win, you will have your promise from me. And I will tell you something of significance regarding your High King."

"I don't want to know anything about him," I snap, too fast and too angrily. I hadn't been expecting her to invoke Cardan.

Her laugh this time is low and rumbling. "Little liar."

We stare at each other for a long moment. Grima Mog's gaze is amiable enough. She knows she has me. I am going to agree to her terms. I know it, too, although it's ridiculous. She's a legend. I don't see how I can win.

But Cardan's name pounds in my ears.

Does he have a new seneschal? Does he have a new lover? Is he going to Council meetings himself? Does he talk about me? Do he and Locke mock me together? Does Taryn laugh?

"We spar until first blood," I say, shoving everything else out of my head. It's a pleasure to have someone to focus my anger on. "I'm not giving you my finger," I say. "You win, you get your cap. Period. And I walk out of here. The concession I am making is fighting you at all."

"First blood is dull." Grima Mog leans forward, her body alert. "Let's agree to fight until one of us cries off. Let it end somewhere between bloodshed and crawling away to die on the way home." She sighs, as if thinking a happy thought. "Give me a chance to break every bone in your scrawny body."

"You're betting on my pride." I tuck her cap into one pocket and the lighter into the other.

She doesn't deny it. "Did I bet right?"

First blood *is* dull. It's all dancing around each other, looking for an opening. It's not real fighting. When I answer her, the word rushes out of me. "Yes."

"Good." She lifts the tip of the cane toward the ceiling. "Let's go to the roof."

"Well, this is very civilized," I say.

"You better have brought a weapon, because I'll loan you nothing." She heads toward the door with a heavy sigh, as though she really is the old woman she's glamoured to be.

I follow her out of her apartment, down the dimly lit hall, and into the even darker stairway, my nerves firing. I hope I know what I'm doing. She goes up the steps two at a time, eager now, slamming open a metal door at the top. I hear the clatter of steel as she draws a thin sword out of her cane. A greedy smile pulls her lips too wide, showing off her sharp teeth.

I draw the long knife I have hidden in my boot. It doesn't have the best reach, but I don't have the ability to glamour things; I can't very well ride my bike around with Nightfell on my back.

Still, right now, I really wish I'd figured out a way to do just that.

I step onto the asphalt roof of the building. The sun is starting to rise, tinting the sky pink and gold. A chill breeze blows through the air, bringing with it the scents of concrete and garbage, along with goldenrod from the nearby park.

My heart speeds with some combination of terror and eagerness. When Grima Mog comes at me, I am ready. I parry and move out of the way. I do it again and again, which annoys her.

"You promised me a threat," she growls, but at least I have a sense of how she moves. I know she's hungry for blood, hungry for violence. I know she's used to hunting prey. I just hope she's overconfident. It's possible she will make mistakes facing someone who can fight back.

Unlikely, but possible.

When she comes at me again, I spin and kick the back of her knee hard enough to send her crashing to the ground. She roars, scrambling up and coming at me full speed. For a moment, the fury in her face and those fearsome teeth send a horrible, paralyzing jolt through me.

Monster! my mind screams.

I clench my jaw against the urge to keep dodging. Our blades shine, fish-scale bright in the new light of the day. The metal slams together, ringing like a bell. We battle across the roof, my feet clever as we scuff back and forth. Sweat starts on my brow and under my arms. My breath comes hot, clouding in the chill air.

It feels good to be fighting someone other than myself.

Grima Mog's eyes narrow, watching me, looking for weaknesses. I am conscious of every correction Madoc ever gave me, every bad habit the Ghost tried to train out of me. She begins a series of brutal blows, trying to drive me to the edge of the building. I give ground, attempting to defend myself against the flurry, against the longer reach of her blade. She was holding back before, but she's not holding back now.

Again and again she pushes me toward a drop through the open air. I fight with grim determination. Perspiration slicks my skin, beads between my shoulder blades.

Then my foot smacks into a metal pipe sticking up through the asphalt. I stumble, and she strikes. It's all I can do to avoid getting speared, and it costs me my knife, which goes hurtling off the roof. I hear it hit the street below with a dull thud.

I should never have taken this assignment. I should never have agreed to this fight. I should never have taken up Cardan's offer of marriage and never been exiled to the mortal world.

Anger gives me a burst of energy, and I use it to get out of Grima Mog's way, letting the momentum of her strike carry her blade down past me. Then I elbow her hard in the arm and grab for the hilt of her sword.

It's not a very honorable move, but I haven't been honorable for a long time. Grima Mog is very strong, but she's also surprised. For a moment, she hesitates, but then she slams her forehead into mine. I go reeling, but I almost had her weapon.

I almost had it.

My head is pounding, and I feel a little dizzy.

"That's cheating, girl," she tells me. We're both breathing hard. I feel like my lungs are made of lead.

"I'm no knight." As though to emphasize the point, I pick up the only weapon I can see: a metal pole. It's heavy and has no edge whatsoever, but it's all there is. At least it's longer than the knife.

She laughs. "You ought to concede, but I'm delighted you haven't."

"I'm an optimist," I say. Now when she runs at me, she has all the speed, although I have more reach. We spin around each other, her striking and my parrying with something that swings like a baseball bat. I wish for a lot of things, but mostly to make it off this roof.

My energy is flagging. I am not used to the weight of the pipe, and it's hard to maneuver.

Give up, my whirling brain supplies. *Cry off while you're still standing. Give her the cap, forget the money, and go home. Vivi can magic leaves into extra cash. Just this time, it wouldn't be so bad. You're not fighting for a kingdom. That, you already lost.*

Grima Mog comes toward me as though she can scent my despair. She puts me through my paces, a few fast, aggressive strikes in the hopes of getting under my guard.

Sweat drips down my forehead, stinging my eyes.

Madoc described fighting as a lot of things, as a game of strategy played at speed, as a dance, but right now it feels like an argument. Like an argument where she's keeping me too busy defending myself to score any points.

Despite the strain on my muscles, I switch to holding the pipe in one hand and pull her cap from my pocket with the other.

"What are you doing? You promised—" she begins.

I throw the cap at her face. She grabs for it, distracted. In that moment, I swing the pipe at her side with all the strength in my body.

I catch her in the shoulder, and she falls with a howl of pain. I hit her again, bringing the metal rod down in an arc onto her outstretched arm, sending her sword spinning across the roof.

I raise the pipe to swing again.

"Enough." Grima Mog looks up at me from the asphalt, blood on her pointed teeth, astonishment in her face. "I yield."

"You do?" The pipe sags in my hand.

"Yes, little cheat," she grits out, pushing herself into a sitting position. "You bested me. Now help me up."

I drop the pipe and walk closer, half-expecting her to pull out a knife and sink it into my side. But she only lifts a hand and allows me to haul her to her feet. She puts her cap on her head and cradles the arm I struck in the other.

"The Court of Teeth have thrown in their lot with the old Grand General—your father—and a whole host of other traitors. I have it on good authority that your High King is to be dethroned before the next full moon. How do you like those apples?"

"Is that why you left?" I ask her. "Because you're not a traitor?"

"I left because of another little goat. Now be off with you. This was more fun than I expected, but I think our game is at a close."

Her words ring in my ears. *Your High King. Dethroned.* "You still owe me a promise," I say, my voice coming out like a croak.

And to my surprise, Grima Mog gives me one. She vows to hunt no more in the mortal lands.

"Come fight me again," she calls after me as I head for the stairs. "I have secrets aplenty. There are so many things you don't know, daughter of Madoc. And I think you crave a little violence yourself."

CHAPTER 3

My muscles stiffen up almost immediately, and the idea of pedaling home makes me feel so tired I'd rather just lie down on the sidewalk, so I take the bus. I get a lot of dirty looks from impatient commuters while strapping my bike to the rack on the front, but when people notice I'm bleeding, they decide in favor of ignoring me.

My sense of a day's shape sits oddly with the human world. In Faerie, staggering home at dawn is the equivalent of staggering home at midnight for mortals. But in the human world, the bright light of morning is supposed to banish shadows. It's a virtuous time, for early risers, not ne'er-do-wells. An elderly woman in a jaunty pink hat passes me a few tissues without comment, which I appreciate. I use them to clean myself up the best I can. For the rest of the ride, I look out the window at the blue sky, hurting and feeling sorry for myself. Raiding my pockets yields four aspirin. I take them in a single bitter mouthful.

Your High King is to be dethroned before the next full moon. How do you like those apples?

I try to tell myself that I don't care. That I should be glad if Elfhame winds up conquered. Cardan has plenty of other people to warn him of what's coming. There's the Court of Shadows and half of his military. The rulers of the low Courts, all sworn to him. The whole Living Council. Even a new seneschal, should he bother to appoint one.

I don't want to think of someone else standing beside Cardan in my place, but my mind turns idly through all the worst choices anyway. He can't choose Nicasia, because she's already the Ambassador of the Undersea. He won't pick Locke, because he's already the Master of Revels and because he's insufferable. And not Lady Asha because...because she'd be *awful.* She'd find the job boring, and she'd trade his influence for whatever benefited her the most. Surely he knows better than to choose her. But maybe he doesn't. Cardan can be reckless. Maybe he and his wicked, heedless mother will make a mockery of the Greenbriar line and the Blood Crown. I hope they do. I hope everybody will be sorry, and him, most of all him.

And then Madoc will march in and take over.

I press my forehead against the cool glass and remind myself that it's no longer my problem. Instead of trying—and failing—not to think about Cardan, I try not to think at all.

I wake to someone shaking my shoulder. "Hey, kid," the bus driver says, worry etched in the lines of his face. "Kid?"

There was a time when my knife would have been in my hand and pressed to his throat before he finished speaking. I realize groggily that I don't even *have* my knife. I forgot to scout around the outside of Grima Mog's building and retrieve it.

"I'm up," I say unconvincingly, rubbing my face with one hand.

"For a minute there, I thought you'd kicked it." He frowns. "That's a lot of blood. You want me to call someone?"

"I'm fine," I say. I realize the bus is mostly empty. "Did I miss my stop?"

"We're here." He looks as though he wants to insist on getting me help. Then he shakes his head with a sigh. "Don't forget that bike."

I was stiff before, but nothing like now. I creak down the aisle like a root woman pulling her limbs from the ground for the first time. My fingers fumble with the mechanics of getting my bike off the front, and I notice the rusty stain on my fingers. I wonder if I just wiped blood across my face in front of the bus driver and touched my cheek self-consciously. I can't tell.

But then my bike is down, and I am able to shuffle across the grass toward the apartment building. I am going to drop the bike in the bushes and take my chances with its getting stolen. That promise to myself gets me most of the way home when I spot someone sitting on the stoop. Pink hair glowing in the sunlight. She lifts a paper coffee cup in salute.

"Heather?" I say, keeping my distance. Considering how the bus driver looked at me, showing off my fresh cuts and bruises seems like a bad idea.

"I'm trying to get up the bravery to knock."

"Ah," I say, leaning my bike down on the grass. The bushes are too far off. "Well, you can just come in with me and—"

"No!" she says, and then realizing how loud that came out, lowers her voice. "I don't know if I'm going in today."

I look at her again, realizing how tired she seems, how faded the pink in her hair is, as though she hasn't bothered to re-dye it. "How long have you been out here?"

"Not long." She glances away from me and shrugs. "I come here sometimes. To check how I feel."

With a sigh, I give up on the idea that I am going to hide that I got hurt. I walk to the stairs, then slump down on a step, too tired to keep standing.

Heather stands. "Jude? Oh no, oh holy—what the—*what happened to you*?" she demands. I wince. Her voice is much too loud.

"Shhhh! I thought you didn't want Vivi to know you're here," I remind her. "Anyway, it looks worse than it is. I just need a shower and some bandages. And a good day's sleep."

"Okay," she says in a way that makes me think she doesn't believe me. "Let me help you go in. Please don't worry about me tripping over seeing your sister or whatever. You're actually hurt. You shouldn't have stood there talking to me!"

I shake my head, holding up a hand to ward off her offer. "I'll be fine. Just let me sit for a minute."

She gazes at me, worry warring with her desire to put off the inevitable confrontation with Vivi a little longer. "I thought you were still in that place? Did you get hurt there?"

"Faerieland?" I like Heather, but I am not going to pretend away the world I grew up in because she hates the idea of it. "No. This happened here. I've been staying with Vivi. Trying to figure things out. But if you move back in, I can make myself scarce."

She looks down at her knees. Bites a corner of a fingernail. Shakes her head. "Love is stupid. All we do is break one another's hearts."

"Yeah," I say, thinking again of Cardan and how I walked right into the trap he set for me, as though I were some fool who'd never heard a ballad in her life. No matter how much happiness I wish for Vivi, I don't want Heather to be the same kind of fool. "Yeah, *no*. Love might be stupid, but you're not. I know about the message you sent Vivi. You can't go through with it."

Heather takes a long sip from her cup. "I have nightmares. About that place. Faerie. I can't sleep. I look at people on the street, and I wonder if they're glamoured. This world already has enough monsters, enough people who want to take advantage of me or hurt me or take away my rights. I don't need to know there's a whole *other* world full of monsters."

"So not knowing is better?" I ask.

She scowls and is silent. Then, when she speaks again, she looks out past me, as though she's looking at the parking lot. "I can't even explain to my parents what Vee and I are fighting about. They keep asking me if she was kicking it with someone else or if having Oak around was just too much, like I can't handle him being a *kid*, instead of whatever he is."

"He's still a kid," I say.

"I *hate* being afraid of Oak," she says. "I know it hurts his feelings. But I also hate that he and Vee have magic, magic that she could use to win every argument that we could ever have. Magic to make me obsessed with her. Or turn me into a duck. And that's not even considering why I'm attracted to her in the first place."

I frown. "Wait, what?"

Heather turns toward me. "Do you know what makes people love one another? Well, no one else does, either. But scientists study it, and there's all this bizarre stuff about pheromones and facial symmetry and the circumstances under which you first met. People are weird. Our bodies are weird. Maybe I can't help being attracted to her the same way flies can't help being attracted to carnivorous plants."

I make an incredulous sound, but Balekin's words echo in my ears. *I have heard that for mortals, the feeling of falling in love is very like the feeling of fear.* Maybe he was more right than I wanted to believe.

Especially when I consider my feelings for Cardan, since there was no good reason I should have had any feelings for him at all.

"Okay," Heather says, "I know I sound ridiculous. I feel ridiculous. But I also feel afraid. And I still think we should go inside and bandage you up."

"Make Vivi promise not to use magic on you," I say. "I can help you say the exact right words to bind her and then—" I stop speaking when I see that Heather is looking at me sadly, maybe because believing in promises sounds childish. Or maybe the idea of binding Vivi with a promise sounds magical enough to freak her out more.

Heather takes a deep breath. "Vee told me that she grew up here, before your parents were murdered. I'm sorry to even mention it, but I know she's messed up about it. I mean, of course she is. Anyone would be." She takes a breath. She's waiting to see how I react.

I think about her words as I sit on the stairs, bruises coming up beside sluggishly bleeding slashes. *Anyone would be.* Nope, not me, not messed up at all.

I remember a much younger Vivi, who was furious all the time, who screamed and broke whatever she touched. Who slapped me every time I let Madoc hold me in the crook of his arm. Who seemed as though she would bring down his entire hall with her rage. But that was so long ago. We all gave in to our new life; it was just a matter of when.

I don't say any of that. Heather takes a shaky breath. "The thing is, I wonder if she's, you know, playing house with me. Pretending her life went the way she wanted. Pretending she never found out who she was and where she was from."

I reach out and take Heather's hand. "Vivi stayed so long in Faerie for me and Taryn," I say. "She didn't want to be there. And the reason she finally left was because of you. Because she loved you. So yeah, Vivi took the easy way out in not explaining stuff. She should definitely have told you the truth about Faerie. And she should have never, ever used magic on you, even if it was out of panic. But now you know. And I guess you have to decide if you can forgive her."

She starts to say something, then stops herself. "Would *you*?" she asks finally.

"I don't know," I say, looking at my knees. "I am not a very forgiving person these days."

Heather stands. "Okay. You rested. Now get up. You need to go inside and take a bath in Neosporin. You probably should see a doctor, but I know what you're going to say about that."

"You're right," I say. "Right about everything. No doctor." I roll onto my side to try to push myself to my feet, and when Heather comes over to help me, I let her. I even lean my weight on her as we limp together to the door. I have given up on being proud. As Bryern reminded me, I am no one special.

Heather and I go together through the kitchen, past the table with Oak's cereal bowl sitting on it, still half-full of pink milk. Two empty coffee mugs rest beside a box of Froot Loops. I note the number of mugs before my brain gives meaning to that detail. Just as Heather helps me into the living room, I realize we must have a guest.

Vivi is sitting on the couch. Her face lights up when she sees Heather. She looks at her like someone who just stole a giant's magnificent talking harp and knows consequences are on the horizon but can't bring herself to care. My gaze goes to the person beside her, sitting primly in a fanciful Elfhame court dress of gossamer and spun glass. My twin sister, Taryn.

CHAPTER 4

Adrenaline floods my body, despite my stiffness and soreness and bruises. I'd like to put my hands around Taryn's neck and squeeze until her head pops off.

Vivi stands, maybe because of my murderous look, but probably because Heather is right beside me.

"You," I say to my twin. "Get out."

"Wait," Taryn says, standing, too. "Please." Now we're all up, looking at one another across the small living room as though we're about to brawl.

"There's nothing I want to hear out of your lying mouth." I'm glad to have a target for all the feelings Grima Mog and Heather stirred up. A deserving target. "Get out, or I'll throw you out."

"This is Vivi's apartment," Taryn counters.

"This is *my* apartment," Heather reminds us. "And you're hurt, Jude."

"I don't care! And if you all want her here, then I can go!" With that, I turn and force myself to walk back to the door and down the stairs.

The screen door bangs. Then Taryn rushes in front of me, her gown blowing in the morning breeze. If I didn't know what a real princess of Faerie looked like, I might think she resembled one. For a moment, it seems impossible that we're related, no less identical.

"What happened to you?" she asks. "You look like you got into a fight."

I don't speak. I just keep walking. I am not even sure where I am going, as slow and stiff and sore as I am. Maybe to Bryern. He'll find me a place to crash, even if I won't like the price later. Even bunking with Grima Mog would be better than this.

"I need your help," Taryn says.

"No," I say. "No. Absolutely not. Never. If that's why you came here, now you've got your answer and you can leave."

"Jude, just hear me out." She walks in front of me, causing me to have to look at her. I glance up and then start to circle the billowing skirts of her dress.

"Also no," I say. "No, I won't help you. No, I won't hear you explain why I should. It really is a magical word: *no.* You say whatever bullshit you want, and I just say no."

"Locke is dead," she blurts out.

I wheel around. Above us, the sky is bright and blue and clear. Birds call to one another from nearby trees. In the distance, there's the sound of construction and road traffic. In this moment, the juxtaposition of standing in the mortal world and hearing about the demise of an immortal being—one that I knew, one that I kissed—is especially surreal.

"Dead?" It seems impossible, even after everything I've seen. "Are you sure?"

The night before his wedding, Locke and his friends tried to ride me down like a pack of dogs chasing a fox. I promised to pay him back for that. If he's dead, I never will.

Nor will he ever plan another party for the purpose of humiliating Cardan. He won't laugh with Nicasia nor play Taryn and me against each other again. Maybe I should be relieved, for all the trouble he caused. But I am surprised by feeling grief instead.

Taryn takes a breath, as if steeling herself. "He's dead because I killed him."

I shake my head, as though that's going to help me understand what she's saying. *"What?"*

She looks more embarrassed than anything else, as though she were confessing to some kind of dumb accident instead of to *murdering her husband.* I am uncomfortably reminded of Madoc, standing over three screaming children a moment after cutting down their parents, surprise on his face. As though he hadn't quite meant for it to go so far. I wonder if that's how Taryn feels.

I knew I'd grown up to be more like Madoc than I was comfortable with, but I never thought she and he were anything alike.

"And I need you to pretend to be me," she finishes, with no apparent worry that suggesting the very trick that allowed Madoc to march off with half of Cardan's army, the very trick that doomed me to agreeing to the plan that got me exiled, is in poor taste. "Just for a few hours."

"Why?" I start, and then realize I am not being clear. "Not the pretending part. I mean, *why did you kill him?*"

She takes a breath, then looks back at the apartment. "Come inside, and I'll tell you. I'll tell you everything. Please, Jude."

I look toward the apartment and reluctantly admit to myself I have nowhere else to go. I don't want to go to Bryern. I want to go back inside and rest in my own bed. And despite being exhausted, I can't deny that the prospect of sneaking into Elfhame as Taryn has an unsettling appeal. The very thought of being there, of seeing Cardan, speeds my heart.

At least no one is privy to my thoughts. Stupid as they are, they remain my own.

Inside, Heather and Vivi are standing in a corner of the kitchen near the coffeepot, having an intense conversation that I don't want to disturb. At least they're finally talking. That's one good thing. I head into Oak's room, where the few clothes I have are shoved in the bottom drawer of his dresser. Taryn follows, frowning.

"I'm going to take a shower," I tell her. "And smear some ointment on myself. You're going to make me some magical healing yarrow tea from the kitchen. Then I'll be ready to hear your confession."

"Let me help you out of that," Taryn says with an exasperated shake of her head when I'm about to object. "You have no squire."

"Nor any armor for her to polish," I say, but I don't fight when she lifts my shirt over sore limbs. It's stiff with blood, and I wince when she tugs it free. I inspect my cuts for the first time, raw and red and puffy. I suspect Grima Mog of not keeping her knife as clean as I'd like.

Taryn turns on the shower, adjusting the taps and then guiding me over the tub's edge to stand in the warming spray. Being sisters, we've seen each other naked a bajillion times over the years, but as her gaze goes to the messy scar on my leg, I recall she's never seen it before.

"Vivi said something," Taryn says slowly. "About the night before my wedding. You were late, and when you came, you were quiet and pale. Sick. I worried it was because you still loved him, but Vivi insists that isn't true. She says you got hurt."

I nod. "I remember that night."

"Did Locke...do something?" She isn't looking at me now. Her gaze is on the tiles, then on a framed drawing Oak did of Heather, brown crayon for her skin bleeding into pink for her hair.

I grab the body wash that Vivi buys at the organic store, the one that's supposed to be naturally antibacterial, and smear it liberally over the dried blood. It smells bleachy and stings like hell. "You mean, did he try to kill me?"

Taryn nods. I catch her eye. She already knows the answer. "Why didn't you say something? Why did you let me marry him?" she demands.

"I didn't know," I admit. "I didn't know it was Locke who'd led a hunt for me until I saw you wearing the earrings I lost that night. And then I got taken by the Undersea. And soon after I got back, you *betrayed* me, so I figured it didn't matter."

Taryn frowns, clearly torn between the urge to argue and an effort to stay quiet to win me over. A moment later, arguing triumphs. We're twins, after all. "I just did what Dad said! I didn't think it mattered. You had all that power and you wouldn't use it. But I never wanted to hurt you."

"I think I prefer Locke and his friends chasing me around the woods to you stabbing me in the back. Again."

I can see her visibly stopping herself from saying anything more, taking a breath, biting her tongue. "I'm sorry," she says, and slips out of the bathroom, leaving me to finish my shower alone.

I turn up the heat and take a long time.

When I come out, Heather has left, and Taryn has gone through the fridge and constructed some kind of nervous-energy tea party out of our leftovers. A big pot of tea sits at the center of the table, along with a smaller pot of the yarrow. She has taken our last half sleeve of gingersnap cookies and arranged them on a tray. Our bread got turned into two kinds of sandwiches: ham and celery, peanut butter and Cheerios.

Vivi is brewing a pot of coffee and watching Taryn with a worried expression. I pour myself a mug of the healing tea and drink it down, then pour myself another. Clean, bandaged, and dressed in new clothes, I feel a lot more clearheaded and ready to deal with the news that Locke is dead and that my twin sister murdered him.

I pick up a ham sandwich and take a bite. The celery is crunchy and a little weird, but not bad. Suddenly, I am aware of how hungry I am. I shove the rest of the sandwich into my mouth and pile two more onto a plate.

Taryn wrings her hands, pressing them together and then against her dress. "I snapped," she says. Neither Vivi nor I speak. I try to crunch my celery more quietly.

"He promised he would love me until he died, but his love didn't protect me from his unkindness. He warned me that the Folk don't love as we do. I didn't understand until he left me alone in his great, awful house for weeks on end. I cultivated hybrid roses in the garden and commissioned new curtains and hosted month-long revels for his friends. It didn't matter. I was sometimes louche and sometimes chaste. I gave him *everything*. But he said that all the story had gone out of me."

I raise my eyebrows. That was an awful thing for him to say, but not necessarily what I expected to be his last words. "I guess you showed him."

Vivi laughs abruptly and then glares at me for making her laugh.

Taryn's eyelashes sparkle with unshed tears. "I guess so," she says in a flat, dull voice that I find hard to interpret. "I tried to explain how things had to change—they *had to*—but he acted as though I was being ridiculous. He kept *talking*, as if he could talk me out of my own feelings. There was a jeweled letter opener on the desk and—you remember all those lessons Madoc gave us? The next thing I knew, the point of it was in Locke's throat. And then he was finally quiet, but when I took it out, there was so much blood."

"So you didn't mean to kill him?" Vivi asks.

Taryn doesn't answer.

I get what it feels like to shove things down for long enough that they erupt. I also get what it's like to shove a knife in somebody. "It's okay," I say, not sure if that's true.

She turns to me. "I thought we were nothing alike, you and I. But it turns out we're just the same."

I don't think she believes that to be a good thing.

"Where's his body now?" I ask, trying to focus on the practical. "We need to get rid of it and—"

Taryn shakes her head. "His body was already discovered."

"How? What did you do?" Before, I was frustrated she came to ask for help, but now I'm annoyed she didn't come sooner, when I could have taken care of this.

"I dragged his body down to the waves. I thought the tide would carry him away, but he just washed up again on another beach. At least, um, at least some of him was chewed. It was harder for them to tell how he died." She looks at me helplessly, as though she still can't conceive how any of this is happening to her. "I'm not a bad person."

I take a sip of my yarrow tea. "I didn't say you were."

"There's going to be an inquest," Taryn goes on. "They're going to glamour me and ask questions. I won't be able to lie. But if you answer in my place, you can say honestly that you didn't kill him."

"Jude is exiled," Vivi says. "Banished until she gets the crown's forgiveness or some other high-handed crap. If they catch her, they'll kill her."

"It will just be a few hours," Taryn says, looking from one of us to the other. "And no one will know. Please."

Vivi groans. "It's too risky."

I say nothing, which seems to be the thing that tips her off that I am considering it. "You want to go, don't you?" Vivi asks, fixing me with a shrewd look. "You want an excuse to go back there. But once they glamour you, they'll ask your name. Or ask something else that will tip them off when you don't answer the way Taryn would. And then you'll be screwed."

I shake my head. "I had a geas placed on me. It protects me from glamours." I hate how much the idea of returning to Elfhame thrills me, hate how much I want another bite at the everapple, another chance at power, another shot at him. Maybe there's a way around my exile, too, if only I can find it.

Taryn frowns. "A geas? Why?"

Vivi fixes me with a glare. "Tell her. Tell her what you really did. Tell her what you are and why you can't go back there."

There's something in Taryn's face, a little like fear. Madoc must have explained that I'd gained a promise of obedience from Cardan—otherwise, how would she have known to order him to release half the army from their vows? Since I've been back in the mortal world, I've had a lot of time to go over what happened between us. I am sure Taryn was angry with me for not telling her about my hold over Cardan. I am sure Taryn was even angrier that I pretended I couldn't persuade Cardan to dismiss Locke from being Master of Revels, when, in fact, I could have commanded him. But she had a lot of other reasons to help Madoc. After all, he was our father, too. Maybe she wanted to play the great game. Maybe she thought of all the things he could do for her if he were sitting on the throne.

"I should have told you everything, about Dain and the Court of Shadows, but—" I begin, but Vivi interrupts me.

"Skip that part," she says. "Cut to the chase. *Tell her what you are.*"

"I've heard of the Court of Shadows," says Taryn quickly. "They're spies. Are you saying you're a spy?"

I shake my head because I finally understand what Vivi wants me to explain. She wants me to say that Cardan married me and made me, effectively, High Queen of Elfhame. But I can't. Every time I even think about it, I feel a rush of shame for believing he wasn't going to play me. I don't think I can explain any part of it without seeming like a fool, and I am not ready to be that vulnerable with Taryn.

I need to end this conversation, so I say the one thing I know will distract them both, for very different reasons. "I've decided to go and be Taryn in the inquest. I'll be back in a day or two, and then I'll explain everything to her. I promise."

"Can't you both just stay here in the mortal world?" Vivi asks. "Screw Faerie. Screw all this. We'll get a bigger place."

"Even if Taryn stays with us, it would be better for her not to skip out on the High King's inquest," I say. "And I can bring back stuff we can pawn for some easy cash. We've got to pay for that bigger place somehow."

Vivi gives me an exasperated look. "We could stop living in apartments and playing at being mortal whenever you like. I did this for Heather. If it's just us, we can take over one of the abandoned warehouses by the waterfront and glamour it so no one ever comes inside. We can steal all the money we need to buy anything at all. Just say the word, Jude."

I take the five hundred dollars I fought for out of my jacket and place it on the table. "Bryern will be by with the other half later today. Since we're still playing at being mortal. And since Heather is apparently still around. Now I am going to go take a nap. When I get up, I'm going to Faerie."

Taryn looks at the money on the table with some confusion. "If you needed—"

"If you get caught, you'll be executed, Jude," Vivi reminds me, interrupting whatever offer Taryn was about to make. I'm glad. I might be willing to do this, but it certainly doesn't mean I forgive her. Or that we're close now. And I don't want her acting as though it does.

"Then I won't get caught," I tell them both.

CHAPTER 5

Since Oak is at school, I curl up in his bed. As hurt as I am, sleep overtakes me quickly, sucking me down into darkness.

And dreams.

I am at lessons in the palace grove, sitting in the long shadows of the late afternoon. The moon has already risen, a sharp crescent in the cloudless blue sky. I draw a star chart from memory, my ink a dark red that clots on the paper. It's blood, I realize. I am dabbing my quill into an inkpot full of blood.

Across the grove, I see Prince Cardan, sitting with his usual companions. Valerian and Locke look strange: their clothing moth-eaten, their skin pallid, and only inky smudges where their eyes ought to be. Nicasia doesn't seem to notice. Her sea-colored hair hangs down her back in heavy coils; her lips are twisted into a mocking smile, as though nothing in the world is wrong. Cardan wears a bloodstained crown, tilted at an angle, the sharp planes of his face as hauntingly beautiful as ever.

"Do you remember what I said before I died?" Valerian calls to me in his taunting voice. "*I curse you. Three times, I curse you. As you've murdered me, may your hands always be stained with blood. May death be your only companion. May you*—That's when I died, so I never got to say the rest. Would you like to hear it now? *May your life be brief and shrouded in sorrow, and when you die, may you go unmourned.*"

I shudder. "Yeah, that last bit really was the zinger."

Cardan comes over, stepping on my star chart, kicking over the inkpot with his silver-tipped boots, sending the blood spilling across the paper, blotting out my marks. "Come with me," he says imperiously.

"I knew you liked her," says Locke. "That's why I had to have her first. Do you remember the party in my maze garden? How I kissed her while you watched?"

"I recall that your hands were on her, but her eyes were on me," Cardan returns.

"That's not true!" I insist, but I remember Cardan on a blanket with a daffodil-haired faerie girl. She pressed her lips to the edge of his boot, and another girl kissed his throat. His gaze had turned to me when one of them began kissing his mouth. His eyes were coal-bright, as wet as tar.

The memory comes with the slide of Locke's palm over my back, heat in my cheeks, and the feeling my skin was too tight, that everything was too much.

"Come with me," Cardan says again, drawing me away from the blood-soaked star chart and the others taking their lessons. "I am a prince of Faerie. You have to do what I want."

He leads me to the dappled shade of an oak tree, then lifts me up so I am seated on a low branch. He keeps his hands on my waist and moves closer, so that he's standing between my thighs.

"Isn't this better?" he says, gazing up at me.

I am not sure what he means, but I nod.

"You're so beautiful." He begins to trace patterns on my arms, then runs his hands down my sides. "So very beautiful."

His voice is soft, and I make the mistake of looking into his black eyes, at his wicked, curving mouth.

"But your beauty will fade," he continues, just as softly, speaking like a lover. His hands linger, making my stomach tighten and warmth pool in my belly. "This smooth skin will wrinkle and spot. It will become as thin as cobwebs. These breasts will droop. Your hair will grow dull and thin. Your teeth will yellow. And all you have and all you are will rot away to nothing. You will be nothing. You are nothing."

"I'm nothing," I echo, feeling helpless in the face of his words.

"You come from nothing, and it is to nothing you will return," he whispers against my neck.

A sudden panic overtakes me. I need to get away from him. I push off the edge of the branch, but I don't hit the ground. I just fall and fall and fall through the air, dropping like Alice down the rabbit hole.

Then the dream changes. I am on a slab of stone, wrapped in fabric. I try to get up, but I can't move. It's as though I am a carved doll made of wood. My eyes are open, but I can't shift my head, can't blink, can't do anything. All I can do is stare at the same cloudless sky, the same sharp scythe of a moon.

Madoc comes into view, standing over me, looking down with his cat eyes. "It's a shame," he says, as though I am beyond hearing. "If only she stopped fighting me, I would have given her everything she ever wanted."

"She was never an obedient girl," says Oriana beside him. "Not like her sister."

Taryn is there, too, a delicate tear running over her cheek. "They were only ever going to let one of us survive. It was always going to be me. You're the sister who spits out toads and snakes. I'm the sister who spits out rubies and diamonds."

The three of them leave. Vivi stands beside me next, pressing her long fingers to my shoulder.

"I should have saved you," Vivi says. "It was always my job to save you."

"My funeral will be next," Oak whispers a moment later.

Nicasia's voice travels, as though she is speaking from far away. "They say faeries weep at weddings and laugh at funerals, but I thought your wedding and funeral were equally funny."

Then Cardan comes into view, a fond smile on his lips. When he speaks, he does so in a conspiratorial whisper. "When I was a child, we would stage burials, like little plays. The mortals were dead, of course, or at least they were by the end."

At that, I can finally speak. "You're lying," I say.

"Of course I'm lying," he returns. "This is your dream. Let me show you." He presses a warm hand against my cheek. "I love you, Jude. I've loved you for a long time. I will never stop loving you."

"Stop it!" I say.

Then it's Locke standing over me, water spilling from his mouth. "Let's be sure she's really dead." A moment later, he plunges a knife into my chest. It goes in over and over and over again.

At that, I wake, my face wet with tears and a scream in my throat.

I kick off my covers. Outside, it's dark. I must have slept the whole day away. Flicking on the lights, I take deep breaths, check my brow for fever. I wait for my jangling nerves to settle. The more I think about the dream, the more disturbed I am.

I go out to the living room, where I find a pizza box open on the coffee table. Someone has placed dandelion heads beside the pepperoni on a few of the slices. Oak is trying to explain *Rocket League* to Taryn.

Both of them look over at me warily.

"Hey," I say to my twin. "Can I talk to you?"

"Sure," Taryn says, getting up from the couch.

I walk back into Oak's bedroom and perch on the edge of his bed. "I need to know if you came here because you were told to come," I say. "I need to know if this is a trap set by the High King to lure me into violating the terms of my exile."

Taryn looks surprised, but to her credit, she doesn't ask me why I would think such a thing. One of her hands goes to her stomach, fingers spreading over her belly. "No," she says. "But I didn't tell you everything."

I wait, unsure what she's talking about.

"I've been thinking about Mom," she says finally. "I always thought she left Elfhame because she fell in love with our mortal dad, but now I'm not so sure."

"I don't understand," I say.

"I'm pregnant," she says, her voice a whisper.

For centuries, mortals have been valued for their ability to conceive faerie children. Our blood is less sluggish than that of the Folk. Faerie women would be fortunate to bear a single child over the course of their long lives. Most never will. But a mortal wife is another matter. I knew all that, and yet it never occurred to me that Taryn and Locke would conceive a child.

"Wow," I say, my gaze going to her hand spread protectively over her stomach. "Oh."

"No one should have the childhood we had," she says.

Had she imagined bringing up a child in that house, with Locke messing with both of their heads? Or was it because she imagined that if she left, he might hunt her down as Madoc hunted down our mother? I am not sure. And I am not sure I should push her, either. Now that I am better rested, I can see in her the signs of exhaustion I missed before. The red-rimmed eyes. A certain sharpness to her features that marks forgetting to eat.

I realize that she has come to us because she has nowhere else to go—and she had to believe there was every chance I wouldn't help her.

"Did he know?" I ask finally.

"Yes," she says, and pauses as though she's recalling that conversation. And possibly the murder. "But I haven't told anyone else. No one but you. And telling Locke went—well, you already heard how it went."

I don't know what to say to that, but when she makes a helpless gesture toward me, I come into her arms, leaning my head on her shoulder. I know there are a lot of things I ought to have told her and a lot she ought to have told me. I know we haven't been kind. I know she's hurt me, more than she can guess. But for all that, she's still my sister. My widowed, murderer sister with a baby on the way.

An hour later, I am packed and ready to leave. Taryn has drilled me in the details of her day, about the Folk she talks to regularly, about the running of Locke's estate. She has given me a pair of gloves to disguise my missing finger. She has changed out of her elegant dress of gossamer and spun glass. I am wearing it now, my hair arranged in a rough estimation of hers while she wears my black leggings and sweater.

"Thank you," she says, a thing the Folk never say. Thanks are considered rude, trivializing the complicated dance of debt and repayment. But that's not what mortals mean by thanking one another. That's not what they mean at all.

Still, I shrug off her words. "No worries."

Oak comes over to be picked up, even though at eight he is all long limbs and gangly boy body. "Squeeze hug," he says, which means he jumps up and wraps his arms around your neck, half-strangling you. I submit to this and squeeze him back hard, slightly out of breath.

Setting him down, I pull off my ruby ring—the one Cardan stole and then returned to me during our exchange of vows. One I can definitely not have with me while posing as Taryn. "Will you keep this safe? Just until I get back."

"I will," Oak says solemnly. "Come back soon. I'll miss you."

I am surprised by his sweetness, especially after our last encounter.

"Soon as I can," I promise, pressing a kiss to his brow. Then I go to the kitchen. Vivi is waiting for me. Together, we walk out onto the grass, where she has cultivated a small patch of ragwort.

Taryn trails after us, pulling at the sleeve of the sweater she's wearing.

"You're sure about this?" Vivi asks, plucking a plant at the root. I look at her, shrouded in shadows, her hair lit by the streetlamp. It usually looks brown like mine, but in the right light it is woven through with strands of a gold that is almost green.

Vivi has never hungered for Faerie as I have. How can she, when she carries it with her wherever she goes?

"You know I'm sure," I say. "Now, are you going to tell me what happened with Heather?"

She shakes her head. "Stay alive if you want to find out." Then she blows on the ragwort. "Steed, rise and bear my sister where she commands." By the time the flowering stem falls to the ground, it is already changing into an emaciated yellow pony with emerald eyes and a mane of lacy fronds.

It snorts at the air and strikes the ground with its hooves, almost as eager to fly as I am.

Locke's estate is as I remembered it—tall spires and mossy tiles, covered in a thick curtain of honeysuckle and ivy. A hedge maze crosses the grounds in a dizzying pattern. The whole place looks straight out of a fairy tale, the kind where love is a simple thing, never the cause of pain.

At night, the human world looks as though it's full of fallen stars. The words come to me suddenly, what Locke said when we stood together at the top of his tallest tower.

I urge the ragwort horse to land, and swing down from its back, leaving it pawing the ground as I head toward the grand front doors. They slide open at my approach. A pair of servants stand just inside, mushroomy skin so pale that their veins are visible, giving them the appearance of a matched set of old marble statues. Small, powdery wings sag from their shoulders. They regard my approach with their cold, inkdrop eyes, recalling to me all at once the inhumanity of the Folk.

I take a deep breath and draw myself to my full height. Then I head inside.

"Welcome back, my lady," the female says. They are brother and sister, Taryn informed me. Nera and Neve. Their debt was to Locke's father, but they were left behind when he departed, to serve out the rest of their time taking care of his son. They snuck around before, staying out of sight, but Taryn forbade them from doing so after she came to live there.

In the mortal world, I have become acclimated to thanking people for small services and now have to bite back the words. "It's good to be home," I say instead, and sweep past them into the hall.

It's changed from what I remember. Before, the rooms were largely empty, and where they were not, the furniture was old and heavy, the upholstery stiff with age. The long dining table had been bare, as had been the floors. Not anymore.

Cushions and rugs, goblets and trays and half-full decanters cover every surface—all of them in a riot of colors: vermilion and umber, peacock blue and bottle green, gold and damson plum. The coverlet of a daybed is smeared with a thin golden powder, perhaps from a recent guest. I frown a moment too long, my reflection mirrored back to me in a polished silver urn.

The servants are watching, and I have no cause to study rooms with which I am supposed to be familiar. So I try to smooth out my expression. To hide that I am puzzling out the parts of Taryn's life she didn't tell me about.

She designed these rooms, I am sure. Her bed in Madoc's stronghold was always massed with bright pillows. She loves beautiful things. And yet, I cannot miss that this is a place made for bacchanalia, for decadence. She spoke of hosting month-long revels, but only now do I imagine her spread out on the pillows, drunk and laughing and maybe kissing people. Maybe doing more than kissing people.

My sister, my twin, was always more lark than grackle, more shy than sensualist. Or at least I thought she was. While I walked the path of daggers and poison, she walked the no-less-fraught path of desire.

I turn toward the stairs, unsure that I am going to pull this off after all. I go back over what I know, over the explanation that Taryn and I came up with together for the last time I saw Locke. He had been planning to meet with a selkie, I will say, with whom he was carrying on an affair. It was plausible, after all. And the Undersea had so recently been at odds with the land that I hope Folk will be inclined against them.

"Will you take dinner in the grand hall?" Neve asks, trailing behind me.

"I'd prefer a tray in my room," I say, unwilling to eat alone at that long table and be waited on in conspicuous silence.

Up I go, fairly sure I recall the way. I open a door with trepidation. For a moment, I think I am in the wrong place, but it is only that Locke's room has changed, too. The bed is bedecked in curtains embroidered with foxes stalking through tall trees. A low divan sits in front of the bed, where a few gowns are scattered, and a small desk is cluttered with paper and pens.

I go to Taryn's dressing chamber and look at her dresses—a collection less riotous in color than the furnishings she chose, but no less beautiful. I choose a shift and a heavy satin robe to wear over it, then strip off her dress of gossamer and glass.

The fabric shivers against my skin. I stand in front of the mirror in her bedroom and comb out my hair. I stare at myself, trying to see what might give me away. I am more muscular, but clothes can hide that. My hair is shorter, but not by much. And then, of course, there's my temper.

"Greetings, Your Majesty," I say, trying to imagine myself in the High Court again. What would Taryn do? I sink into a low curtsy. "It's been too long."

Of course, Taryn probably saw him quite recently. For her, it hasn't been long at all. Panic drums in my chest. I am going to have to do more than answer questions at the inquest. I am going to have to pretend that I am a cordial acquaintance of High King Cardan *to his face.*

I fix myself with a look in the mirror, trying to summon the correct expression of deference, trying not to scowl. "Greetings, Your Majesty, you betraying toad."

No, that wouldn't work, no matter how good it felt.

"Greetings, Your Majesty," I try again. "I didn't kill my husband, even though he richly deserved it."

There is a knock on the door, and I startle.

Nera has brought a large wooden tray, which he sets on the bed and then departs with a bow, barely making a sound as he goes. On it are toast and a marmalade with a cloying, strange scent that makes my mouth water. It takes longer than it ought for me to realize it's *faerie fruit.* And they've brought it as though it's nothing to Taryn, as though she eats it regularly. Did Locke give it to her without her knowing? Or did she take it deliberately, as a sort of recreational blurring of the senses? Once again, I am lost.

At least there's also a pot of nettle tea, soft cheese, and three hard-boiled duck eggs. It's a simple dinner, other than the weirdness of the faerie fruit.

I drink the tea and eat the eggs and toast. The marmalade, I hide in a napkin that I tuck in the very back of the closet. If Taryn finds it moldering weeks from now, well, that's a small price to pay for the favor she's getting out of me.

I look at the dresses again, try to choose one for the day ahead. Nothing whimsical. My husband is supposed to be dead, and I am supposed to be sad. Unfortunately, while Taryn's commissions for me were almost entirely black, her own closet is empty of the color. I push past silk and satin, past brocade in the pattern of forests with animals peeking out from between the leaves, and embroidered velvets of sage green and sky blue. Finally, I settle on a dark bronze dress and drag it over to the divan, along with a pair of midnight blue gloves. I rifle through her jewelry box and pull out the earrings I gave her. One a moon, the other a star, crafted by the master smith Grimsen, magicked to make the wearer more beautiful.

I itch to sneak out of Locke's demesne and back into the Court of Shadows. I want nothing more than to visit the Roach and the Bomb, to hear gossip from the Court, to be in those familiar underground rooms.

But those rooms are gone—destroyed by the Ghost when he betrayed us to the Undersea. I don't know where the Court of Shadows operates out of now.

And I can't risk it.

Opening the window, I sit at Taryn's desk and sip nettle tea, drinking in the sharp salt scent of the sea and the wild honeysuckle and the distant breeze through fir trees. I take a deep breath, at home and homesick all at the same time.

CHAPTER 6

The inquest is set to happen when the first of the stars is visible in the sky. I arrive at the High Court in Taryn's bronze dress, with a shawl over my shoulders, gloves on my fingers, and my hair swept into a loose chignon. My heart races, and I hope that no one can sense the nervous sweat starting under my arms.

As the High King's seneschal, I was accorded a certain kind of deference. Although I lived eight years in Elfhame without it, I got very used to it very quickly.

As Taryn, I am watched with suspicion when I push my way through a crowd that no longer automatically parts for me. She is the daughter of a traitor, the sister of an outcast, and the suspected murderer of her husband. Their gazes are greedy, as though they hope for the spectacle of her guilt and punishment. But they still are not afraid of her. Even with her alleged crime, they see her as a mortal and weak.

Good, I suppose. The weaker she seems, the more believable her innocence.

My gaze darts away from the dais even as I move toward it. High King Cardan's presence seems to infect the very air I breathe. For a wild moment, I consider turning and getting out of there before he spots me.

I don't know if I can do this.

I feel a little dizzy.

I don't know if I can look at him and not show on my face any of what I am feeling.

I take a deep breath and let it out again, reminding myself that he won't know I'm the one standing in front of him. He didn't recognize Taryn when she dressed in my clothes, and he won't recognize me now.

Plus, I tell myself, *if you don't pull this off, you and Taryn are both in a lot of trouble.*

I am suddenly reminded of all the reasons Vivi told me this was a bad idea. She's right. This is ridiculous. I am supposed to be exiled until such time as I am pardoned by the crown, on pain of death.

It occurs to me that maybe he made a mistake with that phrasing. Maybe I can pardon myself. But then I remember when I insisted I was the Queen of Faerie, and the guards laughed. Cardan didn't need to deny me. He only had to say nothing. And if I pardoned myself, he would only have to say nothing again.

No, if he recognizes me, I will have to run and hide and hope that my training with the Court of Shadows wins out over the training of the guard. But then the Court will know that Taryn is guilty—otherwise, why have me stand in her stead? And if I don't manage to escape…

Idly, I wonder what sort of execution Cardan might order. Maybe he'd strap me to some rocks and let the sea do the work. Nicasia would like that. If he's not in the mood, though, there's also beheading, hanging, exsanguination, drawn and quartered, fed whole to a riding toad...

"Taryn Duarte," says a knight, interrupting my morose thoughts. His voice is cold, his chased silver armor marking him as one of Cardan's personal guard. "Wife of Locke. You must stand in the place of petitioners."

I move there, disoriented at the thought of standing where I had seen so many before when I was the seneschal. Then I remember myself and make the deep curtsy of someone comfortable with submission to the High King's will. Since I cannot do that while looking at his face, I make sure that I keep my gaze on the ground.

"Taryn?" Cardan asks, and the sound of his voice, the familiarity of it, is shocking.

With no more excuses, I raise my eyes to his.

He is even more horrifically beautiful than I was able to recall. They're all beautiful, unless they're hideous. That's the nature of the Folk. Our mortal minds cannot conceive of them; our memory blunts their power.

His every finger sparks with a ring. An etched and jeweled breastplate in polished gold hangs from his shoulders, covering a frothy white shirt. Boots curl up at his toes and rise high over his knees. His tail is visible, curled to one side of his leg. I suppose he has decided it is no longer something he needs to hide. At his brow, of course, is the Blood Crown.

He regards me with gold-rimmed black eyes, a smirk hovering at the corners of his mouth. His black hair tumbles around his face, unbound and a little messy, as though he's recently risen from someone's bed.

I can't stop marveling at how I once had power over him, over *the*

High King of Faerie. How I once was arrogant enough to believe I could keep it.

I remember the slide of his mouth on mine. I remember how he tricked me.

"Your Majesty," I say, because I have to say something and because everything I practiced began with that.

"We recognize your grief," he says, sounding annoyingly regal. "We would not disturb your mourning were it not for questions over the cause of your husband's death."

"Do you really think she's sad?" asks Nicasia. She is standing beside a woman it takes me a moment to place: Cardan's mother, Lady Asha, done up in a silvery dress, jeweled tips covering the points of her horns. Lady Asha's face has been highlighted in silver as well—silver along her cheekbones and shining on her lips. Nicasia, meanwhile, wears the colors of the sea. Her gown is the green of kelp, deep and rich. Her aqua hair is braided up and adorned with a cunning crown made of fish bones and jaws.

At least neither of them is on the dais beside the High King. The position of seneschal appears still to be open.

I want to snap at Nicasia, but Taryn wouldn't, so I don't. I say nothing, cursing myself for knowing what Taryn *wouldn't* do, but being less sure what she *would*.

Nicasia steps closer, and I am surprised to see sorrow in her face. Locke was her friend, once, and her lover. I don't think he was particularly good at either, but I guess that doesn't mean she wanted him dead. "Did you kill Locke yourself?" she asks. "Or did you get your sister to do it for you?"

"Jude is in exile," I say, my words coming out dangerously soft instead of the regular kind of soft they were intended to be. "And I've never hurt Locke."

"No?" Cardan says, leaning forward on his throne. Vines shiver behind him. His tail twitches.

"I lov..." I can't quite make my mouth say the words, but they are waiting. I force them out and try to force out a little sob, too. "I loved him."

"Sometimes I believed that you did, yes," Cardan says absently. "But you could well be lying. I am going to put a glamour on you. All it will do is force you to tell us the truth." He curves his hand, and magic shimmers in the air.

I feel nothing. Such is the power of Dain's geas, I suppose. Not even the High King's glamour can ensorcell me.

"Now," says Cardan. "Tell me only the truth. What is your name?"

"Taryn Duarte," I say with a curtsy, grateful at how easy the lie comes. "Daughter of Madoc, wife of Locke, subject of the High King of Elfhame."

His mouth curves. "What fine courtly manners."

"I was well instructed." He ought to know. We were instructed together.

"Did you murder Locke?" he asks. Around me, the hum of conversation slows. There are no songs, little laughter, few clinks of cups. The Folk are intent, wondering if I am about to confess.

"No," I say, and give a pointed look to Nicasia. "Nor did I orchestrate his death. Perhaps we ought to look to the *sea*, where he was found."

Nicasia turns her attention to Cardan. "We know that Jude murdered Balekin. She confessed as much. And I have long suspected her of killing Valerian. If Taryn isn't the culprit, then Jude must be. Queen

Orlagh, my mother, swore a truce with you. What possible gain could she have from the murder of your Master of Revels? She knew he was your friend—and mine." Her voice breaks at the end, although she tries to mask it. Her grief is obviously genuine.

I try to summon tears. It would be useful to cry right now, but standing in front of Cardan, I cannot weep.

He peers down at me, black brows drawn together. "Well, what do you think? Did your sister do it? And don't tell me what I already know. Yes, I sent Jude into exile. That may or may not have deterred her."

I wish I could punch him in his smug face and show him how undeterred I am by his exile. "She had no reason to hate Locke," I lie. "I don't think she wished him ill."

"Is that so?" Cardan says.

"Perhaps it is only Court gossip, but there is a popular tale about you, your sister, and Locke," Lady Asha ventures. "She loved him, but he chose you. Some sisters cannot bear to see the other happy."

Cardan glances at his mother. I wonder what has drawn her to Nicasia, unless it is only that they are both awful. And I wonder what Nicasia makes of her. Orlagh might be a ferocious and terrifying Queen of the Undersea, and I never want to spend another moment in her presence, but I believe she cherishes Nicasia. Surely Nicasia would expect more of Cardan's mother than the thin gruel of emotion she has served her son.

"Jude never loved Locke." My face feels hot, but my shame is an excellent cover to hide behind. "She loved someone else. He's the one she'd want dead."

I am pleased to see Cardan flinch. "Enough," he says before I can go on. "I have heard all I care to on this subject—"

"No!" Nicasia interrupts, causing everyone under the hill to stir a little. It is immense presumption to interrupt the High King. Even for a princess. Especially for an ambassador. A moment after she speaks, she seems to realize it, but she goes on anyway. "Taryn could have a charm on her, something that makes her resistant to glamours."

Cardan gives Nicasia a scathing look. He does not like her undermining his authority. And yet, after a moment, his anger gives way to something else. He gives me one of his most awful smiles. "I suppose she'll have to be searched."

Nicasia's mouth curves to match his. It feels like being back at lessons on the palace grounds, conspired against by the children of the Gentry.

I recall the more recent humiliation of being crowned the Queen of Mirth, stripped in front of revelers. If they take my gown now, they will see the bandages on my arms, the fresh slashes on my skin for which I have no good explanation. They will guess I am not Taryn.

I can't let that happen. I summon all the dignity I can muster, trying to imitate my stepmother, Oriana, and the way she projects authority. "My husband was murdered," I say. "And whether or not you believe me, I do mourn him. I will not make a spectacle of myself for the Court's amusement when his body is barely cold."

Unfortunately, the High King's smile only grows. "As you wish. Then I suppose I will have to examine you alone in my chambers."

CHAPTER 7

I am furious as I walk through the corridors of the palace, steps behind Cardan, followed by his guard to keep me from trying to slip away.

My choices now are not good.

He will take me back to his enormous chambers and then what? Will he force a guard to hold me and divest me of anything that might protect me from glamour—jewelry, clothing—until I am stripped bare? If so, he cannot fail to notice my scars, scars he has seen before. And if he peels off my gloves, there can be no doubt. The missing half digit will give me away.

If I am undressed, he will know me.

I am going to have to make a break for it. There's the secret passageway in his rooms. From there, I can get out through one of the crystal windows.

I glance at the guards. If they were dismissed, I could get past Cardan, through the secret passageway, and out. But how to get rid of them?

I consider the smile Cardan wore on the dais when he announced what he was going to do to me. Maybe he *wants* to see Taryn naked. He desired *me*, after all, and Taryn and I are identical. Perhaps if I volunteer to undress myself, he'll agree to dismiss his guard. He did say he'd examine me alone.

Which leads me to an even more daring thought. Maybe I could distract him thoroughly enough that he wouldn't know me at all. Perhaps I could blow out the candles and be naked only in the half light....

Those thoughts occupy me so completely that I barely notice a hooved servant carrying a tray supporting a carafe of a pale celery-green wine and a collection of blown-glass goblets. She is coming from the opposite direction, and when we pass, the tray digs into my side. She gives a cry, I feel a shove, and we both tumble to the floor, glass shattering around us.

The guards halt. Cardan turns. I look over at the girl, baffled and surprised. My dress is soaked with wine. The Folk are seldom clumsy, and this doesn't feel like an accident. Then the girl's fingers touch one of my gloved hands. I feel the press of leather and steel against the inside of my wrist. She is pushing a sheathed knife up my sleeve under cover of cleaning up the spilled contents of the tray. Her head dips close to mine as she brushes shards of glass from my hair.

"Your father is coming for you," she whispers. "Wait for a signal. Then stab the guard closest to the door and run."

"What signal?" I whisper back, pretending to help her sweep up the debris.

"Oh no, my lady, your pardon," she says in a normal voice with a bob of her head. "You ought not lower yourself."

One of the High King's personal guard catches my arm. "Come

along," he says, lifting me to my feet. I press my hands to my heart to keep the knife from slipping out my sleeve.

I resume my walk toward Cardan's rooms, my thoughts thrown into even more confusion.

Madoc is coming to save Taryn. It's a reminder that while I am no longer in his good graces, she helped him wriggle out of his vows of service to the High King. She gave him half an army. I wonder what plans he has for her, what rewards he's promised. I imagine he will be pleased to have her no longer encumbered with Locke.

But when Madoc comes, what's his plan? Whom is he expecting to fight? And what will he do when he comes for her and finds me instead?

Two servants open heavy double doors to the High King's chambers, and he goes inside, throwing himself down on a low couch. I follow, standing awkwardly in the middle of the carpet. None of the guards so much as enter his chambers. As soon as I step over the threshold, the doors shut behind me, this time with a grim finality. I don't have to worry about persuading Cardan to dismiss the guard; they never lingered.

At least I have a knife.

The parlor is as I remember it from Council meetings. It carries the scent of smoke and verbena and clover. Cardan himself lounges, his booted feet resting on a stone table carved in the shape of a griffin, claws raised to strike. He gives me a quicksilver, conspiratorial grin that seems completely at odds with the way he spoke to me from his throne.

"Well," he says, patting the couch beside him. "Didn't you get my letters?"

"What?" I am confused enough that the word comes out like a croak.

"You never replied to a one," he goes on. "I began to wonder if you'd misplaced your ambition in the mortal world."

This must be a test. This must be a trap.

"Your Majesty," I say stiffly. "I thought you brought me here to assure yourself I had neither charm nor amulet."

A single eyebrow rises, and his smile deepens. "I will if you like. Shall I command you to remove your clothes? I don't mind."

"What are you *doing*?" I say finally, desperately. "What are you playing at?"

He's looking at me as though somehow I am the one who's behaving strangely. "Jude, you can't really think I don't know it's you. I knew you from the moment you walked into the brugh."

I shake my head, reeling. "That's not possible." If he knew it was me, then I wouldn't be here. I would be imprisoned in the Tower of Forgetting. I would be preparing for my execution.

But maybe he's *pleased* I violated the terms of the exile. Maybe he's glad I put myself in his power by doing so. Maybe that's his game.

He stands up from the couch, his gaze intense. "Come closer."

I take a step backward.

He frowns. "My councilors told me that you met with an ambassador from the Court of Teeth, that you must be working with Madoc now. I was unwilling to believe it, but seeing the way you look at me, perhaps I must. Tell me it's not true."

For a moment, I don't understand, but then I do. Grima Mog. "I'm not the betrayer here," I say, but I am suddenly conscious of the blade in my sleeve.

"Are you angry about—" He cuts himself off, looking at my face more carefully. "No, you're *afraid*. But why would you be afraid of me?"

I am trembling with a feeling that I barely understand. "I'm not," I lie. "I hate you. You sent me into exile. Everything you say to me, everything you promise, it's all a trick. And I, stupid enough to believe you once." The sheathed knife slides easily to my hand.

"Of course it was a trick—" he begins, then sees the weapon and bites off whatever he was about to say.

Everything shakes. An explosion, close by and intense enough that we both stumble. Books fall and scatter over the floor. Crystal orbs slip off their stands to roll across floorboards. Cardan and I look at each other in shared surprise. Then his eyes narrow in accusation.

This is the part where I am supposed to stab him and run.

A moment later, there's the unmistakable sound of metal striking metal. Close by.

"Stay here," I say, drawing the blade and tossing the sheath onto the ground.

"Jude, don't—" he calls after me as I slip into the hall.

One of his guard lies dead, a polearm jutting out of her rib cage. Others clash with Madoc's handpicked soldiers, battle-hardened and deadly. I know them, know that they fight without pity, without mercy, and if they've made it this close to the High King, Cardan is in terrible danger.

I think again of the passageway I was planning to slip through. I can get him out that way—in exchange for a pardon. Either Cardan can end my exile and live or hope his guard wins against Madoc's soldiers. I am about to head back to put that deal to him when one of the helmeted soldiers grabs hold of me.

"I have Taryn," she calls gruffly. I recognize her: Silja. Part huldra and entirely terrifying. I'd seen her carve up a partridge in a way that made her delight in slaughter very clear.

I stab at her hand, but the thick hide of her gloves turns my blade. A steel-covered arm wraps around my waist.

"Daughter," Madoc says in his gravelly voice. "Daughter, don't be afraid—"

His hand comes up with a cloth smelling of cloying sweetness. He presses it over my nose and mouth. I feel my limbs go loose, and a moment later, I feel nothing at all.

CHAPTER 8

When I wake, I am in woods I don't recognize. I don't smell the ubiquitous salt of the sea, and I don't hear the crash of the waves. Everything is ferns, leaf mold, the crackle of a fire, and the hum of distant voices. I sit up. I am lying on heavy blankets, with more on top of me—horse blankets, albeit elegant ones. I see a solidly built carriage nearby, the door hanging open.

I am still in Taryn's dress, still wearing her gloves.

"Don't mind the dizziness," says a kind voice. Oriana. She is sitting nearby, dressed in a gown of what appears to be felted wool over several layers of skirts. Her hair is pulled back into a green cap. She looks nothing like the diaphanous courtier she's been the whole time I've known her. "It will pass."

I run a hand through my hair, come loose now, the pins still in it. "Where are we? What happened?"

"Your father didn't like the thought of your staying on the isles to begin with, but without Locke's protection, it was only a matter of time before the High King came up with an excuse to make you his hostage."

I rub a hand over my face. By the fire, a spindly, insectile faerie stirs a big pot. "You want soup, mortal?"

I shake my head.

"You want to be soup?" it asks hopefully. Oriana waves it off and takes a kettle from the ground beside the fire. She pours the steaming contents into a wooden cup. The liquid is redolent of bark and mushrooms.

I take a sip and abruptly feel less dizzy.

"Was the High King captured?" I ask, recalling when I was taken. "Is he alive?"

"Madoc was unable to get to him," she says, as though his being alive is a disappointment.

I hate how relieved I feel.

"But—" I start, meaning to ask how the battle ended. I remember myself in time to bite my tongue. Over the years, Taryn and I have occasionally pretended to be each other at home. We mostly got away with it, so long as it didn't go on for too long or we weren't too obvious about it. If I don't do anything stupid, I have a good chance of pulling this off until I can escape.

And then what?

Cardan was so disarmingly casual, as though sentencing me to death was some shared joke between us. And talking of messages, messages I never got. What could they have said? Could he have intended to pardon me? Could he have offered me some kind of bargain?

I cannot imagine a letter from Cardan. Would it have been short and formal? Full of gossip? Wine-stained? Another trick?

Of course it was a trick.

Whatever he intended, he must believe I am working with Madoc now. And though it shouldn't bother me, it does.

"Your father's priority was to get you out," Oriana reminds me.

"Not just that, right?" I say. "He can't have attacked the Palace of Elfhame for me alone." My thoughts are unruly, chasing one another around. I am no longer sure of anything.

"I don't question Madoc's plans," she says neutrally. "Nor should you."

I forgot how it felt to be bossed around by Oriana, always treated as though my curiosity would immediately create some scandal for our family. It's especially galling to be treated this way now, when her husband stole half an army from the High King and is planning a coup against him.

Grima Mog's words echo in my mind. *The Court of Teeth have thrown in their lot with the old Grand General—your father—and a whole host of other traitors. I have it on good authority that your High King is to be dethroned before the next full moon.*

That seems a lot more pressing now.

But since I am supposed to be Taryn, I don't respond. After a moment, she looks repentant. "The important thing is for you to rest. I am sure being dragged out here is a lot to take in on top of losing Locke."

"Yes," I say. "It is a lot. I think I do want to rest awhile, if that's all right."

Oriana reaches over and smooths my hair back from my brow, a fond gesture that I am sure she wouldn't have made if she knew it was me, Jude, that she was touching. Taryn admires Oriana, and they're close in a way that she and I are not—for many reasons, not the least of which is that I helped hide Oak in the mortal world, away from the crown. Since then, Oriana has been both grateful and resentful. But in Taryn, I think, Oriana sees someone she understands. And maybe Taryn *is* like Oriana, although the murder of Locke has called that and everything else I thought I knew about my twin sister into question.

I close my eyes. Although I mean to puzzle through how to get away, instead I sleep.

The next time I wake, I am in a carriage, and we are on the move. Madoc and Oriana sit on the opposite bench. The curtains are drawn, but I hear the sounds of a traveling camp, of mounts and soldiers. I hear the distinctive growl of goblins calling to one another.

I look over at the redcap who raised me, my father and the murderer of my father. I take in the whiskers from a few days of not shaving. His familiar, inhuman face. He looks exhausted.

"Finally up?" he says with a smile that shows too many teeth. I am uncomfortably reminded of Grima Mog.

I try to smile back as I straighten. I don't know whether something in the soup knocked me out or the deathsweet Madoc made me inhale isn't out of my system, but I don't remember being loaded into the carriage. "How long was I asleep?"

Madoc makes a negligent gesture. "The High King's trumped-up inquest is three days past."

I feel fuzzy-headed, afraid I will say the wrong thing and be discovered. At least my easy slide into unconsciousness must have made me seem to be my sister. Before I became a captive of the Undersea, I'd trained my body to be immune to poisons. But now I am exactly as vulnerable as Taryn.

If I keep my wits about me, I can get away without either of them knowing. I consider what part of Madoc's conversation Taryn would focus on. Probably the matter of Locke. I take a deep breath. "I told them I hadn't done it. Even glamoured, I insisted."

Madoc doesn't look as though he sees through my disguise, but he does look as though he thinks I am being an idiot. "I doubt that boy king ever intended to let you walk out of the Palace of Elfhame alive. He fought hard to keep you."

"Cardan?" That doesn't sound like him.

"Half my knights never made it out," he informs me grimly. "We got in easily enough, but the brugh itself closed around us. Doorways cracked and shrank. Vines and roots and leaves obstructed our way, closed like vises on our necks, crushed and strangled us."

I stare at him for a long moment. "And the High King caused that?" I can't believe it of Cardan, whom I left in his chambers, as though he was the one in need of protecting.

"His guard were neither poorly trained nor poorly chosen, and he knows his power. I am glad to have tested him before going against him in earnest."

"Are you sure it's wise to go against him at all, then?" I ask carefully. It is perhaps not exactly what Taryn would say, but it's not exactly what I would say, either.

"Wisdom is for the meek," he returns. "And it seldom helps them as much as they believe it will. After all, as wise as you are, you still married Locke. Of course, perhaps you are wiser than even that—perhaps you're so wise you made yourself a widow, too."

Oriana puts her hand on his knee, a cautioning gesture.

He gives a great laugh. "What? I made no secret of how little I liked the boy. You can hardly expect me to mourn him."

I wonder if he would laugh so hard if he knew Taryn had actually done it. Who am I kidding? He would probably laugh even harder. He would probably laugh himself sick.

Eventually, the carriage stops, and Madoc jumps down, calling to his soldiers. I slide out and look around, at first disoriented by the unfamiliar landscape and then by the sight of the army before me.

Snow covers the ground, and huge bonfires dot it, along with a maze of tents. Some are made of animal skins. Others are elaborate affairs of painted canvas and wool and silk. But what is most astonishing is how big the camp is, full of soldiers armed and ready to move against the High King. Behind the encampment, a little to the west, is a mountain girded in a thick green pelt of fir trees. And beside it, another tiny outpost—a single tent and a few soldiers.

I feel very far away from the mortal world.

"Where are we?" I ask Oriana, who steps out of the carriage behind me, carrying a cloak to place over my shoulders.

"Near the Court of Teeth," she says. "It's mostly trolls and huldra up this far north."

The Court of Teeth is the Unseelie Court that held the Roach and the Bomb prisoner, and who exiled Grima Mog. The absolute last place I want to be—and with no clear path to escape.

"Come," Oriana says. "Let's get you settled."

She leads me through the camp, past a group of trolls skinning a moose, past elves and goblins singing war songs, past a tailor repairing a pile of hide armor before a fire. In the distance, I hear the clang of steel, raised voices, and animal sounds. The air is thick with smoke, and the ground is muddy from trampling boots and snowmelt. Disoriented, I focus on not losing Oriana in the throng. Finally, we come to a large but practical-looking tent, with a pair of sturdy wooden chairs in front, both covered in sheepskin.

My gaze is drawn to an elaborate pavilion nearby. It sits off the ground on golden clawed feet, looking for all the world as though it could scuttle off if its owner gave the command. As I stare, Grimsen steps out. Grimsen the Smith, who created the Blood Crown and many more artifacts of Faerie yet hungers for greater and greater fame. He's arrayed so finely that he might be a prince himself. When he sees me, he gives me a sly look. I avert my eyes.

The inside of Madoc and Oriana's tent reminds me uncomfortably of home. A corner of it works as a makeshift kitchen, where dried herbs hang in garlands beside dried sausages and butter and cheese.

"You can have a bath," Oriana says, indicating a copper tub in another corner, half-filled with snow. "We place a metal bar on the fire, then plunge it into the melt, and everything heats up swiftly enough."

I shake my head, thinking of how I need to continue to hide my hands. At least in this cold, it will be no surprise for me to keep my gloves on. "I just want to wash my face. And maybe put on some warmer clothes?"

"Of course," she says, and bustles around the small space to gather up a sturdy blue dress, some hose, and boots. She goes out and comes back.

After a few minutes, a servant arrives with steaming water in a bowl and places it on a table, along with a cloth. The water is scented with juniper.

"I will leave you to freshen up," Oriana says, putting on a cloak. "Tonight we dine with the Court of Teeth."

"I don't mean to inconvenience you," I say, awkward in the face of her kindness, knowing that it isn't for me.

She smiles and touches my cheek. "You're a good girl," she says, making me flush with embarrassment.

I am never that.

Still, when she is gone, I am glad to be alone. I snoop around the tent but find no maps or battle plans. I eat a little cheese. I wash my face and pits and everywhere else I can reach, then rinse my mouth with a little peppermint oil and scrape my tongue.

Finally, I put on the new heavier, warmer clothes and rebraid my hair simply, into two tight plaits. I replace my velvet gloves with woolen ones—checking to make sure the stuffing at the tip of my finger looks convincing.

By the time I am done, Oriana has returned. She has brought with her several soldiers carrying a pallet of furs and blankets, which she has them arrange into a bed for me, curtained with a screen.

"I think this will do for now," she says, looking at me for confirmation.

I swallow the urge to thank her. "Better than I could have asked."

As the soldiers depart, I follow them through the tent flap. Outside, I orient myself by the sun as it is about to set and look over the sea of tents again. I am able to pick out factions. Madoc's people, flying his sigil, the crescent moon turned like a bowl. Those from the Court of Teeth have their tents marked with a device that seems to suggest an ominous mountain range. And two or three other Courts, either smaller ones or ones that sent fewer soldiers. *A whole host of other traitors*, Grima Mog said.

I can't help but think like the spy I was, cannot help but see that I am perfectly positioned to discover Madoc's plan. I am in his camp, in his very tent. I could uncover everything.

But that's absolute madness. How long before Oriana or Madoc realizes that I am Jude and not Taryn? I remember the vow Madoc made to me: *And when I best you, I will make sure I do it as thoroughly as I would any opponent who has shown themselves to be my equal.* It was a backhanded compliment, but it was also a straightforward threat. I know exactly what Madoc does to his enemies—he kills them and then washes his cap in their blood.

And what does it matter? I am in exile, pushed out.

But if I had Madoc's plans, I could trade them for the end of my exile. Surely Cardan would agree to that, if I gave him the means to save Elfhame. Unless, of course, he thought I was lying.

Vivi would say I ought to stop worrying about kings and wars and worry instead about getting home. After my fight with Grima Mog, I could demand better jobs from Bryern. Vivi is right that if we gave up the pretense of living like other humans, we could have a much bigger place. And given the results of the inquest, Taryn probably can't return to Faerie.

At least until Madoc takes over.

Maybe I should just let it happen.

But that brings me to the thing I cannot get past. Even though it's ridiculous, I can't stop the anger that rises in me, lighting a fire in my heart.

I am the *Queen of Elfhame.*

Even though I am the queen in exile, I am still the queen.

And that means Madoc isn't just trying to take Cardan's throne. He's trying to take mine.

CHAPTER 9

We dine in the tent of the Court of Teeth, which is easily three times the size of Madoc's and decorated as elaborately as any palace. The floor is covered in rugs and furs. Lamps hang from the ceilings, and fat pillar candles burn atop tables beside decanters of some pale libation and bowls of frost-covered white berries of a type I have never seen before. A harpist plays in a corner, the strains of her music carrying through the buzz of conversation.

At the center of the tent rests three thrones—two large and one small. They seem to be sculptures of ice, with flowers and leaves frozen inside them. The large thrones are unoccupied, but a blue-skinned girl sits on the small one, a crown of icicles on her head and a golden bridle around her mouth and throat. She looks to be only a year or two older than Oak and is dressed in a column of gray silk. Her gaze is on her fingers, which move restlessly against one another. Her nails are bitten short and crusted with a thin rime of blood.

If she is the princess, then it is not hard to pick out the king and queen. They wear even more elaborate icicle crowns. Their skin is gray, the color of stone or corpses. Their eyes are a bright and clear yellow, like wine. And their garments are the blue of her skin. A matching trio.

"This is Lady Nore and Lord Jarel and their daughter, Queen Suren," Oriana says to me quietly. So the little girl is the ruler?

Unfortunately, Lady Nore notices my staring. "A mortal," she says with a familiar contempt. "Whatever for?"

Madoc shoots an apologetic look in my direction. "Allow me to present one of my foster daughters, Taryn. I am sure I mentioned her."

"Perhaps," says Lord Jarel, joining us. His gaze is intense, the way an owl looks at a misguided mouse climbing directly into its nest.

I give my best curtsy. "I am glad to have a place at your hearth tonight."

He turns his cold gaze on Madoc. "Diverting. It speaks as though it thinks it's one of us."

I forgot how it felt, all those years of being utterly powerless. Having Madoc alone for protection. And now that protection depends on his not guessing which of his daughters stands beside him. I look up at Lord Jarel with fear in my eyes, fear I don't have to fake. And I hate how obviously it pleases him.

I think of the Bomb's words about what the Court of Teeth did to her and to the Roach: *The Court carved us up and filled us full of curses and geases. Changed us. Forced us to serve them.*

I remind myself I am no longer the girl I was before. I might be surrounded, but that doesn't mean I'm powerless. I vow that one day it is Lord Jarel who will be afraid.

But for now, I edge myself toward a corner, where I sit on a hide-covered tuffet and survey the room. I recall the Living Council warning that Courts were evading swearing fealty by hiding their children as changelings in the mortal world, then elevating them to rulers. I wonder if that's what's happened here. If so, it must gall Lord Jarel and Lady Nore to give up their titles. And make them nervous enough to bridle her.

Interesting to see their ostentation on display—their crowns and thrones and luxurious tent—as they support Madoc's bid to elevate himself to High King, which would put him far above them. I don't buy it. They might back him now, but I bet they hope to eliminate him later.

It is then that Grimsen enters the tent, wearing a scarlet cloak with an enormous pin in the shape of a metal-and-blown-glass heart that seems to beat. Lady Nore and Lord Jarel turn their attention to him, their stiff faces moving to chilly smiles.

I look over at Madoc. He appears less pleased to see the smith.

After a few more pleasantries, Lady Nore and Lord Jarel usher us to the table. Lady Nore leads Queen Suren by her bridle. As the child queen is led to the table, I notice that the straps sit oddly against her skin, as though they have partially sunken into it. Something in the shimmer of the leather makes me think of enchantment.

I wonder if this horrible thing is Grimsen's work.

Seeing her bound, I can't help but think about Oak. I glance at Oriana, wondering if she's reminded of him, too, but her expression is as calm and remote as the surface of a frozen lake.

We go to the table. I am seated beside Oriana, across the table from Grimsen. He spots the sun-and-moon earrings I am still wearing and gestures at them.

"I wasn't sure your sister would give those up," he says.

I lean in and touch my gloved fingers to my earlobes. "Your work is exquisite," I tell him, knowing how fond he is of flattery.

He gives me an admiring look that I suspect is pride in his own art. If he finds me pretty, it's a compliment to his craft.

But it's also to my advantage to keep him talking. No one else here is likely to tell me much. I try to imagine what Taryn might say, but all I can come up with is more of what I think Grimsen wants to hear. I drop my voice to a whisper. "I can hardly bear to take them off, even at night."

He preens. "Mere trinkets."

"You must think I am very silly," I say. "I know you have made far greater things, but these have made me very happy."

Oriana gives me an odd look. Did I make a mistake? Does she suspect me? My heart speeds.

"You ought to visit my forge," Grimsen says. "Allow me to show you what truly potent magic looks like."

"I should like that very much," I manage, but I am distracted with worry over being caught and frustrated by the smith's invitation. If only he'd been willing to brag *here*, tonight, instead of setting up some assignation! I don't want to go to his forge. I want to get out of this camp. It is only a matter of time before I'm caught. If I am to learn anything, I need to do it quickly.

My frustration mounts as further conversation is cut off by the arrival of servants bringing dinner, which turns out to be a massive cut of roasted bear meat, served with cloudberries. One of the soldiers draws Grimsen into a discussion about his brooch. Beside me, Oriana is speaking of a poem I don't know to a courtier from the Court of Teeth. Left to myself, I concentrate on picking out the voices of Madoc and Lady Nore. They are debating which Courts can be brought over to their side.

"Have you spoken with the Court of Termites?"

Madoc nods. "Lord Roiben is wroth with the Undersea, and he cannot like that the High King denied him his revenge."

My fingers clench on my knife. I made a deal with Roiben. I killed Balekin to honor it. That was Cardan's excuse for *exiling* me. It is a bitter draught to consider that after all that, Lord Roiben might prefer to join with Madoc.

But whatever Lord Roiben wants, he still swore an oath of loyalty to the Blood Crown. And while some Courts—like the Court of Teeth—may have schemed their way free of their ancestors' promises, most are still bound by them. Including Roiben. So how does Madoc think he is going to dissolve those bonds? Without some means of doing that, it doesn't matter whom the low Courts prefer. They must follow the only ruler with the Blood Crown on his head: High King Cardan.

But since Taryn would say none of that, I bite my tongue as the conversations swirl around me. Later, back at our tent, I carry pitchers of honey wine and refill the cups of Madoc's generals. I am not particularly memorable—merely Madoc's human daughter, someone most of them have met in passing and thought little upon. Oriana gives me no more odd looks. If she thought my behavior with Grimsen was strange, I don't think I have given her further reason to doubt me.

I feel the gravitational pull of my old role, the ease of it, ready to enfold me like a heavy blanket.

Tonight it seems impossible that I was ever anyone other than this dutiful child.

When I go to sleep, it is with a bitterness in my throat, one I haven't felt in a long time, one that comes from not being able to affect the things that matter, even though they are happening right in front of me.

I wake on the cot, loaded with blankets and furs. I drink strong tea near the fire, walking around to loosen my limbs. To my relief, Madoc has already gone.

Today, I tell myself, *today I must find a way out of here.*

I'd noticed horses when we made our way through the camp. I could probably steal one. But I am an indifferent rider, and without a map, I could quickly become lost. Those are probably kept all together in a war tent. Perhaps I could invent a reason to visit my father.

"Do you think Madoc would like some tea?" I ask Oriana hopefully.

"If so, he can send a servant to prepare it," she tells me kindly. "But there are many useful tasks to occupy your time. We Court ladies gather and stitch banners, if you're feeling up to it."

Nothing will give away my identity faster than my needlecraft. To call it poor is flattery.

"I don't think I'm ready to answer questions about Locke," I warn.

She nods sympathetically. Gossip passes the time at such gatherings, and it's not unreasonable to think a dead husband would provoke talk.

"You may take a little basket and go foraging," she suggests. "Just be careful to stay to the woods and away from the camp. If you see sentries, show them Madoc's sigil."

I try to contain my eagerness. "I can do that."

As I draw on a borrowed cloak, she puts a hand on my arm.

"I heard you speaking with Grimsen last night," Oriana says. "You must be careful of him." I recall her many cautions over the years at revels. She made us promise not to dance, not to eat anything, not to *do anything* that could result in embarrassment for Madoc. It's not that she doesn't have her reasons, either. Before she was Madoc's wife, she was High King Eldred's lover and saw another of his lovers—and her dear friend—poisoned. But it's still annoying.

"I will. I'll be careful," I say.

Oriana looks into my eyes. "Grimsen wants many things. If you are too kind, he may decide he wants you, too. He could desire you for your loveliness as one covets a rare jewel. Or he could desire you just to see if Madoc would give you up."

"I understand," I say, trying to seem like someone she doesn't need to worry over.

She lets go of me with a wan smile, seeming to believe we understand each other.

Outside, I head toward the woods with my little basket. Once I hit the tree line, I stop, overwhelmed with the relief of no longer playing a role. For a moment, here, I can relax. I take some steadying breaths and consider my options. Again and again, I come back to Grimsen. Despite Oriana's warning, he's my best bet to find a way out of here. With all his magic trinkets, maybe he's got a pair of metal wings to fly me home or a magical sled pulled by obsidian lions. Even if not, at least he doesn't know Taryn well enough to doubt that I'm her.

And if he wants something that I don't want to give him, well, he has a bad habit of leaving knives just lying about.

I hike through the woods to higher ground. From there, I can see the camp and all its pavilions. I spot the makeshift forge, set back from everything else, smoke rising in great quantities from its three chimneys. I spot an area of the camp where a large, round tent is a hub of activity. Maybe that's where Madoc is and where the maps are.

And I spot something else. When I first took stock of the camp, I noticed a small outpost at the base of the mountain, far from the other tents. But from here I can see there's also a cave. Two guards stand as sentries by the entrance.

Odd, that. It seems inconveniently far from everything else. But depending on what's in there, maybe that's the point. It's far enough to muffle even the loudest of screams.

With a shudder, I head down toward the forge.

I get a few looks from goblins and grigs and sharp-toothed members of the Folk with powdery wings as I cut through the outer edge of the camp. I hear a little hiss as I pass, and one of the ogres licks his lips in what is not at all a come-on. No one stops me, though.

The door to Grimsen's forge is propped open, and I see the smith inside, shirtless, his wiry, hairy form bent over the blade he's hammering. The forge is scorchingly hot, the air thick with heat, stinking of creosote. Around him are an array of weapons and trinkets that are far more than what they seem: little metal boats, brooches, silver heels for boots, a key that looks as though it was carved from crystal.

I think of the offer Grimsen wanted me to convey to Cardan before he decided greater glory lay in betrayal: *I will make him armor of ice to shatter every blade that strikes it and that will make his heart too cold to feel pity. Tell him I will make him three swords that, when used in the same battle, will fight with the might of thirty soldiers.*

I hate to think of all that in Madoc's hands.

Steeling myself, I knock on the doorframe.

Grimsen spots me and puts down his hammer. "The girl with the earrings," he says.

"You invited me to come," I remind him. "I hope this isn't too soon, but I was so curious. Can I ask what you're making, or is it a secret?"

That seems to please him. He indicates with a smile the enormous bar of metal he's working on. "I am crafting a sword to crack the firmament of the isles. What do you think of that, mortal girl?"

On one hand, Grimsen has forged some of the greatest weapons ever made. But can Madoc's plan truly be to cut through the armies of Elfhame? I think of Cardan, causing the sea to boil, storms to come, and trees to wither. Cardan, who has the sworn loyalty of dozens of low Court rulers and the command of all their armies. Can any one sword be great enough to stand against that, even if it is the greatest blade Grimsen has ever forged?

"Madoc must be grateful to have you on his side," I say neutrally. "And to have such a weapon promised to him."

"Hmph," he says, fixing me with a beady eye. "He ought to be, but *is* he? You'd have to ask him yourself, since he makes no mention of gratitude. And if they *happen* to make songs about me, well, is he interested in hearing them? No. No time for songs, he says. I wonder if he'd feel differently if there were songs about him."

Apparently, it wasn't encouraging his bragging that got him to talk, but stoking his resentment.

"If he becomes the next High King, there will be plenty of songs about him," I say, pressing the point.

A cloud passes over Grimsen's face, his mouth moving into a slight expression of disgust.

"But you, who has been a master smith through Mab's reign and all those who followed, your story must be more interesting than his—better fodder for ballads." I fear I am laying it on too thick, but he brightens.

"Ah, Mab," he says, reminiscing. "When she came to me to forge the Blood Crown, she entrusted me with a great honor. And I cursed it to protect it for all time."

I smile encouragingly. I know this part. "The murder of the wearer causes death for the person responsible."

He snorts. "I want my *work* to endure just as Queen Mab wanted her *line* to endure. But I care for even the least of my creations." He reaches out to touch the earrings with his sooty fingers. He brushes the lobe of my ear, his skin warm and rough. I duck out of his grasp with what I hope is a demure laugh and not a snarl.

"Take these, for example," he says. "Prize out the gems, and your beauty would fade—not just the extra smidge they grant, but all your beauty, until you were so wretched that the sight of you would set even the Folk to screaming."

I try to control the urge to rip the earrings from my ears. "You cursed them, too?"

His grin is sly. "Not everyone is properly respectful of a craftsman the way you are, Taryn, daughter of Madoc. Not everyone deserves my gifts."

I ponder that for a long moment, wondering at the array of creations that have come from his forge. Wondering how many of them were cursed.

"Is that why you were exiled?" I ask.

"The High Queen disliked my taking quite so much artistic license, so I was not much in favor when I followed the Alderking into exile," he says, and I figure that means yes, pretty much. "She liked to be the clever one."

I nod, as though there is nothing at all alarming about that story. My mind is racing, trying to recall all the things he's made. "Didn't you gift an earring to Cardan when you first came to Elfhame?"

"You have a good memory," he says. Hopefully, I have a better memory than he does, because Taryn didn't attend the Blood Moon revel. "It allowed him to overhear those speaking just outside of range. A wonderful device for eavesdropping."

I wait expectantly.

He laughs. "That's not what you want to know, is it? Yes, it was cursed. With a word, I could turn it into a ruby spider that would bite him until he died."

"Did you use it?" I ask, recalling the globe I saw in Cardan's study, in which a glittering red spider scrabbled restlessly at the glass. I am filled with cold horror at a tragedy already averted—and then blinding anger.

Grimsen shrugs. "He's still alive, isn't he?"

A very faerie answer. It sounds like *no*, when the truth is that the smith *tried* and *it didn't work*.

I ought to press him for more, ought to ask him about a way for me to escape the camp, but I can't bear to speak with him for another minute and not stab him with one of his own weapons. "Can I visit again?" I grit out, the false smile I am wearing feeling a lot more like a grimace.

I don't like the look he gives me, as though I am a gemstone he wishes to set into metal. "I would like that," he says, sweeping his hand around the forge, at all the objects there. "As you can see, I like beautiful things."

CHAPTER 10

After my visit to Grimsen, I tromp back into the woods to do the promised foraging with satisfying aggressiveness, collecting rowan berries, wood sorrel, nettles, a bit of deathsweet, and enormous cep mushrooms. I kick a rock, sending it skittering deeper into the woods. Then I kick another. It takes a lot of rocks before I feel even a little bit better.

I am no closer to finding a way to get out of here and no clearer on my father's plans. The only thing I am closer to is getting caught.

With that grim thought in mind, I discover Madoc sitting by the fire outside the tent, cleaning and sharpening the set of daggers he keeps on his person. Habit urges me to help him with the job, and I have to remind myself that Taryn wouldn't do that.

"Come sit," he urges, patting a bare side of a log on which he's perched. "You aren't used to campaigning, and you've been thrust into the thick of it."

Does he suspect me? I sit, resting my overfull basket near the fire, and reassure myself that he wouldn't sound nearly as friendly if he thought he was talking to Jude. I know I don't have long, though, so I chance it and ask him what I want to ask. "Do you really think you can defeat him?"

He laughs as though it's the question of a small child. *If you could reach your hand up far enough, could you pluck the moon from the sky?* "I wouldn't play the game if I couldn't win."

I feel oddly emboldened by his laughter. He really believes that I'm Taryn and that I know nothing of war. "But *how*?"

"I will spare you the whole of the strategy," he says. "But I am going to challenge him to a duel—and after I win, I will split his melon of a head."

"A duel?" I am flummoxed. "Why would *he* fight *you*?" Cardan is the High King. He has armies to stand between them.

Madoc grins. "For love," he says. "And for duty."

"Love of whom?" I can't believe that Taryn would be any less confused than I am right now.

"There is no banquet too abundant for a starving man," he says.

I don't know what to say to that. After a moment, he takes pity on me. "I know you don't care for lessons on tactics, but I think this one will appeal even to you. For what we want most, we will take almost any chance. There is a prophecy that he would make a poor king. It hangs over his head, but he believes he can charm his way free of fate. Let's see him try. I am going to give him a chance to prove he's a good ruler."

"And then?" I prompt.

But he only laughs again. "Then the Folk will call you Princess Taryn."

All my life I have heard of the great conquests of Faerie. As one might expect of an immortal people with few births, most battles are highly formalized, as are lines of succession. The Folk like to avoid all-out war, which means it's not unusual to settle an issue with some mutually agreed-upon contest. Still, Cardan never cared much for sword fighting and isn't particularly good at it. Why would he agree to a duel?

If I ask that, though, I am terrified Madoc will know me. Yet I must say *something*. I can't just sit here staring at him with my mouth hanging open.

"Jude got control of Cardan somehow," I pose. "Maybe you could do the same and—"

He shakes his head. "Look what became of your sister. Whatever power she had, he took back from her. No, I don't intend to continue even the pretense of serving any longer. Now I would rule." He stops sharpening his dagger and looks over at me with a dangerous gleam in his eye. "I gave Jude chance after chance to be a help to the family. Every opportunity to tell me the game she was playing. Had she done so, things would have come out very different."

A shiver goes through me. Does he guess I am sitting beside him?

"Jude is pretty sad," I say in what I hope is a neutral way. "At least according to Vivi."

"And you do not wish me to punish her further when I am High King, is that it?" he asks. "It's not as though I am not proud. What she achieved was no small thing. She's perhaps the most like me of all my children. And like children the world over, she was rebellious, and her grasp exceeded her reach. But *you*..."

"Me?" My gaze goes to the fire. It's jarring to hear him talk about me, but the idea of hearing something meant for Taryn alone is worse. I feel as though I am taking something from her. I can think of no way to stop it, though, no way that doesn't involve giving myself away.

He reaches over to grip my shoulder. It would be reassuring, except that the pressure is a little too hard, his claws a little too sharp. This is the moment he's going to grab me by the throat and tell me I am caught. My heart speeds.

"You must have felt as though I favored her, despite her ingratitude," he says. "But it was only that I understood her better. And yet, you and I have something in common—we both made a poor marriage."

I give him a sideways look, relief and incredulity warring with each other. Is he really saying his marriage to our mother was like Taryn's marriage to Locke?

He draws away from me to add another log to the fire. "And both ended tragically."

I suck in a breath. "You don't really think..." But I don't know what lie to give. I don't even know if Taryn would lie.

"No?" Madoc asks. "Who killed Locke, if not you?"

For too long, I can't think of any good answer.

He barks out a laugh and points a clawed finger at me, absolutely delighted. "It *was* you! Truly, Taryn, I always thought you were soft and meek, but I see now how wrong I have been."

"Are you *glad* I killed him?" He seems prouder of Taryn for murdering Locke than for all her other graces and skills combined—her ability to put people at ease, to choose just the right garment, and to tell just the right kind of lie to make people love her.

He shrugs, still smiling. "Alive or dead, I never cared about him. I only cared for you. If you're sorrowful that he's gone, then I am sorry for that. If you wish he were returned to life so you could kill him again, I recognize that feeling. But perhaps you dispensed justice and are only troubled that justice can be cruel."

"What do you think he did to me to deserve to die?" I ask.

He stokes the fire. Sparks fly up. "I assumed he broke your heart. An eye for an eye, a heart for a heart."

I remember what it was like to have a knife pressed to Cardan's throat. To panic at the thought of the power he had over me, to realize there was an easy way to end it. "Is that why you killed Mom?"

He sighs. "I honed my instincts in battle," he says. "Sometimes those instincts are still there when there is no more war."

I consider that, wondering what it takes to harden yourself to fight and kill over and over again. Wondering if some part of him is cold inside, a kind of cold that can never be warmed, like a shard of ice through the heart. Wondering if I have a shard like that, too.

For a moment, we sit quietly together, listening to the crackle and pop of the flames. Then he speaks again. "When I murdered your mother—your mother *and* your father—I changed you. Their deaths were a crucible, the fire in which all three of you girls were forged. Plunge a heated sword into oil, and any small flaw will turn into a crack. But quenched in blood as you were, none of you broke. You were only hardened. Perhaps what led you to end Locke's life is more my fault than yours. If it's hard for you to bear what you did, give me the weight."

I think of Taryn's words: *No one should have the childhood we had.*

And yet I find myself wanting to reassure Madoc, even if I can never forgive him. What would Taryn say? I don't know, but it would be unfair to comfort him with her voice.

"I should take this to Oriana," I say, indicating the basket of foraged food. I rise, but he catches my hand.

"Do not think I will forget your loyalty." He looks up at me meditatively. "You put our family's interests above your own. When all this is over, you can name your reward, and I will make sure you get it."

I feel a pang that I am no longer the daughter to whom he makes offers like this. I am not the one welcomed to his hearth, not the one he would care for and cherish.

I wonder what Taryn would ask for herself and the baby in her belly. Safety, I'd wager, the one thing Madoc believes he has already given us, the one thing he can never truly provide. No matter what promises he would make, he is too ruthless to ever keep anyone safe for long.

As for me, safety is not even on offer. He hasn't caught me yet, but my ability to sustain this masquerade is wearing thin. Although I am not sure how I will manage the trek across the ice, I resolve that I must run tonight.

CHAPTER 11

Oriana oversees the preparation of dinner for the company, and I stay by her side. I observe the making of nettle soup, stewed with potatoes until the sting is removed, and the butchering of deer, their freshly shot bodies steaming in the cold, their fat used to flavor tender greens. Each of the company has their own bowl and cup, clanking on their belts like ornamentation, and these are presented to the servers and filled with a ration of food and watered wine.

Madoc eats with his generals, laughing and talking. The Court of Teeth keep to their tents, sending a servant out to prepare their meal over a different fire. Grimsen sits apart from the generals, at a table of knights who listen with rapt attention to his stories of exile with the Alderking. It is impossible not to notice that the Folk who surround him wear perhaps more ornament than is typical.

The area where the cookpots and tables are is on the far side of the camp, closer to the mountain. In the distance, I see two guards standing sentry near the cave, not leaving their shift to eat with us. Near them, two reindeer nuzzle the snow, looking for buried roots.

I chew my nettle soup, an idea forming in my mind. By the time Oriana urges me back to our tent, I have come to a decision. I will steal one of the mounts from the soldiers near the cave. It will be easier to do that than take one from the main camp, and if something goes wrong, I will be more difficult to pursue. I still don't have a map, but I can navigate by the stars well enough to go south, at least. Hopefully, I will find a mortal settlement.

We share a cup of tea and shake off the snow. I warm my stiff fingers on the cup impatiently. I don't want to make her suspicious, but I need to get moving. I've got to pack up food and any other supplies I can manage.

"You must be quite cold," says Oriana, studying me. With her white hair and ghostly pale skin, she looks to be made of snow herself.

"Mortal weakness." I smile. "Another reason to miss the isles of Elfhame."

"We'll be home soon," she assures me. She cannot lie, so she must believe that. She must believe that Madoc will win, that he will be made High King.

Finally, she seems ready to retire. I wash my face, then stuff matches in one pocket and a knife in another. After I get into bed, I wait until I figure Oriana is probably asleep, counting off the seconds until a half hour has passed. Then I slip out from the coverlets as quietly as I can and shove my feet into boots. I dump some cheese into a bag, along with a heel of bread and three withered apples. I take the deathsweet I found while foraging and wrap it up in a little paper. Then I pad to the exit of the tent, taking up my cloak along the way. There is a single knight there, amusing himself by carving a flute before the fire. I nod to him as I pass.

"My lady?" he says, rising.

I turn my most withering glare on him. I am no prisoner, after all. I am the daughter of the Grand General. "Yes?"

"Where should I tell your father he can find you, should he ask?" The question is phrased in a deferential manner, but no doubt answering it wrong could lead him to less deferential questions.

"Tell him that I am busy using the woods for a chamber pot," I say, and he flinches, as I hoped he would. He asks me no more questions as I settle the cloak over my shoulders and head out, aware that the more time I take, the more suspicious he will become.

The walk to the cave is not overlong, but I stumble frequently in the dark, the cold wind more cutting with every step. Music and revelry rise from the camp, goblin songs about loss and longing and violence. Ballads of queens and knights and fools.

Close to the cave, I see three guards standing at attention around the wide opening—one more than I had hoped. The cave entrance is long and wide, like a smile, and the darkness beyond flickers occasionally, as though it's lit from somewhere deep within. Two pale reindeer doze nearby, curled in the snow like cats. A third scratches its antlers against a nearby tree.

That one, then. I can sneak deeper into the trees and lure him with one of the apples. As I begin to head into the woods, I hear a cry from the cave. The dense, cold air carries the sound to me, making me turn back.

Madoc has someone imprisoned.

I try to convince myself this isn't my problem, but another sound of distress cuts through all those clever thoughts. Someone is in there, in pain. I've got to make sure it isn't someone I know. My muscles are already stiff with cold, so I go slowly, circling the cave and climbing the rocks directly above it.

My impromptu plan is to drop down into the cave entrance since the guards are mostly looking in the other direction. It has the advantage of hiding me on my way to the drop, but then the actual dropping needs to be done really, really well or the combination of sound and motion is going to alert them immediately.

I grit my teeth and remember the Ghost's lessons—go slowly, make every step sure, keep to the shadows. Of course, that comes with the memory of the betrayal that followed, but I tell myself that doesn't make the lessons any less useful. I lower myself slowly from a jagged bit of a boulder. Even in gloves, my fingers feel frozen.

Then, hanging there, I realize I have made a terrible miscalculation. Even fully extended, my body cannot reach the ground. When I drop, there's no way to avoid making some sound. I am just going to have to be as quiet as I can and move as swiftly as I am able. I take a breath and let myself fall the short distance. At the inevitable crunch of my feet in the snow, one of the guards turns. I slip into the shadows.

"What is it?" asks one of the other two guards.

The first is staring into the cave. I can't tell if he spotted me or not.

I keep myself as still as possible, holding my breath, hoping he didn't see me, hoping that he can't *smell* me. At least, cold as it is, I'm not sweating.

My knife is near to hand. I remind myself that I fought Grima Mog. If it comes to it, I can fight them, too.

But after a moment, the guard shakes his head and goes back to listening to goblin songs. I wait and then wait some more, just to be sure. It gives my eyes time to adjust. There is a mineral scent in the air, along with that of burning lamp oil. Shadows dance at the end of a slanted passageway, tempting me on with the promise of light.

I make my way along between stalagmites and stalactites, as though I am stepping through the jagged teeth of a giant. I step into a new chamber and have to blink against the glow of torchlight.

"Jude?" says a soft voice. A voice I know. The Ghost.

Thin, with bruises blooming along his collarbones, he rests on the floor of the cave, his wrists manacled and chained to plates in the ground. Torches blaze in a circle surrounding him. He looks up at me with wide hazel eyes.

Cold as I am, I suddenly feel colder. The last thing he said to me was *I served Prince Dain. Not you.* That was right before I got dragged off to the Undersea and held there for weeks, terrified, starved, and alone. And yet, despite that, despite his betrayal, despite destroying the Court of Shadows, he speaks my name with all the wonder of someone who thinks I might be coming to save him.

I consider pretending to be Taryn, but he could hardly believe it was my twin who snuck past those guards. After all, he's the one who taught me to move like that. "I wanted to see what Madoc was hiding out here," I say, drawing out my knife. "And if you're thinking of calling the guards, know that the only reason I have for not stabbing you in the throat is the fear that you might die loudly."

The Ghost gives me a small, wry smile. "I would, you know. Very loudly. Just to spite you."

"So here are the wages for your service," I say with a pointed look around the cave. "I hope betrayal was its own reward."

"Gloat all you like." His voice is mild. "I deserve it. I know what I did, Jude. I was a fool."

"Then why did you do it?" It makes me feel uncomfortably vulnerable even to ask. But I'd trusted the Ghost, and I wanted to know how stupid I'd been. Had he hated me the whole time I'd considered us friends? Had he and Cardan laughed together at my trusting nature?

"Do you remember when I told you that I killed Oak's mother?"

I nod. Liriope had been poisoned with blusher mushroom to hide that while she was the lover of the High King, she was pregnant with Prince Dain's child. If Oriana hadn't cut Oak from Liriope's womb, the baby would have died, too. It's an awful story, and one I wouldn't be likely to forget, even if it didn't concern my brother.

"Do you remember how you looked at me when you discovered what I'd done?" he asks.

It had been a day or two after the coronation. I had taken Prince Cardan prisoner. I was still in shock. I was trying to piece together Madoc's plot. I'd been horrified to learn that the Ghost did such a horrendous thing, but I was horrified a lot then. Still, blusher mushroom is a nightmarish way to die, and my brother was almost murdered, too. "I was surprised."

He shakes his head. "Even the Roach was appalled. He never knew."

"And that's why you betrayed us? You thought we were too judgmental?" I ask, incredulous.

"No. Just listen one moment more." The Ghost sighs. "I killed Liriope because Prince Dain brought me to Faerie, provided for me, and gave me purpose. Because I was loyal, I did it, but afterward, I was shaken by what I had done. In despair, I went to the boy I thought was Liriope's only living child."

"Locke," I say numbly. I wonder if Locke realized, after Cardan's coronation, that Oak must be his half brother. I wonder if he felt anything about it, if he ever mentioned it to Taryn.

"Stricken with guilt," the Ghost goes on, "I offered him my protection. And my name."

"Your—" I begin, but he cuts me off.

"My *true name*," says the Ghost.

Among the Folk, true names are closely guarded secrets. A faerie can be controlled by their true name, surer than by any vow. It's hard to believe the Ghost would give so much of himself away.

"What did he make you do?" I ask, cutting to the chase.

"For many years, nothing," the Ghost said. "Then little things. Spying on people. Ferreting out their secrets. But until he ordered that I take you to the Tower of Forgetting and let the Undersea abduct you, I believed he meant mischief, never danger."

Nicasia must have known to ask him for a favor. No wonder Locke and his friends felt safe enough to hunt me the night before his wedding. He knew I would be gone the next day.

And yet, I still understand what the Ghost means. I thought Locke always meant mischief, too, even when it seemed possible I would die of it.

I shake my head. "But that doesn't explain how you came to be here."

The Ghost looks as though he is struggling to keep his voice even, to keep his temper in check. "After the Tower, I tried to put enough distance between myself and Locke that he wouldn't be able to order me to do anything again. Knights caught me leaving Insmire. That's when I found out the scope of what Locke had done. He gave my name to your father. It was his dowry for your twin sister's hand and a seat at the table when Balekin came to power."

I suck in my breath. "*Madoc* knows your *true name*?"

"Bad, right?" He gives a hollow laugh. "Your stumbling in here is the first good fortune I've had in a long time. And it is good fortune, even if we both know what needs to happen next."

I remember how carefully I gave Cardan commands, ones that meant he couldn't avoid or escape me. Madoc has doubtless done that and more, so that the Ghost believes only one path is open to him.

"I'm going to get you out of here," I say. "And then—"

The Ghost cuts me off. "I can show you where to cause me the least pain. I can show you how to make it seem like I did it myself."

"You said that you'd die loudly, just to spite me," I repeat, pretending he's not serious.

"I would have, too," he says with a little smile. "I needed to tell you—I needed to tell *someone* the truth before I died. Now that's done. Let me teach you one last lesson."

"Wait," I say, holding up a hand. I need to stall him. I need to think.

He goes on relentlessly. "It is no life to be always under someone's control, subject to their will and whim. I know the geas you asked for from Prince Dain. I know you were willing to murder to receive it. No glamour touches you. Remember when it was otherwise? Remember what it felt like to be powerless?"

Of course I do. And I can't help thinking of the mortal servant in Balekin's household, Sophie, with her pockets full of stones. Sophie, lost to the Undersea. A shudder goes through me before I can shrug it off.

"Stop being dramatic." I draw out the bag of food I had with me and sit down in the dirt to cut up wedges of cheese, apples, and bread. "We're not out of options yet. You look half-starved, and I need you alive. You could enchant a ragwort stalk and get us out of here—and you owe me that much help, at least."

He grabs pieces of cheese and apple and shoves them into his mouth. As he eats, I consider the chains holding him. Could I pry apart the links? I note a hole on the plate that seems just the size for a key.

"You're scheming," the Ghost says, noticing my gaze. "Grimsen made my restraints to resist all but the most magical of blades."

"I'm *always* scheming," I return. "How much of Madoc's plan do you know?"

"Very little. Knights bring me food and changes of clothing. I have been allowed to bathe only under a heavy guard. Once, Grimsen came to peer at me, but he was entirely silent, even when I shouted at him." It is not like the Ghost to shout. Or to scream the way he must have for me to have heard him, to scream out of misery and despair and hopelessness. "Several times, Madoc has come to interrogate me about the Court of Shadows, about the palace, about Cardan and Lady Asha and Dain, even about you. I know he's searching for weaknesses, for the means to manipulate everyone."

The Ghost reaches for another slice of the apple and hesitates, looking at the food as though seeing it for the first time. "Why did you have any of this with you? Why bring a picnic to explore a cave?"

"I was planning on running away," I admit. "Tonight. Before they discover I am not the sister I am pretending to be."

He looks up at me in horror. "Then go, Jude. Run. You can't stay for my sake."

"I'm not—you're going to help me get out of here," I insist, cutting him off when he starts to argue. "I can manage for one more day. Tell me how to open your chains."

Something in my face seems to convince him of my seriousness. "Grimsen has the key," he says, not meeting my eyes. "But you'd be better served if you used the knife."

The worst part is, he's probably right.

CHAPTER 12

When I get back to the tent, the guard isn't there. Feeling lucky, I slip under the flap, hoping to creep to my bed before Madoc gets home from whatever he's plotting with his generals.

What I do not expect is for the candles to be lit and Oriana to be sitting at the table, entirely awake. I freeze.

She stands, folding her arms. "Where were you?"

"Uh," I say, scrambling to figure out what she already knows—and what she'd believe. "There was a knight who asked me to meet him under the stars and—"

Oriana holds up her hand. "I covered for you. I dismissed the guard before he could carry tales. Do not insult me by lying anymore. You are not Taryn."

The cold horror of discovery settles over me. I want to run back out the way I came, but I think of the Ghost. If I run now, my chances of getting the key are pitiful. He will not be saved. And I will have very little chance of saving myself.

"Don't tell Madoc," I say, hoping against hope I can persuade her to be on my side in this. "Please. I never planned on coming here. Madoc rendered me unconscious and dragged me to this camp. I only pretended to be Taryn because I was already pretending to be her in Elfhame."

"How do I know you're not lying?" she demands, her unblinking pink eyes gazing at me warily. "How do I know you're not here to murder him?"

"There's no way I could have known Madoc would come for Taryn," I insist. "The only reason I'm still here is that I don't know how to leave—I tried tonight, but I couldn't. Help me get away," I say. "Help me, and you will never have to see me again."

She looks as though that's an enormously compelling promise. "If you're gone, he will guess I had a hand in it."

I shake my head, scrambling for a plan. "Write to Vivi. She can get me. I'll leave a note that I went to visit her and Oak. He never needs to know Taryn wasn't here."

Oriana turns away, pouring a deep green herbal liquor into tiny glasses. "Oak. I do not like how different he is becoming in the mortal world."

I want to scream in frustration at her abrupt subject change, but I force myself to be calm. I imagine him stirring his brightly colored cereal. "I don't always like it, either."

She passes me a delicate cup. "If Madoc can make himself High King, then Oak can come home. He won't be between Madoc and the crown. He will be safe."

"Remember your warning about how it was dangerous to be near a king?" I wait until she sips before I do. It is bitter and grassy and explodes on my tongue with the flavors of rosemary and nettle and thyme. I wince but don't dislike it.

She gives me an annoyed look. "You certainly have not behaved as though *you* recalled it."

"Fair," I admit. "And I paid the price."

"I will keep your secret, Jude. And I will send Vivi a message. But I won't work against Madoc, and you shouldn't, either. I want you to promise."

As the Queen of Elfhame, I am the one Madoc is against. It would give me such satisfaction for Oriana to know, when she thinks so little of me. It's a petty thought, followed by the realization that if Madoc found out, I would be in a whole different kind of trouble than I have been in before. He would use me. As frightened as I have been, here by his side, I ought to have been even more afraid.

I look Oriana in the eyes and lie as sincerely as I have ever done. "I promise."

"Good," she says. "Now, why were you sneaking around Elfhame, masquerading as Taryn?"

"She asked me to," I say, raising my brows and waiting for her to understand.

"Why would she—" Oriana begins, and then stops herself. When she speaks, it seems as though she is talking mostly to herself. "For the inquest. Ah."

I take another sip of the herbal liquor.

"I worried about your sister, alone in that Court," Oriana says, her pale brows drawing together. "Her family reputation in tatters and Lady Asha back, no doubt seeing an opportunity to exert influence over the courtiers, now that her son was on the throne."

"Lady Asha?" I echo, surprised that Oriana would think of her as a threat to Taryn, specifically.

Oriana rises and gathers writing materials. When she sits again, she begins penning a note to Vivi. After a few lines, she looks up. "I never supposed she would return."

That's what happens when people get tossed into the Tower of Forgetting. They get forgotten. "She was a courtier around the time that you were, right?" That's the closest I can say to what I mean, that Oriana was also the High King's lover. And while she never gave him a child, she has reason to know *a lot* of gossip. Something led her to make the comment she did.

"Your mother was once a friend to Lady Asha, you know. Eva had a great appreciation for wickedness. I do not say that to hurt you, Jude. It is a trait worthy of neither scorn nor pride."

I knew your mother. That was the first thing Lady Asha ever said to me. *Knew so many of her little secrets.*

"I didn't realize *you* knew my mom," I say.

"Not well. And it's hardly my place to talk about her," Oriana says.

"Nor am I asking you to," I return, although I wish that I could.

Ink drips from the tip of Oriana's pen before she sets it down and seals up the letter to Vivienne. "Lady Asha was beautiful and eager for the High King's favor. Their dalliance was brief, and I am sure Eldred thought bedding her would come to nothing. He rather too obviously regretted that she bore him a child—but that may have had something to do with the prophecy."

"Prophecy?" I prompt. I have a memory of Madoc saying something similar regarding his fortune when he was trying to convince me that we should join forces.

She gives a minute shrug of her shoulders. "The youngest prince was born under an ill-favored star. But he was still a prince, and once Asha had him, her place in the Court was secure. She was a disruptive force. She craved admiration. She wanted experiences, sensations, triumphs, things that required conflict—and enemies. She would not have been kind to someone as friendless as your sister must have been."

I wonder if she was unkind to Oriana, once. "I understand she didn't take very good care of Prince Cardan." I am thinking of the crystal globe in Eldred's rooms and the memory trapped inside.

"It wasn't as though she didn't dress him in velvets or furs; it's that she left them on until they grew ragged. Nor was it that she didn't feed him the most delectable cuts of meat and cake; but she forgot him for long enough that he had to scavenge for food in between. I don't think she loved him, but then I don't think she loved anyone. He was petted and fed wine and adored, then forgotten. But for all that, if he was bad with her, he was worse without her. They are cut from the same cloth."

I shudder, imagining the loneliness of that life, the anger. That desire for love.

There is no banquet too abundant for a starving man.

"If you're looking for reasons why he disappointed you," Oriana says, "by all accounts, Prince Cardan was a disappointment from the beginning."

That night, Oriana releases a snowy owl with a letter attached to its claws. As it flies up into the cold sky, I am hopeful.

And later, lying in bed, I scheme as I have not done since my exile. Tomorrow, I will steal the key from Grimsen, and when I leave, I will take the Ghost with me. With what I know about Madoc's plans and allies and the location of his army, I will force a bargain with Cardan to rescind my exile and to end the inquest into Taryn. I'm not going to let myself get distracted by letters I never received or the way he looked at me when we were alone in his rooms or my father's theories about his weaknesses.

Unfortunately, from the time I wake, Oriana will not let me leave her side. While she trusts me enough to keep my secret, she doesn't trust me enough to let me walk around the camp, now that she knows who I truly am.

She gives me wet laundry to spread before the fire, beans to pick from stones, and blankets to fold. I try not to rush through the tasks. I try to appear annoyed only because there seems to be a lot of work for me, though there was never so much work when I was Taryn. I don't want her to know how frustrated I am as the day wears on. My fingers itch to steal the key from Grimsen.

Finally, as evening sets in, I catch a break. "Take this to your father," Oriana tells me, setting down a tray bearing a pot of nettle tea, a wrapped-up bundle of biscuits, and a crock of jam to go with them. "In the generals' tent. He asked for you specifically."

I grab my cloak, hoping not to seem obviously eager, when the second half of what she said sinks in. A soldier is waiting for me outside the door, amping up my nerves. Oriana said she wouldn't tell Madoc about me, but that doesn't mean she couldn't have given me away somehow. And it doesn't mean that Madoc couldn't have figured it out himself.

The generals' tent is large and cluttered with all the maps I couldn't find in his tent. It's also filled with soldiers sitting on goat-hide camp stools, some armored and some not. When I come in, a few of them glance up, and then their gazes slide away from me as from a servant.

I set down the tray and pour a cup, forcing myself not to look too carefully at the map unfurled in front of them. It's impossible not to notice that they're moving little wooden boats across the sea, toward Elfhame.

"Pardon," I say, setting the nettle tea in front of Madoc.

He gives me an indulgent smile. "Taryn," he says. "Good. I have been thinking you ought to have your own tent. You're a widow, not a child."

"Tha—that's very kind," I say, surprised. It *is* kind, and yet I cannot help wondering if it's like one of those chess moves that looks innocuous at first but turns out to be the one setting up checkmate.

As he sips his tea, he projects the satisfaction of someone who obviously has more important matters to take care of yet is pleased to have a chance to play the doting father. "I promised your loyalty would be rewarded."

I cannot help seeing how everything he says and does could be double-edged.

"Come here," Madoc calls to one of his knights. A goblin in shining golden armor makes an elegant bow. "Find my daughter a tent and supplies to outfit it. Anything she needs." Then to me. "This is Alver. Do not be too great a torment to him."

It is not custom to thank the Folk, but I kiss Madoc on his cheek. "You're too good to me."

He snorts, a small smile showing a sharp canine. I let my gaze flicker to the map—and the models of boats floating on the paper sea—one more time before I follow Alver out the door.

An hour later, I am setting up a spacious tent erected not far from Madoc's. Oriana is suspicious when I arrive to move my things, but she allows it to be done. She even brings cheese and bread, placing them on the painted table that was found for me.

"I don't see why you're going to all this trouble to decorate," she says when Alver has finally left. "You'll be gone tomorrow."

"Tomorrow?" I echo.

"I received word from your sister. She will be here near dawn to pick you up. You're to meet her just outside the camp. There's an outcrop of rocks where Vivi can safely wait for you. And when you leave a note for your father, I expect it to be convincing."

"I will do my best," I say.

She presses her lips into a fine line. Maybe I should feel grateful to her, but I am too annoyed. If only she hadn't wasted the better part of my day, my evening would go a lot easier.

I will have to deal with the Ghost's guards. There will be no sneaking past them this time. "Will you give me some of your paper?" I ask, and when she agrees, I take a wineskin as well.

Alone in my new tent, I crush the deathsweet and add a little bit to the wine so it can infuse for at least an hour before I strain the vegetal bits. That should be strong enough to cause them to sleep for at least a day and a night but not kill them. I am aware, however, that time to prepare is not on my side. My fingers fumble as I go, nerves getting the better of me.

"Taryn?" Madoc sweeps back the flap of my tent, making me jump. He looks around, admiring his own generosity. Then his gaze returns to me, and he frowns. "Is all well?"

"You surprised me," I say.

"Come dine with the company," he says.

For a moment, I try to dream up an excuse, to give him some reason for me to stay behind so that I can slip out to Grimsen's forge. But I can't afford his suspicion, not now, when my escape is so close. I resolve to get up in the night, long before dawn, and go then.

And so I eat with Madoc one final time. I pinch some color into my cheeks and rake back my hair into a fresh braid. And if I am particularly kind that evening, particularly deferential, if I laugh particularly loudly, it is because I know I will never do this again. I will never have him behave like this with me again. But for one final night, he's the father I remember best, the one in whose shadow I have—for better or worse—become what I am.

CHAPTER 13

I wake to the press of a hand over my mouth. I slam my elbow into where I think the person holding me must be and am satisfied to hear a sharp intake of breath, as though I connected with a vulnerable part. There's a hushed laugh from my left. Two people, then. And one of them is not too worried about me, which is worrisome. I reach under my pillow for my knife.

"Jude," says the Roach, still laughing. "We've come to save you. Screaming would really hurt the plan."

"You're lucky I didn't stab you!" My voice comes out harsher than I intend, anger masking how terrified I was.

"I told him to watch out," the Roach says. There's a sharp sound, and light flares from a little box, illuminating the jagged planes of the Roach's goblin face. He's grinning. "But would he listen? I'd have ordered him, if not for the little matter of his being the High King."

"Cardan sent you?" I ask.

"Not exactly," says the Roach, moving the light so that I can see the person with him, the one I elbowed. The High King of Elfhame, in plain brown wool, a cloak on his back of a fabric so dark it seems to absorb light, leaf blade in the scabbard on his hip. He wears no crown on his brow, no rings on his fingers, nor gold paint limning his cheekbones. He looks every inch a spy from the Court of Shadows, down to the sneaky smile pulling at a corner of his beautiful mouth.

Looking at him, I feel a little light-headed from some combination of shock and disbelief. "You shouldn't be here."

"I said that, too," the Roach goes on. "Really, I miss the days when you were in charge. High Kings shouldn't be gallivanting around like common ruffians."

Cardan laughs. "What about uncommon ruffians?"

I swing my legs over the edge of the bed, and his laugh gutters out. The Roach turns his gaze to the ceiling. I am abruptly aware that I am in a nightgown Oriana lent me, one that is entirely too diaphanous.

My cheeks go hot enough with anger that I barely feel the cold. "How did you find me?" Padding across the tent, I feel my way to where I put my dress and fumble it on, pulling it on straight over my nightclothes. I tuck my knife into a sheath.

The Roach cuts a glance at Cardan. "Your sister Vivienne. She came to the High King with a message from your stepmother. She worried it was a trap. I was worried it was a trap, too. A trap for *him*. Maybe even for myself."

Which is why they took pains to catch me at my most vulnerable. But why come at all? And given all the disparaging things my older sister said about Cardan, why would she trust him with any of this? "Vivi went to *you*?"

"We spoke after Madoc carried you off from the palace," Cardan begins. "And whom did I find in her little dwelling but Taryn? We all had quite a lot to say to one another."

I try to imagine the High King in the mortal world, standing in front of our apartment complex, knocking on our door. What ridiculous thing had he worn? Had he sat down on the lumpy couch and drank coffee as though he didn't despise everything around him?

Did he pardon Taryn when he wouldn't pardon me?

I think of Madoc's believing that Cardan desires to be loved. It seemed like nonsense then and seems like even more nonsense now. He charms everyone, even my own sisters. He is a gravitational force, pulling everything toward him.

But I am not so easily taken in now. If he's here, it's to his own purpose. Maybe allowing his queen to fall into the hands of his enemies is dangerous to him. Which means I have power. I just have to discover it and then find a way to wield it against him.

"I can't go with you yet," I say, drawing on thick hose and jamming my foot into a heavy boot. "There's something I have to do. And something I need you to give me."

"Perhaps you could just allow yourself to be rescued," Cardan says. "For once." Even in his plain clothes, his head bare of any crown, he cannot pretend away how much he has grown into his royal role. When a king tries to give you a gift, you're not allowed to refuse it.

"Perhaps you could just give me what I want," I say.

"What?" the Roach asks. "Let's put our cards on the table, Jude. Your sisters and their friend are waiting with the horses. We need to be swift."

My *sisters*? Both of them? And a friend—Heather? "You let them come?"

"They insisted, and since they were the ones who knew where you were, we had no choice." The Roach is obviously frustrated with the whole situation. It's risky to work with people who have no training. Risky to have the High King acting as your foot soldier. Risky to have the person you're trying to extract—who might be a traitor—start backseat-driving your plan.

But that's his problem, not mine. I walk over and take his light from him, using it to find my wineskin. "This is dosed with a sleeping draught. I was going to take this to some guards, steal a key, and free a prisoner. We were supposed to escape together."

"Prisoner?" the Roach echoes warily.

"I saw the maps in Madoc's war room," I tell them. "I know the formation in which he means to sail against Elfhame, and I know the number of his ships. I know the soldiers in this encampment and which Courts are on his side. I know what Grimsen is making in his forge. If Cardan will promise me safe passage to Elfhame and to lift my exile once we're there, I will give all that to you. Plus, you will have the prisoner delivered into your hands before he can be used against you."

"If you're telling the truth," the Roach says. "And not leading us into a net of Madoc's making."

"I'm on my own side," I tell him. "You of all people should understand that."

The Roach gives Cardan a look. The High King is staring at me strangely, as though he wishes to say something and is holding himself back from it.

Finally, he clears his throat. "Since you're mortal, Jude, I cannot hold you to your promises. But you can hold me to mine: I guarantee you safe passage. Come back to Elfhame with me, and I will give you the means to end your exile."

"The *means* to end it?" I ask. If he thinks I don't know better than to agree to that, he's forgotten everything worth knowing about me.

"Come back to Elfhame, tell me what you would tell me, and your exile will end," he says. "I promise."

Triumph sweeps through me, followed by wariness. He tricked me once. Standing in front of him, recalling that I believed his offer of marriage was made in earnest, makes me feel small and scrubby and very, very mortal. I cannot allow myself to be tricked again.

I nod. "Madoc is keeping the Ghost prisoner. Grimsen has the key we need—"

The Roach interrupts me. "You want to *free* him? Let's gut him like a haddock. Quicker and far more satisfying."

"Madoc has his true name. He got it from Locke," I tell them. "Whatever punishment the Ghost deserves, you can dole it out once he's back in the Court of Shadows. But it's not death."

"Locke?" Cardan echoes, then sighs. "Yes, all right. What do we have to do?"

"I was planning to sneak into Grimsen's forge and steal the key to the Ghost's chains," I say.

"I'll help you," says the Roach, then turns to Cardan. "But you, sire, will absolutely not. Wait for us with Vivienne and the others."

"I am coming," Cardan begins. "You cannot order me otherwise."

The Roach shakes his head. "I can learn from Jude's example, though. I can ask for a promise. If we're spotted, if we're set upon, promise to go back to Elfhame immediately. You must do everything in your power to get to safety, no matter what."

Cardan glances toward me, as though for help. When I am silent, he frowns, annoyed with both of us. "Although I am wearing the cloak Mother Marrow made me, the one that will turn any blade, I still promise to run, tail between my legs. And since I have a tail, that should be amusing for everyone. Are you satisfied?"

The Roach grunts his approval, and we sneak from the tent. A wineskin full of poison sloshes softly at my hip as we slide through the shadows. Though it is late, a few soldiers move between tents, some gathered to drink or play dice and riddle games. A few sing along to a tune strummed on a lute by a goblin in leathers.

The Roach moves with perfect ease, slipping from shadow to shadow. Cardan moves behind him, more silently than I might have supposed. It gives me no pleasure to admit that he's grown better at slyfooting than I am. I could pretend that it's because the Folk have a natural ability, but I suspect that he also has practiced more than I have. I spread my learning too thin, although, to be fair, I'd like to know how much time he spent studying all the things he ought to know to be *the ruler of Elfhame*. No, those studies fell to me.

With those resentful thoughts circling in my head, we approach the forge. It is quiet, its embers cold. No smoke comes from its metal chimneys.

"So you've *seen* this key?" the Roach asks, going to a window and wiping away the grime to try to peer through the pane.

"It's crystal and hanging on the wall," I say in return, seeing nothing through the cloudy glass. It's too dark inside for my eyes. "And he's begun a new sword for Madoc."

"I wouldn't mind ruining that before it's put to my throat," says Cardan.

"Look for the big one," I say. "That'll be it."

The Roach gives me a frown. I can't help not having a better description; the last time I saw it, it was barely more than a bar of metal.

"Really big," I say.

Cardan snorts.

"And we ought to be careful," I say, thinking of the jeweled spider, of Grimsen's earrings that can give beauty or steal it. "There are bound to be traps."

"We'll go in and out fast," says the Roach. "But I would feel a lot better if the both of you stayed out and let me be the one to go in."

When neither of us reply, the goblin squats down to pick the lock on the door. After applying a bit of oil to the joints, they swing open silently.

I follow him inside. The moonlight reflects off the snow in such a way that even my poor, mortal eyes can see around the workshop. A jumble of items—some jeweled, some sharp, all piled up on one another. A collection of swords rests on a hat rack, one with a handle that is coiled like a snake. But there is no mistaking Madoc's blade. It sits on a table, not yet sharpened or polished, its tang raw. Pale bone-like fragments of root rest beside it, waiting to be carved and fitted into a handle.

I lift the crystal key from the wall gingerly. Cardan stands by me, looking over the array of objects. The Roach crosses the floor toward the sword.

He's halfway there when a sound like the chime of a clock rings out. High up the wall, two inset doors open, revealing a round hole. All I have time to do before a spray of darts shoots out is point and make a sound of warning.

Cardan steps in front of me, pulling his cloak up. The metal needles glance off the fabric, falling to the floor. For a moment, we stare at each other, wide-eyed. He looks as surprised as I am that he protected me.

Then, from the hole where the darts shot, comes a metal bird. Its beak opens and closes. "Thieves!" it cries. "Thieves! Thieves!"

Outside, I hear shouts.

Then I spot the Roach across the room. His skin has turned pale. He's about to say something, his face anguished, when he slides to one knee. The darts must have struck him. I rush over. "What was he hit with?" Cardan calls.

"Deathsweet," I say. Probably plucked from the same patch I found in the woods. "The Bomb can help him. She can make an antidote."

I hope she can, at least. I hope there's time.

With surprising ease, Cardan lifts the Roach in his arms. "Tell me this wasn't your plan," he pleads. "Tell me."

"No," I say. "Of course not. I swear it."

"Come then," he says. "My pocket is full of ragwort. We can fly."

I shake my head.

"*Jude*," he warns.

We don't have time to argue. "Vivi and Taryn are still waiting for me. They won't know what's happened. If I don't go to them, they'll be caught."

I can tell he's not sure if he should believe me, but all he does is shift the Roach so that he can untie his cloak with one hand. "Take this, and *do not stop*," he orders, his expression fierce. Then he heads into the night, bearing the Roach in his arms.

I set out for the woods, neither running nor hiding, exactly, but moving swiftly, tying his cloak over my shoulders as I go. I glance back once and see the soldiers swarming around the forge—a few entering Madoc's tent.

I said I was going straight to Vivi, but I lied. I head for the cave. There's still time, I tell myself. The incident at the forge is an excellent distraction. If they're looking for intruders there, they won't be looking for me here with the Ghost.

My optimism seems borne out as I draw close. The guards aren't at their posts. Letting out a sigh of relief, I rush inside.

But the Ghost is no longer in chains. He's not there at all. In his place is Madoc, outfitted in his full suit of armor.

"I'm afraid you're too late," he says. "Much too late."

Then he draws his sword.

CHAPTER 14

Fear steals my breath. Not only do I not have a weapon with the range of his sword, but it's unimaginable to win in battle against the person who taught me nearly everything I know. And looking at him, I can tell he's come to fight.

I draw the cloak more closely around me, inexpressibly glad for it. Without it, I would have no chance.

"When did you know it was me and not Taryn?" I ask.

"Later than I ought," he says conversationally, taking a step toward me. "But I wasn't *looking*, was I? No, it was a little thing. Your expression when you saw that map of the isles of Elfhame. Just that and every other thing you'd said and done went slant, and I saw they all belonged to you."

I am grateful to know he didn't guess from the start. Whatever he's planned, he had to do it hastily, at least. "Where's the Ghost?"

"*Garrett*," he corrects, mocking me with part of the Ghost's true name, the name the Ghost never told me, even when I might have used it to countermand the orders he'd received from Madoc. "Even if you live, you'll never stop him in time."

"Whom did you send him after?" My voice shakes a little, imagining Cardan escaping from Madoc's camp only to be shot in his own palace as he was once almost shot in his own bed.

Madoc's smile is all sharp teeth and satisfaction, as though I am being taught a lesson. "You're still loyal to that puppet. Why, Jude? Wouldn't it be better if he took an arrow through the heart in his own hall? You cannot believe he makes a better High King than I would."

I look Madoc in the eye, and my mouth makes the words before I can snatch them back. "Maybe I believe that it's time for Elfhame to be ruled by a queen."

He laughs at that, a bark of surprise. "You think Cardan will just hand over his power? To you? Mortal child, surely you know better. He exiled you. He reviled you. He will never see you as anything but beneath him."

It's nothing I haven't thought myself, yet his words still fall like blows.

"That boy is your weakness. But worry not," Madoc continues. "His reign will be short."

I take some satisfaction in the fact that Cardan was here, under his nose, and that he got away. But everything else is awful. The Ghost is gone. The Roach is poisoned. I've made mistakes. Even now, Vivi and Taryn and possibly Heather wait for me across the snow, growing more and more worried the closer dawn creeps to the horizon.

"Surrender, child," Madoc says, looking as though he feels a little sorry for me. "It's time to submit to your punishment."

I take a step backward. My hand goes to my knife on instinct, but fighting him when he is in armor *and* his weapon has the superior reach is a bad idea.

He gives me an incredulous look. "Will you defy me to the last? When I get ahold of you, I am going to keep you in chains."

"I never wanted to be your enemy," I say. "But I didn't want to be in your power, either." With that, I take off through the snow. I do the one thing I told myself I would never do.

"Do not run from me!" he shouts, a horrible echo of his final words to my mother.

The memory of her death makes my legs go faster. Clouds of air gasp from my lungs. I hear him barreling after me, hear the grunt of his breaths.

As I run, my hopes of losing him in the woods diminish. No matter how I zig and zag, he doesn't let up. My heart thunders in my chest, and I know that, above all things, I can't lead him to my sisters.

It turns out I am far from done with making mistakes.

One breath, two breaths. I draw my knife. Three breaths. I turn.

Because he isn't expecting it, he crashes toward me. I get under his guard, stabbing him in his side, striking where the plates of his armor meet. The metal still takes the better part of the blow, but I see him wince.

Cocking back his arm, he backhands me into the snow.

"You were always good," he says, looking down at me. "Just never good enough."

He's right. I learned a lot about swordplay from him, from the Ghost, but I didn't study it *for the better part of an immortal life.* And over most of the last year, I was busy learning to be a seneschal. The only reason I made it as long as I did in our last fight is that he was poisoned. The only reason I beat Grima Mog is that she didn't expect me to be very good at all. Madoc has my measure.

Also, against Grima Mog, I was wielding a much longer knife.

"I don't suppose you're willing to make this more sportsmanlike?" I say, rolling to my feet. "Maybe you could fight with one hand behind your back, to even the odds."

He grins, circling me.

Then he swings, leaving me only to block. I feel the effort all down my arm. It's obvious what he's doing, but it's still devastatingly effective. He's wearing me down, making me block and dodge again and again, while never letting me close enough to strike him. By keeping me focused on defense, he's exhausting me.

Despair starts to creep in. I could turn and run again, but I'd be in the same situation as before, running without anywhere to run to. As I meet his blows with my pathetic dagger, I realize how few choices I have and how they will continue to shrink.

It's not long before I falter. His sword slices against the cloak covering my shoulder. Mother Marrow's fabric is unscathed.

He pauses in surprise, and I strike for his hand. It's a cheat move. But I draw blood, and he roars.

Grabbing the cloak, he winds it around his hand, hauling me toward him. The ties choke me, then rip free. His sword sinks into my side, into my stomach.

I look up at him for a moment, eyes wide.

He seems as surprised as I feel.

Somehow, despite knowing better, part of me still believed he would pull a killing blow.

Madoc, who was my father ever since he murdered my father. Madoc, who taught me how to swing a sword to actually hit someone and not just their blade. Madoc, who sat me on his knee and read to me and told me he loved me.

I fall to my knees. My legs have collapsed under me. His blade comes free, slick with my blood. My leg is wet with it. I am bleeding out.

I know what happens next. He's going to deliver the final blow. Lopping off my head. Stabbing through my heart. The strike that's a kindness, really. After all, who wants to die slowly when you can die fast?

Me.

I don't want to die fast. I don't want to die at all.

He raises his sword, hesitates. My animal instincts kick in, pushing me to my feet. My vision swims a little, but adrenaline is on my side.

"Jude," Madoc says, and for the first time that I can recall, there's fear in his voice. Fear I don't understand.

Then three black arrows fly past me across the icy field. Two whiz over him, and the other strikes him in the shoulder of his sword arm. He howls, switches hands, and looks for his attacker. For a moment, I am forgotten.

Another arrow comes out of the darkness. This one hits him square in the chest. It strikes through his armor. Not deeply enough to kill him, but it's got to hurt.

From behind a tree, Vivi steps into view. Beside her is Taryn, wearing Nightfell on her hip. And with them, another person, who turns out not to be Heather at all.

Grima Mog, sword drawn, sits astride a ragwort pony.

CHAPTER 15

I force myself to move. Step after step, each one making my side scream with pain.

"Dad," Vivi says. "Stay where you are. If you try to stop her, I've got plenty more arrows, and I've been waiting half my life to put you in the ground."

"You?" Madoc sneers. "The only way you'd be the end of me is by accident." He reaches down to snap the shaft sticking out of his chest. "Have a care. My army is just over the hill."

"Go get them, then," Vivi says, sounding half hysterical. "Get your whole damn army."

Madoc looks in my direction. I must be quite a sight, blood-soaked, hand on my side. He hesitates again. "She's not going to make it. Let me—"

Three more arrows fly toward him in answer. None of them hit, not a great sign for Vivi's marksmanship. I just hope that he believes her missing is intentional.

A bout of dizziness overcomes me. I sag to one knee.

"Jude." My sister's voice comes from close by. Not Vivi. Taryn. She's got Nightfell drawn, holding the sword in one hand and reaching toward me with the other. "Jude, you have to stand up. Stay with me."

I must have looked as though I was going to faint. "I'm here," I say, reaching for her hand, letting her support my weight. I stagger forward.

"Ah, Madoc," comes Grima Mog's tart voice. "Your child challenged me just a week back. Now I know who she really wanted to kill."

"Grima Mog," Madoc says, dipping his head slightly, indicating respect. "However you have come to be here, this is nothing to do with you."

"Oh, no?" she counters, sniffing the air. Probably catching the scent of my blood. I should have warned Vivi about her when I had the chance, but however she has come to be here, I am glad of it. "I am out of work, and it seems the High Court is in need of a general."

Madoc looks momentarily confused, not realizing that she has traveled here with Cardan himself. But then he sees his opportunity. "My daughters are out of favor with the High Court, but I have work for you, Grima Mog. I will heap you with rewards, and you will help me win a throne. Just bring my girls to me." The last was a growl, not actually in my direction but at the lot of us. His betraying daughters.

Grima Mog looks past him, toward where the mass of his army is assembled. There's a wistful expression on her face, probably thinking of her own troops.

"Have you cleared that offer with the Court of Teeth?" I spit out with a backward glance at him.

Grima Mog's expression hardens.

Madoc sends an annoyed look in my direction that turns to

something else, something with a bit more sorrow in it. "Perhaps you'd prefer revenge to reward. But I could give you both. Just help me."

I knew he didn't like Nore and Jarel.

But Grima Mog shakes her head. "Your daughters paid me in gold to protect them and fight for them. And I mean to do just that, Madoc. I have long wondered which one of us would prevail in battle. Shall we find out?"

He hesitates, looking at Grima Mog's sword, at Vivi's large black bow, at Taryn and Nightfell. Finally, he looks at me.

"Let me take you back to the camp, Jude," Madoc says. "You're dying."

I shake my head. "I'm staying here."

"Good-bye, then, daughter," Madoc says. "You would have made a good redcap."

With that, he withdraws through the snow, never turning his back to us. I watch him, too relieved at his retreat to be angry that he's the reason I am in so much pain. I am too tired for anger. All around me the snow looks soft, like heaped-up feather beds. I imagine lying down on it and closing my eyes.

"Come on," Vivi says to me. She sounds a little like she's begging. "We've got to get you back to our camp, where the rest of the horses are. It's not far."

My side is on fire. But I have to move. "Sew me up," I say, trying to shake off the creeping lethargy. "Sew me up here."

"She's bleeding," says Taryn. "A lot."

I am struck with a dull certainty that if I don't do something now, nothing will be left to do. Madoc is right. I will die here, in the snow, in front of my sisters. I will die here, and no one will ever know there was once a mortal Queen of Faerie.

"Pack the wound with earth and leaves and then stitch it," I say.

My voice sounds as though it's coming from far away, and I'm not sure I am making any sense. But I remember the Bomb talking about how the High King is tied to the land, how Cardan had to draw on it to heal himself. I remember she made him take a mouthful of clay.

Maybe I can heal myself, too.

"You'll get an infection," Taryn says. "Jude—"

"I'm not sure it will work. I'm not magic," I tell her. I know I am leaving out parts. I know I am not explaining this the right way, but everything has become a little unmoored. "Even if I am the true queen, the land might not have anything to do with me."

"The true queen?" Taryn echoes.

"Because she married Cardan," Vivi says, sounding frustrated. "That's what she's talking about."

"What?" Taryn says, astonished. "No."

Then Grima Mog's voice comes. Rough and scratchy. "Go on. You heard her. Although she must be the most foolish child ever born to get herself in this fix."

"I don't understand," Taryn says.

"It's not for us to question, is it?" Grima Mog says. "If the High Queen of Elfhame gives us an order, we do it."

I grab for Taryn's hand.

"You're good at needlework," I say with a groan. "Stitch me up. Please."

She nods, looking a bit wild-eyed.

I can do nothing but hope as Grima Mog takes the cape from her own shoulders and spreads it out on the snow. I lie down on it and try not to wince as they rip my dress to expose my side.

I hear someone draw a sharp breath.

I look up at the dawn sky and wonder whether the Ghost has made it to the Palace of Elfhame. I recall the taste of Cardan's fingers pressed against my mouth as fresh pain blooms at my side. I bite back a scream and then another as the needle digs into the wound. Clouds blow by overhead.

"Jude?" Taryn's voice sounds like she's trying to fight back tears. "You're going to be okay, Jude. I think it's working."

But if it's working, why does she sound like that?

"Not..." I get the word out. I make myself smile. "Worried."

"Oh, Jude," she says. I feel a hand against my brow. It's so warm, which makes me think I must be very cold.

"In all my days, I have seen naught the like of this," Grima Mog says in a hushed voice.

"Hey," Vivi says, her voice wavering. She doesn't sound like herself. "Wound's closed. How are you feeling? Because some strange stuff is going on."

My skin has the sensation of being stung all over with nettles, but the fresh, hot pain is gone. I can move. I roll onto my good side and then up onto my knees. The wool beneath me is soaked through with blood. Way more blood than I am ready to believe came from me.

And around the edges of the cloak, I spot tiny white flowers pushing through the snow, most of them still buds, but a few opening as I look. I stare, not sure what I am seeing.

And then when I do understand, I can't quite take it in.

Baphen's words about the High King come to me: *When his blood falls, things grow.*

Grima Mog goes to one knee. "My queen," she says. "Command me."

I can't believe she is speaking those words to me. I can't believe the land chose me.

I had half-convinced myself I was faking being the High Queen, the way I faked my way through being the seneschal.

A moment later, everything else comes roaring back. I push myself to standing. If I don't move now, I will never get there in time. "I've got to get to the palace. Can you watch over my sisters?"

Vivi fixes me with a stern look. "You can barely stand."

"I'll take the ragwort pony." I nod toward it. "You follow with the horses you have at the campsite."

"Where's Cardan? What happened to that goblin he was traveling with?" Vivi looks ready to scream. "They were supposed to take care of you."

"The goblin called himself the Roach," Taryn reminds her.

"He was poisoned," I say, taking a few steps. My dress is open on the side, the wind blowing snow against my bare skin. I force myself to go to the horse, to touch its lacy mane. "And Cardan had to rush him to the antidote. But he doesn't know that Madoc sent the Ghost after him."

"The Ghost," Taryn echoes.

"It's ridiculous the way everyone acts like killing a king is going to make someone better at being one," Vivi says. "Imagine if, in the mortal world, a lawyer passed the bar by killing another lawyer."

I have no idea what my sister is talking about. Grima Mog gives me a sympathetic glance and reaches into her jacket, drawing out a small stoppered flask. "Take a slug of this," she says to me. "It'll help you keep going."

I don't even bother asking her what it is. I am far beyond that. I just toss back a long swallow. The liquid scalds all the way down my throat, making me cough. With it burning in my belly, I heave myself up onto the back of the horse.

"Jude," Taryn says, putting her hand on my leg. "You have to be careful not to pull your stitches." When I nod, she unclasps the sheath from around her waist, then passes it to me. "Take Nightfell," she says.

I feel better already with a weapon in my hand.

"We'll see you there," Vivi warns. "Don't fall off the horse."

"Thank you," I say, reaching out my hands. Vivi takes one, and then Taryn clasps the other. I squeeze.

As the pony kicks its way into the frigid air, I see the mountains below me, along with Madoc's army. I look down at my sisters, hurrying through the snow. My sisters, who, despite everything, came for me.

CHAPTER 16

The sky warms as I fly toward Elfhame. Holding on to the mane of the ragwort horse, I drink in great gulps of salt-spray air and watch the waves peak and roll below me. Although the land kept me from death, I am not entirely whole. When I shift my weight, my side hurts. I feel the stitches holding me together as though I am a rag doll with stuffing trying to leak out.

And the closer I get, the more panicked I become.

Wouldn't it be better if he took an arrow through the heart in his own hall?

It's the Ghost's habit to plan an assassination like a trap-door spider, finding a place to strike from and then waiting for his victim to arrive. He took me to the rafters of the Court of Elfhame for my first murder and showed me how to do it. Despite the success of that assassination, nothing about the inside of the cavernous chamber was changed—I know because shortly after is when I came into power, and I'm the one who changed nothing.

My first impulse is to present myself at the gates and demand to be taken to the High King. Cardan promised to lift my exile, and whatever he intends, at least I could warn him about the Ghost. But I worry that some overeager knight might hasten to decide I should forfeit my life first and he should carry any messages I have second, if at all.

My second thought is to creep into the palace through Cardan's mother's old chamber and the secret passageway to the High King's rooms. But if Cardan isn't there, I will be stuck, unable to sneak past the guards who watch over his door. And sneaking back will waste a lot of time. Time I am already short on.

With the Court of Shadows bombed out and no sense of where they rebuilt, I can't get in that way, either.

Which leaves me a single path—walking right into the brugh. A mortal in servant's livery might normally pass unnoticed, but I am too well known for that trick to work unless I am well disguised. But I have little access to clothes. My rooms, deep in the palace, are impossible to get to. Taryn's home, formerly Locke's and with Locke's servants still around, is too risky. Madoc's stronghold, though—abandoned, with clothing that used to belong to Taryn and Vivi and me still hanging in forgotten closets…

That might work.

I fly low to the tree line, glad to be arriving in the late morning, when most Folk are still abed. I land by the stables and step off the pony. It immediately collapses back into ragwort stalks, the magic already pushed to its full measure. Sore and slow, I head for the house.

In my head, my fears and hopes collide in a loop of words playing over and over again:

Please let the Roach be okay.

Let Cardan not be shot. Let the Ghost be clumsy.

Let me get inside easily. Let me stop him.

I do not pause to ask myself why I am in such a panic to save someone for whom I swore I rooted out every feeling. I will not think about that.

Inside the estate, much of the furniture is gone. Of what remains, the upholstery is ripped open, as though sprites or squirrels were nesting in it. My steps echo as I go up the familiar stairs, made strange by the emptiness of the rooms. I don't bother going to my own old chamber. Instead, I go to Vivi's, where I find that her closets are still full. I suspected she would have left many things behind when she went to live in the human world, and my guess is rewarded.

I find some stretchy hose in dark gray, pants, and a close-fitting jacket. Good enough. As I am changing, a wave of dizziness hits me, and I have to hang on to the doorframe until it passes and I get my balance again. Pushing up my shirt, I do what I've been avoiding thus far—I look at the wound. Dried-blood flecks stick all along the red pucker of where Madoc stabbed me, neat stitching holding the skin together. It's nice, careful work, and I am grateful to Taryn for it. But just a glance at it gives me a cold, unsteady feeling. Especially the reddest spots, where there are already signs of pulling.

I leave my sliced and blood-soaked dress in a corner, along with my boots. With trembling fingers, I scrape back my hair into a tight bun, which I cover with a black scarf wound twice around my head. Once I am climbing, I don't want anything to draw the eye.

In the main part of the house, I find an out-of-tune lute hanging in Oriana's parlor, along with pots of makeup. I darken around my eyes dramatically, drawing them out into a wing, with eyebrows to match. Then I take a mask with gargoyle features that I fit over my own.

In the armory, I find a small bow that breaks down into something I can hide. Regretfully, I leave Nightfell, hidden as best I can among the other swords. I take a piece of paper from Madoc's old desk and use his quill pen to write a note of warning:

> Expect an assassination attempt, most likely in the great hall. Keep the High King in seclusion.

If I give that to someone to pass to Baphen or one of Cardan's personal guard, then perhaps I have a better chance of finding the Ghost before he strikes.

With lute in hand, I head for the palace on foot. It's not far, but by the time I arrive, a cold sweat has started on my brow. It's difficult to guess how hard I can push myself. On one hand, the land healed me, which has made me feel slightly invulnerable. On the other, I nearly died and am still very hurt—and whatever Grima Mog gave me to drink is wearing off.

I find a small knot of musicians and stick close to them through the gates.

"That's a beautiful instrument," says one of the players, a boy with hair the green of new leaves. He looks at me strangely, as though perhaps we know each other.

"I'll give it to you," I say impulsively. "If you will do something for me."

"What is it?" He frowns.

I take his hand and press the note I wrote into it. "Will you take this to one of the members of the Living Council, preferably Baphen? I promise you won't get in any trouble."

He wavers, uncertain.

It is at that unfortunate moment that one of the knights stops me. "You. Mortal girl in the mask," he says. "You smell like blood."

I turn. Frustrated and desperate as I am, I blurt out the first thing that comes to me. "Well, I am a *mortal*. And a *girl*, sir. We bleed every month, just like moon swells."

He waves me on, distaste on his face.

The musician looks a little horrified, too.

"Here," I say to him. "Don't forget the note." Not waiting for a response, I shove the lute into his arms. Then I head into the throng. It doesn't take long before I am swallowed up thoroughly enough by the crowd that I can ditch my mask. I make for a shadowed corner and begin my ascent into the rafters.

The climb is horrible. I keep to the shadows, moving slowly, all the while trying to see where the Ghost might be hiding, all the while dreading that Cardan might enter the hall and make himself a target. Again and again, I have to stop and get my bearings. Bouts of light-headedness come and go. Halfway up, I am sure one of my stitches rips. I touch my hand to my side, and it comes away red. Hiding in a thicket of roots, I unwind the scarf from my head and wrap it around my waist, tying it as tightly as I can bear.

I finally make it to a perch high in the curve of the ceiling where several roots converge.

There I string my bow, arrange arrows, and look across the hollow hill. He may already be here, hidden somewhere close. As the Ghost told me when he taught me how to lie in wait, the tedium is the hardest part. Keeping yourself alert, not getting so bored that you lose focus and stop paying attention to every shift in the shadows. Or, in my case, getting distracted by pain.

I need to spot the Ghost, and once I do, I need to shoot him. I cannot hesitate. The Ghost himself would tell me I'd already missed my one chance to kill him; I better not miss again.

I think of Madoc, who raised me in a house of murder. Madoc, who became so used to war that he killed his wife and would have killed me, too.

Plunge a heated sword into oil and any small flaw will turn into a crack. But quenched in blood as you were, none of you broke. You were only hardened.

If I continue the way I am, will I become like Madoc? Or will I break?

Below me, a few courtiers dance in circles that come together, cross, then part again. Having been swept up in them, they can feel utterly chaotic, but from up here, they are triumphs of geometry. I look down at the banquet tables, piled with platters of fruit, flower-studded cheeses, and decanters of clover wine. My stomach growls as late morning turns to early afternoon and more Folk come to the Court.

Baphen, the Royal Astrologer, arrives with Lady Asha on his arm. I watch them make their way around the dais, not far from the empty throne. Seven circle dances later, Nicasia comes into the hall with a few companions from the Undersea. Then Cardan enters with his guard around him and the Blood Crown gleaming atop his ink-black curls.

When I look at him, I feel a dizzy dissonance.

He does not seem like someone who has been carrying poisoned spies through the snow, someone who has braved an enemy camp. Someone who pushed his magical cloak into my hands. He seems like the person who shoved me into the water and laughed when it closed over my head. Who tricked me.

That boy is your weakness.

I watch toasts I can't hear and see plates heaped with roasted doves on spits, leaf-wrapped sweetmeats, and stuffed plums. I feel strange, light-headed, and when I look, I see that the black scarf is nearly soaked through with blood. I shift my balance.

And I wait. And wait. And try not to bleed on anyone. My vision gets a little blurry, and I force myself to focus.

Below, I see Randalin with something in his hand, something he's waving at Cardan. The note I wrote. The boy must have delivered it after all. I tighten my hand on my crossbow. Finally, they'll get him out of here and out of danger.

Cardan doesn't look at the paper, though. He makes a dismissive gesture, as though perhaps he's already read it. But if he got my note, what is he doing here?

Unless, fool that he is, he's decided to be bait.

Just then I see a flicker of movement near some roots. I think for a second that I am just seeing shadows move. But then I spot the Bomb at the same moment her gaze goes to me and her eyes narrow. She lifts her own bow, arrow already notched.

I realize what's happening a moment too late.

A note told the Court of an assassination attempt, and the Bomb went looking for an assassin. She found someone hiding in the shadows with a weapon. Someone who had every reason to want to kill the king: me.

Wouldn't it be better if he took an arrow through the heart in his own hall?

Madoc set me up. He never sent the Ghost here. He only made me think he did, so I would come and chase after a phantom in the rafters. So I would incriminate myself. Madoc didn't have to deliver the killing blow. He made sure I would march straight to my doom.

The Bomb shoots, and I dodge. Her bolt goes past me, but my foot slips sideways in my own blood, and then I plunge backward. Off the rafter and into the open air.

For a moment, it feels like flying.

I crash onto a banquet table, knocking pomegranates to the floor. They roll in every direction, into puddles of spilled mead and shattered crystal. I am sure I ripped a lot of stitches. Everything hurts. I can't seem to get my breath.

I open my eyes to see people crowded around me. Councilors. Guards. I have no memory of closing my eyes, no idea how long I was unconscious.

"Jude Duarte," someone says. "Broken her exile to murder the High King."

"Your Majesty," says Randalin. "Give the order."

Cardan sweeps across the floor toward me, looking like a ridiculously magnificent fiend. The guards part to let him closer, but if I make a move, I have no doubt they'll stab me through.

"I lost your cloak," I croak up at him, my voice coming out all breath.

He peers down at me. "You're a liar," he says, eyes glittering with fury. "A dirty, mortal liar."

I close my eyes again against the harshness of his words. But he has no reason to believe I haven't come here to kill him.

If he sends me to the Tower of Forgetting, I wonder if he'll visit.

"Clap her in chains," says Randalin.

Never have I so wished there was a way for me to show I was telling the truth. But there isn't. No oath of mine carries any weight.

I feel a guard's hand close on my arm. Then Cardan's voice comes. "Do not touch her."

A terrible silence follows. I wait for him to pronounce judgment on me. Whatever he commands will be done. His power is absolute. I don't even have the strength to fight back.

"Whatever can you mean?" Randalin says. "She's—"

"She is my wife," Cardan says, his voice carrying over the crowd. "The rightful High Queen of Elfhame. And most definitely not in exile."

The shocked roar of the crowd rolls around me, but none of them are more shocked than I am. I try to open my eyes, try to sit up, but darkness crowds in at the edges of my vision and drags me under.

Book Two

'Gainst the fairies of the fire she with
tidal spirits waged
War; and earth, and air, and ocean felt how
fierce the battle raged.
High she shook her shining falchion,
pliant as the rushen plant,
Falchion her dwarf-lover forged her,
hard and bright as adamant;
Fighting by the Elle-King's side,
there she the lord of fireland slew;
All the hosts of fire were routed;
crowned her queen the conquering crew;
Back to fairyland she hasted;
home her train in triumph drew.

—Philip James Bailey,
"A Fairy Tale"

CHAPTER 17

I am on the High King's enormous bed, bleeding on his majestically appointed coverlets. Everything hurts. There's a hot, raw pain in my belly, and my head is pounding.

Cardan stands over me. His jacket is thrown on a nearby chair, the velvet soaked through with some dark substance. His white sleeves are rolled up, and he's washing my hands with a wet cloth. Getting the blood off them.

I try to speak, but my mouth feels like it is full of honey. I slide back into the syrupy dark.

I don't know how long I sleep. All I know is that it's a long time. When I wake, I am afflicted with a powerful thirst. I stumble out of bed, disoriented. Several candles burn around the room. By that light, I can tell that I am still in Cardan's chamber, in his bed, and that I am alone.

I find a pitcher of water and bring it to my lips, not bothering with a glass. I drink and drink and drink, until finally I am satisfied. I sag back onto the mattress and try to think over what's happened. It feels like a fever dream.

I can't stay in bed any longer. Ignoring the aches in my body, I head to the bathing room. The tub is filled, and when I touch it, the water shimmers as my fingers trail through it. There's a chamber pot for me to use as well, something for which I am immensely grateful.

I gingerly peel off my clothes and get into the bath, scrubbing with my nails so the water can wash away the grime and crusted blood of the last several days. I scrub my face and wring out my hair. When I emerge, I feel much better.

Back in the bedroom, I go to the closet. I look through rows and rows of Cardan's absurd garments until I determine that even if they fit me, there'd be no way I could wear any of them. I put on a voluminous puffy-sleeved shirt and take his least ridiculous cloak—black wool trimmed in deer fur and embroidered with a border of leaves—to wrap around myself. Then I make my way through the hall to my old rooms.

The knights outside his door notice my bare feet and bare ankles and the way I am clutching the robe. I am not sure what they suppose, but I refuse to be embarrassed. I summon my newly minted status as the Queen of Elfhame and shoot them such a withering look that they turn their faces away.

When I enter my old rooms, Tatterfell looks startled from where she sits on the couch, playing a game of Uno with Oak.

"Oh," I say. "Whoops."

"Hi," Oak says uncertainly.

"What are you doing here?" He flinches, and I regret the harshness of my words. "I'm sorry," I say, coming around the couch and bending down to pull him into a hug. "I'm happy you're here. I'm just surprised." I do not add that I am worried, although I am. The Court of Elfhame is a dangerous place for everyone, but it is particularly dangerous for Oak.

Still, I lean my head against his neck and drink in the scent of him, loam and pine needles. My little brother, who is squeezing me so tightly that it hurts, one of his horns scraping lightly against my jaw.

"Vivi's here, too," he says, letting me go. "And Taryn. And *Heather.*"

"Really?" For a moment, we share a significant look. I'd hoped Heather might get back together with Vivi, but I am stunned she was willing to make another trip to Elfhame. I figured it was going to be a long time before she was okay with more than a very cursory amount of Faerie. "Where are they?"

"At dinner, with the High King," says Tatterfell. "This one didn't want to go, so he had a tray sent up." She injects the words with a familiar disapproval. I am sure she thinks rejecting the honor of royal company is a sign that Oak is spoiled.

I think it's a sign he's been paying attention.

But I am more interested in the dinner tray, with half-eaten portions of delectable things on silver plates. My stomach growls. I am not sure how long it's been since I had a real meal. Without asking for permission, I go over and begin to gobble up cold strips of duck and chunks of cheese and figs. There's some too-strong tea in a pot, and I drink that, too, straight from the spout.

My hunger is great enough to make me suspicious. "How long have I been asleep?"

"Well, they drugged you," Oak says with a shrug. "So you've woken up before, but not for too long. Not like this."

That's disturbing, partially because I don't remember it and partially because I must have been hogging Cardan's bed this whole time, but I refuse to think too much about it, the way I refused to think about sweeping out of the High King's chambers in nothing but his shirt and cloak. Instead, I pick out one of my old seneschal outfits—a gown that is a long column of black with silver-tipped cuffs and collar. It is perhaps too plain for a queen, but Cardan is extravagant enough for both of us.

When I am dressed, I go back into the living space.

"Will you do my hair?" I ask Tatterfell.

She huffs to her feet. "I should hope so. You can hardly walk around the way you came in here." I am swept back into the bedroom, where she shoos me toward my dressing table. There, she braids my brown locks in a halo around my head. Then she paints my lips and eyelids in a pale rose color.

"I wanted your hair to suggest a crown," she says. "But then I suppose you'll have a real coronation at some point."

The thought makes my head swim, a sense of unreality creeping in. I do not understand Cardan's game, and that worries me.

I think of how Tatterfell once urged me to marry. The memory of that, and my certainty that I wouldn't, makes it even stranger that she is here, doing my hair as she did then. "You made me look regal anyway," I say, and her beetle-black eyes meet mine in the mirror. She smiles.

"Jude?" I hear a soft voice. Taryn.

She's come in from the other room, in a gown of spun gold. She looks magnificent—roses in her cheeks and a brightness in her eyes.

"Hey," I say.

"You're awake!" she says, rushing into the room. "Vivi, she's awake."

Vivi walks in, wearing a suit of bottle-green velvet. "You nearly died, you know? You nearly died *again*."

Heather follows in a pale blue gown with edges of the same pink that sits in her tight curls. She gives me a sympathetic grin, which I appreciate. It's good to have one person who doesn't know me well enough to be angry.

"Yes," I say. "I know."

"You keep rushing into danger," Vivi informs me. "You've got to stop acting as though Court politics is some kind of extreme sport and stop chasing the adrenaline high."

"I couldn't help that Madoc kidnapped me," I point out.

Vivi goes on, ignoring me. "Yeah, and the next thing we know, the High King is on our doorstep looking ready to tear down the whole apartment complex to find you. And when we finally hear from you through Oriana, it's not like we could trust *anyone*. So we had to hire a *cannibal redcap* to come with us, just in case. And it's a good thing we did—"

"Seeing you lie in the snow—you were so pale, Jude," Taryn interrupts. "And when things started budding and blooming around you, I didn't know what to think. Flowers and vines pushed right up through the ice. Then color came back into your skin, and you got up. I couldn't believe it."

"Yeah," I say softly. "I was fairly surprised myself."

"Does this mean you're *magical*?" Heather asks, which is a fair question. Mortals are not supposed to be magical.

"I don't know," I tell her.

"I still can't believe you married Prince Cardan," Taryn says.

I feel an obscure need to justify myself. I want to deny that desire came into it, want to claim that I was entirely practical when I agreed. Who wouldn't want to be the Queen of Faerie? Who wouldn't make the bargain I made?

"It's just—you *hated* him," Taryn says. "And then I found out he was under your control the whole time. So I thought maybe you *still* hated him. I mean—I guess it's possible that you hate him now and that he hates you, too, but it's confusing."

A knock on the door interrupts her. Oak runs over to open it. As though summoned by our discussion, the High King is there, surrounded by his guard.

CHAPTER 18

Cardan is wearing a high jeweled collar of jet on a stiff black doublet. Over the tops of his pointed ears are knifelike caps of gold, matching the gold along his cheekbones. His expression is remote.

"Walk with me," he says, leaving little room for refusal.

"Of course." My heart speeds, despite myself. I hate that he saw me when I was at my most vulnerable, that he let me bleed all over his spider-silk sheets.

Vivi catches my hand. "You're not well enough."

Cardan raises his black brows. "The Living Council is eager to speak with her."

"No doubt," I say, then look at my sisters, Heather and Oak behind them. "And Vivi should be happy, because the only danger anyone has ever been in at a Council meeting is of being bored to death."

I let go of my sister. The guards fall in behind us. Cardan gives me his arm, causing me to walk at his side, instead of behind him the way

I would have as his seneschal. We make our way through the halls, and when we pass courtiers, they bow. It's extremely unnerving.

"Is the Roach okay?" I ask, low enough not to be overheard.

"The Bomb has not yet discovered how to wake him," Cardan says. "But there is hope that she yet will."

At least he's not dead, I remind myself. But if he sleeps for a hundred years, I will be in my grave before he opens his eyes again.

"Your father sent a message," Cardan says, glancing at me sideways. "It was very unfriendly. He seems to blame me for the death of his daughter."

"Ah," I say.

"And he has sent soldiers to the low Courts with promises of a new regime. He urges them to not hesitate, but to come to Elfhame and hear his challenge to the crown." Cardan says all this neutrally. "The Living Council waits to hear all you know about the sword and his maps. They found my descriptions of the camp to be sadly inadequate."

"They can wait a little longer," I say, forcing out the words. "I need to talk to you."

He looks surprised and a little uncertain.

"It won't take long." The last thing I want is to have this conversation, but the longer I put it off, the larger it will loom in my mind. He ended my exile—and while I extracted a promise from him to do that, he had no reason to declare me queen. "Whatever your scheme is, whatever you are planning to hold over me, you might as well tell me now, before we're in front of the whole Council. Make your threats. Do your worst."

"Yes," he says, turning down a corridor in the palace that led outside. "We do need to talk."

It is not long before we come to the royal rose garden. The guards stop at the gate, letting us go on alone. As we make our way down a path of shimmering quartz steps, everything is hushed. The wind carries floral scents through the air, a wild perfume that doesn't exist outside of Faerie and reminds me at once of home and of menace.

"I assume you weren't actually trying to shoot me," Cardan says. "Since the note was in your handwriting."

"Madoc sent the Ghost—" I say, then stop and try again. "I thought that there was going to be an attempt on your life."

Cardan gazes at a rosebush with petals so black and glossy they look like patent leather. "It was terrifying," he says, "watching you fall. I mean, you're generally terrifying, but I am unused to fearing *for* you. And then I was furious. I am not sure I have ever been that angry before."

"Mortals are fragile," I say.

"Not you," he says in a way that sounds a little like a lament. "You never break."

Which is ridiculous, as hurt as I am. I feel like a constellation of wounds, held together with string and stubbornness. Still, I like hearing it. I like everything he's saying all too well.

That boy is your weakness.

"When I came here, pretending to be Taryn, you said you'd sent me messages," I say. "You seemed surprised I hadn't gotten any. What was in them?"

Cardan turns to me, hands clasped behind his back. "Pleading, mostly. Beseeching you to come back. Several indiscreet promises." He's wearing that mocking smile, the one he says comes from nervousness.

I close my eyes against frustration great enough to make me scream. "Stop playing games," I say. "You sent me into exile."

"Yes," he says. "That. I can't stop thinking about what you said to me, before Madoc took you. About it being a trick. You meant marrying you, making you queen, sending you to the mortal world, all of it, didn't you?"

I fold my arms across my chest protectively. "*Of course it was a trick.* Wasn't that what you said in return?"

"But that's what you do," Cardan says. "You trick people. Nicasia, Madoc, Balekin, Orlagh. Me. I thought you'd admire me a little for it, that I could trick *you*. I thought you'd be angry, of course, but not quite like this."

I stare at him, openmouthed. "What?"

"Let me remind you that I didn't know you'd murdered my brother, the ambassador to the Undersea, until that very morning," he says. "My plans were made in haste. And perhaps I was a little annoyed. I thought it would pacify Queen Orlagh, at least until all promises were finalized in the treaty. By the time you guessed the answer, the negotiations would be over. Think of it: *I exile Jude Duarte to the mortal world. Until and unless she is pardoned by the crown.*" He pauses. "*Pardoned by the crown.* Meaning by the King of Faerie. Or its queen. You could have returned anytime you wanted."

Oh.

Oh.

It wasn't an accident, his choice of words. It wasn't infelicitous. It was deliberate. A riddle made just for me.

Maybe I should feel foolish, but instead, I feel furiously angry. I turn away from him and walk, swiftly and completely directionless through the garden. He runs after me, grabbing my arm.

I haul around and slap him. It's a stinging blow, smearing the gold on his cheekbone and causing his skin to redden. We stare at each other for long moments, breathing hard. His eyes are bright with something entirely different from anger.

I am in over my head. I am drowning.

"I didn't mean to hurt you." He grabs my hand, possibly to keep me from hitting him again. Our fingers lace together. "No, it's not that, not exactly. I didn't think I *could* hurt you. And I never thought you would be afraid of me."

"And did you like it?" I ask.

He looks away from me then, and I have my answer. Maybe he doesn't want to admit to that impulse, but he has it.

"Well, I was hurt, and yes, you scare me." Even as I am speaking, I wish I could snatch back the words. Perhaps it is exhaustion or having been so close to death, but the truth pours out of me in a devastating rush. "You've always scared me. You gave me every reason to fear your capriciousness and your cruelty. I was afraid of you even when you were tied to that chair in the Court of Shadows. I was afraid of you when I had a knife to your throat. And I am scared of you now."

Cardan looks more surprised than he did when I slapped him.

He was always a symbol of everything about Elfhame that I couldn't have, everything that would never want me. And telling him this feels a little like throwing off a heavy weight, except that weight is supposed to be my armor, and without it, I am afraid I am going to be entirely exposed. But I keep talking anyway, as though I no longer have control of my tongue. "You despised me. When you said you wanted me, it felt like the world had turned upside down.

"But sending me into exile, that made sense." I meet his gaze. "That was an entirely right-side-up Cardan move. And I hated myself for not seeing it coming. And I hate myself for not seeing what you're going to do to me next."

He closes his eyes. When he opens them, he releases my hand and turns so I can't see his face. "I can see why you thought what you did. I suppose I am not an easy person to trust. And maybe I ought not to be trusted, but let me say this: I trust *you*."

He takes a deep breath. "You may recall that I did not want to be the High King. And that you did not consult me before plopping this crown on my head. You may further recollect that Balekin didn't want me to keep the title and that the Living Council never took a real shine to me."

"I suppose," I say, though none of those things seemed particularly unusual. Balekin wanted the crown for himself, and the Living Council wanted Cardan to show up for meetings, which he seldom did.

"There was a prophecy given when I was born. Usually Baphen is uselessly vague, but in this case, he made it clear that should I rule, I would make a very poor king." He pauses. "The destruction of the crown, the ruination of the throne—a lot of dramatic language."

I recall Oriana said something about Cardan's being ill-fated, and so did Madoc, but this is more than bad luck. It makes me think of the coming battle. It makes me think of my dream of the star charts and the spilled inkpot of blood.

Cardan turns back to me, gazing down at me as he did in my imaginings. "When you forced me into working for the Court of Shadows, I never thought of the things I could do—frightening people, charming people—as *talents*, no less ones that might be valuable. But *you* did. You showed me how to use them to be *useful*. I never minded being a minor villain, but it's possible I might have grown into something else, a High

King as monstrous as Dain. And if I did—if I fulfilled that prophecy—I *ought* to be stopped. And I believe that you would stop me."

"Stop you?" I echo. "Sure. If you're a huge jerk and a threat to Elfhame, I'll pop your head right off."

"Good." His expression is wistful. "That's one reason I didn't want to believe you'd joined up with Madoc. The other is that I want you here by my side, as my queen."

It's a strange speech, and there's little of love in it, but it doesn't seem like a trick, either. And if it stings a little that he admires me primarily for my ruthlessness, well, I suppose there should be some comfort that he admires me at all. He wants me with him, and maybe he wants me in other ways, too. Desiring more than that from him is just greed.

He gives me a half smile. "But now that you're High Queen and back in charge, I won't be doing anything of consequence anyway. If I destroy the crown and ruin the throne, it will only be through neglect."

That startles a laugh out of me. "So that's your excuse for not doing any of the work? You must be draped in decadence at all times because if you aren't kept busy, you might fulfill some half-baked prophecy?"

"Exactly." He touches my arm, his smile fading. "Would you like me to inform the Council that you will see them another time? It will be a novelty to have me make your excuses."

"No. I'm ready." My head swims with everything we've talked about. My palm is smeared with gold. When I look at him, I see the remaining powder has been smudged over his cheekbone by the strike of my hand. I can't stop staring at it, can't stop thinking about the way he looked at me when he caught my fingers. That's the only excuse I have for not noticing that he's led me back to his rooms, which are, I suppose, also mine since we're married.

"They're *here*?" I say.

"I believe it was meant to be an ambush," he informs me with a twist of his mouth. "As you know, they are very nosy and hate the idea of being kept out of anything important, including royal convalescing."

What I am imagining is how terrible it would have been to be awakened by the entire Living Council when I was still rumpled and filthy and naked. I draw on that anger and hope it makes me seem imperious.

Inside, Fala the Grand Fool dozes on the floor beside the fire. The rest of the Council—Randalin with his ram horns, Baphen stroking his blue beard, sinister Mikkel from the Unseelie Court, and insectile Nihuar from the Seelie—are seated around the room, no doubt annoyed by the wait.

"Queen Seneschal," Fala says, leaping to his feet and making an extravagant bow.

Randalin glowers. The others begin to rise. I feel tremendously awkward.

"No, please," I say. "Remain as you are."

The councilors and I have had a contentious relationship. As Cardan's seneschal, I frequently denied them audiences with the High King. I think they suspected my chief qualification for the position was my ability to lie for him.

I doubt they believe I have any qualifications for my new position.

But before they can say so, I launch into a description of Madoc's camp. Soon, I am re-creating the naval maps I saw and making lists of every faction fighting on his side. I explain what I saw in Grimsen's forge; Cardan chimes in with a few items he recalls.

The numbers are on Elfhame's side. And whether or not I can draw on the power of the land, I know that Cardan can. Of course, there's still the matter of the sword.

"A duel?" Mikkel says. "Perhaps he mistakes the High King for someone more bloodthirsty. You, perhaps?"

From him, that's not exactly an insult.

"Well, Jude did get herself tangled up with *Grima Mog*." Randalin has never much liked me, and I don't think recent events have improved his feelings at all. "Leave it to you to spend your exile recruiting infamous butchers."

"So *did* you murder Balekin?" Nihuar asks me, clearly able to put off her curiosity no longer.

"Yes," I say. "After he poisoned the High King."

"Poisoned?" she echoes in astonishment, looking at Cardan.

He shrugs, lounging in a chair, looking bored as ever. "You can hardly expect me to mention every little thing."

Randalin rises to the bait, looking puffed up with annoyance. "Your Majesty, we were led to believe that her exile was justified. And that if you wished to marry, you would consult—"

"Perhaps at least one of you could have told us—" Baphen says, talking over Randalin.

This was what they really wanted to discuss, I suppose. Whether there was any way they could prevent what's already occurred and invalidate my elevation to High Queen.

Cardan puts up a hand. "No, no, enough. It's all too tedious to explain. I declare this meeting at an end." His fingers make a flicking gesture toward the door. "Leave us. I tire of the lot of you."

I have a long way to go before I can manage that level of shameless arrogance.

It works, however. They grumble but rise and go out. Fala blows me a kiss as he departs.

For a moment, we are alone.

Then there is a sharp rap on the secret door to the High King's chamber. Before either of us can get up, the Bomb pushes her way through, striding into the room with a tray of tea things. Her white hair has been pulled up into a topknot, and if she is tired or grieving, none of it shows on her face.

"Long live Jude," she says with a wink, setting down the tray on a table with a clatter of the pots and saucers and whatnot. "No thanks to me."

I grin. "Good thing you're a lousy shot."

She holds up a packet of herbs. "A poultice. To draw any fever from the blood and help the patient heal faster. Unfortunately, it won't draw the sting from your tongue." She takes some bandages from her coat and turns to Cardan. "*You* should go."

"This is *my* room," he points out, affronted. "And that's *my* wife."

"So you keep telling everyone," the Bomb says. "But I am going to take out her stitches, and I don't think you want to watch that."

"Oh, I don't know," I say. "Maybe he'd like to hear me scream."

"I would," Cardan says, standing. "And perhaps one day I will." On the way out, his hand goes to my hair. A light touch, barely there, and then gone.

CHAPTER 19

Taking out stitches is slow and painful. My sister does beautiful needlework, and it seems that she embroidered my stomach and side, leaving the Bomb with an endless stretch of tiny stitches that need to be individually snipped, the threads teased out of the skin, and then salve applied.

"Ow!" I say for what seems like the millionth time. "Do these really need to come out?"

The Bomb gives a long-suffering sigh. "They should have been removed days ago."

I bite my tongue against another howl of pain. When I can speak again, I try to distract myself by asking, "Cardan said you're hopeful about the Roach."

Bent over me, she smells of cordite and bitter herbs. Her expression is wry. "I'm always hopeful when it comes to him."

There is a soft tap on the door. The Bomb looks at me expectantly.

"Come in?" I call, lowering my dress to cover the mess of my stomach.

A messenger with small moth wings and a nervous expression enters the room, granting me a temporary reprieve from being poked. She sinks into a bow, looking a bit like she's going to faint. Maybe it's the small pile of blood-covered thread.

I consider explaining, but that's supposed to be beneath the dignity of a queen, and it would only embarrass us both. Instead, I give her what I hope is an encouraging smile. "Yes?"

"Your Highness," she says. "Lady Asha wishes to see you. She has sent me to bring you directly to the chamber where she languishes."

The Bomb snorts. "Languishes," she mouths.

"You may tell her that I will see her as soon as I am able," I say with as much grandeur as I can muster.

Although it's clearly not the answer her mistress wanted me to give, the messenger can do little to challenge it. She hesitates a moment, then seems to realize it herself. Abashed, she departs with another bow.

"You're the High Queen of Elfhame. Act like it," the Bomb says, fixing me with a serious expression. "You shouldn't let anyone command you. Not even me."

"I told her no!" I protest.

She begins to pick out another stitch, not particularly gently. "Lady Asha doesn't get to be put *next* on your schedule just for asking. And she shouldn't make the queen come to her. Especially when *you* were hurt. She's lying in bed recuperating from the trauma of watching while you fell from the ceiling."

"Ouch," I say, not sure if I am reacting to the tug against my flesh, her completely justified scolding, or her scathing assessment of Lady Asha.

Once the Bomb is finished with me, I ignore her excellent counsel and head toward Lady Asha's chamber. It's not that I disagree with any of her advice. But I would like to say something to Cardan's mother, and now seems like an excellent time to do so.

As I head through the hall, I am stopped by Val Moren, who places his walking stick in my path. The eyes of the last High King's mortal seneschal are lit with malice.

"How does it feel to rise to such dizzying heights?" he asks. "Afraid you'll take another tumble?"

I scowl at him. "I bet you'd like to know how it feels."

"Unfriendly, my queen," he says with a grunt. "Ought not you be kind to the least of your subjects?"

"You want kindness?" I used to be afraid of him, of his dire warnings and wild eyes, but I am not afraid of him now. "All those years, you could have helped me and my sister. You could have taught us how to survive here as mortals. But you left us to figure it out on our own, even though we're the same."

He peers at me through narrowed eyes. "*The same?*" he demands. "Do you think a seed planted in goblin soil grows to be the same plant as it would have in the mortal world? No, little seed. I do not know what you are, but we are not the same. I came here fully grown."

And with that, he walks on, leaving me scowling after him.

I find Lady Asha in a canopied bed, her head propped up on pillows. Her horns don't look as though they make it easy for her to find a comfortable position, but I guess when they're your horns, you're used to them.

Two courtiers, one in a gown and the other in trousers and a coat with an opening for delicate wings in the back, sit in chairs beside her. One reads from a collection of gossipy sonnets. The servant girl who brought me Lady Asha's message lights candles, and the scents of sage, clove, and lavender permeate the air.

When I come in, the courtiers remain seated far longer than they ought, and when they rise to make their bows, they do so with pointed lethargy. Lady Asha stays abed, gazing at me with a slight smile, as though we both know a distasteful secret.

I think of my own mother, as I have not in a long time. I recall the way she threw back her head when she laughed. How she let us stay up late during the summer, chasing one another through the backyard in the moonlight, my hands sticky with melted Popsicle, the stink of Dad's forge heavy in the air. I recall waking in the afternoon, cartoons playing in the living room and mosquito bites blooming on my skin. I think of the way she would bring me in from the car when I fell asleep on long drives. I think of the drowsy, warm feeling of being carried through the air.

Who would I be without any of that?

"Don't worry about getting up," I tell Lady Asha. She looks surprised, and then offended, by the implication that she owes me the courtesies of my new position. The courtier in the coat has a gleam in his eye that makes me think he is going to go and tell absolutely everyone what he's witnessed. I doubt very much that the story will flatter me.

"We will speak later," Lady Asha says to her friends, a frigid tone in her voice. They seem to take being dismissed in stride. With another bow—this one made carefully to both of us—they depart, barely waiting until the door shuts to begin whispering to each other.

"Your visit must be a kindness," Cardan's mother says. "With you so recently returned to us. And so recently coming into a throne."

I force myself not to smile. The inability to lie makes for some interesting sentences.

"Come," she says. "Sit a moment with me."

I know the Bomb would say that this is another instance where I am letting her tell me what to do, but it seems petty to object to such minor high-handedness.

"When I brought you from the Tower of Forgetting to my den of spies," I say, in case she needs reminding of why she should worry about making me angry, "you said you wanted to be away from the High King, your son. But you two seem to have made up. You must be so pleased."

She makes a pout. "Cardan was not an easy child to love, and he's only grown worse with time. He would scream to be held, and then once picked up he would bite and kick his way out of my arms. He would find a game and obsess over it until it was conquered, then burn all the pieces. Once you're no longer a challenge, he will despise you."

I stare at her. "And you're giving me this warning out of the kindness of your heart?"

She smiles. "I am giving you this warning because it doesn't matter. You're already doomed, Queen of Elfhame. You already love him. You already loved him when you questioned me about him instead of your own mother. And you will still love him, mortal girl, long after his feelings evaporate like morning dew."

I can't help thinking of Cardan's silence when I asked if he liked that I was afraid. A part of him will always delight in cruelty. Even if he has changed, he could change again.

I hate being a fool. I hate the idea of my emotions getting the better of me, of making me weak. But my fear of being a fool turned me into one. I should have guessed the answer to Cardan's riddle long before I did. Even if I didn't understand it was a riddle, it was still a loophole to exploit. But I was so shamed by falling for his trick that I stopped looking for ways around it. And even after I discovered one, I made no plan to use it.

Maybe it isn't the worst thing to want to be loved, even if you're not. Even if it hurts. Maybe being human isn't always being weak.

Maybe it was the shame that was the problem.

But it's not as though my own fears are the only reason I was in exile for so long. "Is that why you intercepted the letters he sent? To protect me? Or was it because you're afraid that he won't tire of me? Because, my lady, I will always be a challenge."

I admit, it's a guess about her and the letters. But not many people would have the access and power to stop a message from the High King. No ambassador from a foreign kingdom. Probably not a member of the Living Council. And I don't think Lady Asha likes me very much.

She regards me mildly. "Many things become lost. Or destroyed."

Given that she can't lie, that's practically a confession.

"I see," I say, standing. "In that case, I will take your advice in exactly the spirit with which you gave it." As I look back at her from the door, I say what I believe she will least like to hear. "And next time, I will expect your curtsy."

CHAPTER 20

I am halfway down the hall when a pixie knight rushes up to me, her armor polished to a shine that reflects her cerulean skin. "Your Majesty, you must come quickly," she says, putting her hand to her heart.

"Fand?" When we were at the palace school, we both dreamed of knighthood. It seems that one of us achieved it.

She looks at me as though surprised at being remembered, although it wasn't very long ago. I suppose she, too, believes I have ascended to dizzying and perhaps memory-altering heights.

"*Sir* Fand," I correct myself, and she smiles. I grin back at her. Although we were not friends, we were friend*ly*—and for me, in the High Court, that was a rarity. "Why do I have to come quickly?"

Her expression goes grave again. "A battalion from the Undersea is in the throne room."

"Ah," I say, and let her escort me through the halls. Some Folk bow as I pass. Others quite pointedly do not. Not sure how to behave, I ignore both.

"You ought to have your own guard," Sir Fand says, keeping pace just behind me.

Everyone seems very fond of telling me how I should do this job. But, at least in this case, my silence is apparently enough of an answer for her to fall silent.

When we get to the brugh, it is mostly empty. Randalin is wringing his wizened hands as he studies the soldiers of the Undersea—selkies and the pale-skinned Folk that make me think of those they called *drowned ones*. Nicasia stands in front of them, in armor of iridescent scales, her hair dressed with shark teeth, clasping Cardan's hands in hers. Her eyes are red-rimmed and swollen, as though she's been weeping. His dark head is bent toward hers, and I am reminded that they were once lovers.

She whirls when she sees me, wild with anger. "This is your father's doing!"

I take a step back in surprise. "What?"

"Queen Orlagh," Cardan says with what seems like slightly exaggerated calm. "Apparently, she was struck with something like elf-shot. It burrowed deep into her flesh, but it seems to have stopped short of her heart. When there is an attempt to remove it, it seems to resist magical and nonmagical extraction. It moves as though it's alive, but there may be some iron in it."

I stop, my mind reeling. The Ghost. That's where Madoc sent him, to the sea. Not to *kill* the queen, which would anger the sea Folk and bring them more firmly to Cardan's side, but to wound her in such a way that he could hold her death over her. How could her people risk fighting Madoc when he would stay his hand so long as Orlagh stayed put?

"I'm so sorry." It's an utterly human thing to say and utterly useless, but I blurt it out anyway.

Nicasia curls her lip. "You ought to be." After a moment, she releases Cardan's hand with some apparent regret. She would have married him once. I very much doubt that my appearance has made her give up the notion. "I must go to my mother's side. The Court of the Undersea is in chaos."

Once, Nicasia and her mother held me captive, locked me in a cage, and tried to take my will from me. Sometimes, in dreams, I am still there, still floating in the dark and the cold.

"We are your allies, Nicasia," Cardan reminds her. "Should you need us."

"I count on you to avenge my mother, if nothing else," she says. Then, with another hostile glance in my direction, she turns and leaves the hall. The Undersea soldiers fall into step behind her.

I cannot even be annoyed with her. I am reeling from the success of Madoc's gambit—and the sheer ambition of it. The death of Orlagh would be no small thing to engineer; she is one of the ancient and established powers of Faerie, older even than Eldred. But to wound her in such a way seems harder still.

"Now that Orlagh is weak, it's possible there will be challengers to her throne," Randalin says with a certain amount of regret, as though doubting Nicasia would be up to what was required of her. "The sea is a brutal place."

"Did they catch the would-be assassin?" I ask.

Randalin frowns at me, as he often does when I ask a question to which he doesn't know the answer but doesn't wish to admit it. "I do not believe so. Had they, I am sure they would have told us."

Which means he may come here after all. Which means Cardan is still in danger. And we have far fewer allies than we did before. This is the problem with playing defense—you can never be sure where your enemy will strike, so you expend more resources trying to cover every eventuality.

"The generals will wish to adjust their plans," Randalin says with a significant look in Cardan's direction. "Perhaps we should summon them."

"Yes," says Cardan. "Yes, I suppose we should."

We repair to the strategy rooms and are greeted by a cold dinner of duck eggs, currant bread, and paper-thin slices of roasted boar. The master of servants, a large, spidery woman, waits for us, along with the generals. The discussion quickly takes on a festival air, with half of it turning to entertaining the coming lords and ladies of the low Courts and the other half planning a war.

The new Grand General turns out to be an ogre named Yorn. He was appointed during my exile. I know nothing to his detriment, but he has a nervous demeanor. He sweeps in with three of his generals and a lot of questions about the maps and materials the Living Council passed on from me. Tentatively, he begins to reimagine our naval strategy.

Once more, I try to guess what Madoc's next move might be. I feel as though I have so many pieces of the puzzle but fail to see how they fit together. What I do know is that he's cutting off the exits, pruning the variables, reducing our ability to surprise him, so that his plans are most likely to succeed.

I can only hope that we can surprise him in turn.

"We should just attack the moment his ships appear on the horizon," says Yorn. "Not give him a chance to call for parlay. It will be harder without the aid of the Undersea, but not impossible. We still have the greater force."

Due to the Folk's customs of hospitality, if Madoc requests it, he and a small party will be welcomed into Elfhame for the purpose of discussing alternatives to war. So long as he doesn't raise a weapon, he can eat and drink and talk with us for however much time he likes. When he is ready to depart, the conflict will start right where it left off.

"He'll send a bird ahead," says Baphen. "And his ships may well come shrouded in fog or shadows. We do not know what magic he has at his disposal."

"He wants to duel," I say. "As soon as he draws a weapon, he will break the terms of parlay. And he will not be allowed to bring a large force onto the land for the purposes of discussing peace."

"Better if we ring the isles in ships," Yorn says, once again moving strategy pieces around a beautifully drawn map of Insweal, Insmire, Insmoor, and Insear that lies on the table. "We can prevent Madoc's soldiers from landing. Shoot down any birds that come our way. We have allies from the low Courts to add to our force."

"What if Madoc gets aid from the Undersea?" I ask. The others look at me in astonishment.

"But we have a treaty," Randalin says. "Perhaps you didn't hear that, because—"

"Yes, you have a treaty *now*," I say, not wanting to be reminded of my exile again. "But Orlagh could pass the crown to Nicasia. If she did, a Queen Nicasia would be free to make a new alliance with Madoc, just as once the Court of Teeth put a changeling on their throne, they were free to march against Elfhame. And Nicasia might ally with Madoc if he would make her mother well."

"Do you think that's likely to happen?" Yorn asks Cardan, frowning over his plans.

The High King makes a nonchalant gesture. "Jude likes to suppose the worst of both her enemies and her allies. Her reward is occasionally being wrong about us."

"Hard to remember an occasion of that," I say to him under my breath.

He lifts a single brow.

Fand steps into the room at that moment, looking very aware that she doesn't belong. "Your pardon, but I—I have a message for the queen," she says with a nervous stammer in her voice. "From her sister."

"As you can see, the queen—" Randalin begins.

"Which sister?" I demand, crossing the room to her.

"Taryn," she says, looking a lot calmer now that she is speaking only to me. Her voice drops low. "She said to meet her in the High King's old dwelling."

"When?" I ask, my heart beating double-time. Taryn is a careful person, mindful of proprieties. She is fond neither of cryptic messages nor sinister meeting places. If she wants me to come to Hollow Hall, something is very wrong.

"As soon as you can get away," Fand says.

"I'll come now," I say, and then turn back to the councilors, the generals, and the High King. "There's been a family difficulty. You will excuse me."

"I will accompany you," Cardan says, rising. I open my mouth to explain all the reasons that he can't go. The problem is that as I look up into his gold-rimmed eyes and he blinks mock-innocently down at me, I can't think of a single one that will actually stop him.

"Good," he says, sweeping past me. "We're decided."

Yorn looks a little relieved that we're leaving. Randalin, predictably, looks annoyed. Baphen is busily eating a duck egg while several other generals are deep in conversation about how many of the low Courts will bring boats and what that means for their maps.

In the hall, I am forced to walk faster to catch up with Cardan. "You don't even know where we're going."

He pushes black curls away from his face. "Fand, where are we going?"

The knight looks miserable but answers. "To Hollow Hall."

"Ah," he says. "Then I am already proven useful. You will need me to sweet-talk the door."

Hollow Hall belonged to Cardan's eldest brother, Balekin. Considered to be the most influential of the Grackles—a faction of the High Court most interested in feasts, debauchery, and excess—Balekin was famous for the wildness of his revels. He tricked mortals into serving him, glamouring them so they remembered only what he wanted them to remember. He was awful, and that was before he led a bloody coup against the rest of his family in a bid for the throne.

He's also the person who raised Cardan.

As I consider all this, Cardan sends Fand off to have the royal coach brought around. I want to protest that I can ride, but I am not so healed yet that I am sure I should. A few minutes later, I am being handed up into a beautifully outfitted royal carriage, with embroidered seats in a pattern of vines and beetles. Cardan settles himself opposite me, leaning his head against the window frame as the horses begin to run.

As we leave the palace, I realize it is later than I thought. Dawn is threatening on the horizon. My long sleep has given me a distorted view of time.

I wonder at Taryn's message. What possible reason could she have for bringing me to Balekin's estate? Could it have something to do with Locke's death?

Could it be another betrayal?

Finally, the horses come to a stop. I climb from the carriage as one of the guards jumps down from the front to properly hand me down. He looks flummoxed to find me already standing beside the horses, but I hadn't thought to wait. I am not used to being royalty and worry that I will not get used to it.

Cardan emerges, his gaze going to neither me nor the guard, but to Hollow Hall itself. His tail lashes the air behind him, showing all the emotion that's not on his face.

Covered in a heavy coat of ivy, with a crooked tower and pale and hairy roots hanging from its balconies, this was once his home. I witnessed Cardan's being whipped by a human servant at Balekin's direction. I am sure far worse things happened there, although he has never spoken of them.

I rub my thumb over the stub of my missing finger top, bitten off by one of Madoc's guards, and realize abruptly that if I told Cardan about it, he might understand. Maybe more than anyone, he'd comprehend the odd mingling of fear and shame I feel—even now—when I think of it. For all our conflicts, there are moments when we understand each other entirely too well.

"Why are we here?" he asks.

"This is where Taryn wanted to meet," I say. "I didn't think she even knew the place."

"She doesn't," Cardan says.

The polished wood door is still carved with an enormous and sinister face, still flanked with lanterns, but sprites no longer fly in desperate circles within. A soft glow of magic emanates instead.

"My king," the door says fondly, its eyes opening.

Cardan smiles in return. "My door," he says with a slight hitch in his voice, as though perhaps everything about returning here feels strange.

"Hail and welcome," it says, and swings wide.

"Is there a girl like this one inside?" he asks, indicating me.

"Yes," says the door. "Very like. She's below, with the other."

"Below?" I say as we walk into the echoing hall.

"There are dungeons," Cardan says. "Most Folk thought they were merely decorative. Alas, they were not."

"Why would Taryn be down there?" I ask, but to that, he has no answer. We go down, the royal guard ahead of me. The basement smells strongly of earth. The room we enter contains little, only some furniture that seems unsuitable for sitting upon and chains. Big braziers burn brightly enough to heat my cheeks.

Taryn sits beside an oubliette. She is dressed simply, a cloak over her shift, and without the grandeur of clothes and hair, she looks young. It frightens me to think I might look that young, too.

When she sees Cardan, she pushes herself to her feet, one hand moving to her belly protectively. She sinks into a low curtsy.

"Taryn?" he says.

"He came looking for you," she tells me. "When he saw me in your rooms, he said I had to restrain him because Madoc had given him more commands. He told me about the dungeons and I brought him here. It seemed like a place no one would look."

Walking over to the hole, I peer down into the pit. The Ghost sits perhaps twelve feet down, his back against the curve of the wall, his wrists and ankles bound in shackles. He looks pale and unwell, peering up with haunted eyes.

I want to ask him if he's okay, but he obviously isn't.

Cardan is gazing at my sister as though attempting to puzzle something through. "You know him, don't you?" he asks.

She nods, crossing her arms over her chest. "He would visit Locke sometimes. But he didn't have anything to do with Locke's death, if that's what you're thinking."

"I wasn't thinking that," Cardan says. "Not at all."

No, he would have already been Madoc's prisoner then. But I don't like the way this conversation is going. I am still not sure what Cardan would do if he knew the truth of Locke's death.

"Can you tell us about Queen Orlagh?" I ask the Ghost, attempting to redirect the conversation back toward what's most important. "What did you do?"

"Madoc gave me a bolt," he says. "It was heavy in my hand, and it squirmed as though it was a living thing. Lord Jarel put a magic on me that let me breathe under the waves, but it made my skin burn as though covered always in ice. Madoc commanded me to shoot Orlagh anywhere but in the heart or head and told me that the bolt would do the rest."

"How did you get away?" I ask.

"I slew a shark pursuing me and hid within its corpse until the danger passed. Then I swam to shore."

"Did Madoc give you any other orders?" Cardan asks, frowning.

"Yes," the Ghost says, a strange expression on his face. And that's the only warning we have before he's climbed halfway up the oubliette. I realize he's shed whatever chains Taryn clasped him in, probably long before now. Icy panic rushes through me. I am too stiff to fight him, too sore. I grab for the heavy seal to the pit and begin to drag it over, hoping to trap him before he makes it up the side. Cardan calls for the guard and draws a wicked-looking knife from inside his doublet, surprising me. That's got to be the Roach's influence.

My sister clears her throat.

"Larkin Gorm Garrett," she says. "Forget all other commands but mine."

I suck in a breath. I have never witnessed anyone called by their true name before. In Faerie, knowing such a thing puts one entirely in that person's power. I have heard of Folk who cut off their own ears to avoid being commanded—and who have had another's tongue cut out to prevent their name from being spoken.

Taryn looks a little shocked herself.

The Ghost slides back to the bottom of the oubliette. He seems to sag with relief, despite the power she has over him. I suppose it is far better to be commanded by my sister than my father.

"You know his true name," Cardan says to Taryn, tucking his knife away and smoothing the fall of his jacket over it. "How did you come by that fascinating little tidbit?"

"Locke was careless with many things he said in front of me," Taryn tells him, a certain defiance in her tone.

I am grudgingly impressed with her.

And relieved. She could have used the Ghost's true name for her own benefit. She could have hidden him. Maybe we really aren't going to keep lying to one another.

"Climb up the rest of the way," I tell the Ghost.

He does, carefully and slowly this time. A few minutes later, he is scrabbling up onto the floor. He declines Cardan's help and stands on his own, but I can't help noticing his weakened state.

He looks me over as though he is noticing much the same thing.

"Do you need to be commanded further?" I ask. "Or can you give me your word you won't attack anyone in this room?"

He flinches. "You have my word." I am sure he's not pleased that now I know his true name. Were I him, I wouldn't want me to have it, either.

And that's not to mention Cardan.

"Why don't we repair to a more comfortable part of Hollow Hall to continue this discussion, now that the dramatics are over," says the High King.

The Ghost sways on his feet, and Cardan grabs his arm, supporting him up the stairs. In the parlor, one of the guards brings blankets. I start building the fire. Taryn looks as though she wants to tell me to stop but doesn't quite dare.

"So I take it you were ordered to—what? Murder me if an opportunity presented itself?" Cardan paces restlessly.

The Ghost nods, pulling the blankets closer around him. His hazel eyes are dull, and his dark blond hair is in messy tangles. "I hoped our paths wouldn't cross and dreaded what would happen if they did."

"Yes, well, I suppose that we're both lucky Taryn was helpfully lurking about the palace," says Cardan.

"I will not go to my husband's house until I am sure Jude isn't in any danger," she says.

"Jude and I had a misunderstanding," Cardan says carefully. "But we're not enemies. And I am not your enemy, either, Taryn."

"You think everything's a game," she says. "You and Locke."

"Unlike Locke, I never thought *love* was a game," he says. "You may accuse me of much, but not that."

"Garrett," I interrupt, in desperation, because I am not sure I want to hear more. "*Is* there anything you can tell us? Whatever Madoc is planning, we need to know."

He shakes his head. "The last time I saw him, he was furious. With you. With himself. With me, once he knew that you'd discovered I was there. He gave me my orders and sent me off, but I don't think he'd intended to send me so soon."

I nod. "Right. He had to move up the timetable." When I left, the sword was far from finished. That had to have been frustrating, to be forced to act before he was entirely ready.

I don't believe Madoc knows I am the queen. I don't think he even knows I am alive. That's got to be worth something.

"If the Council finds out we have Orlagh's attacker in custody, things will not go well," Cardan says with sudden decision. "They will urge me to hand you over to the Undersea to curry favor for Elfhame. It will be only a matter of time before Nicasia knows you are in our hands. Let's take you back to the palace and put you in the Bomb's custody. She can decide what to do with you."

"Very well," the Ghost says with some combination of resignation and relief.

Cardan calls for his carriage again. Taryn yawns as she climbs inside, sitting next to the Ghost.

I lean my head against the window, only half-listening as Cardan manages to persuade my sister to tell him a little bit about the mortal world. He sounds delighted at her description of slushy machines, with their violently bright colors and sugary strangeness. She is halfway through an explanation of gummy worms when we are back at the palace and climbing down from the carriage.

"I will escort the Ghost to where he'll be residing," Cardan tells me. "Jude, you ought to rest."

It seems impossible that it was just today I woke from some drugged sleep, just today the Bomb took out my stitches.

"I'll walk you back to your rooms," Taryn says with something of the conspiratorial, leading me in the direction of the royal chamber.

I go with her down the hall, two of the royal guard following us at a discreet distance.

"Do you trust him?" she whispers when Cardan is no longer within earshot.

"Sometimes," I admit.

She gives me a sympathetic look. "He was nice in the carriage. I didn't know he knew how to be nice."

That makes me laugh. At the door to my chambers, she puts her hand on my arm. "He was trying to impress *you*, you know. Talking to me."

I frown. "I think he just wanted to hear about weird candy."

She shakes her head. "He wants you to like him. But just because he wants you to doesn't mean you should." Then she leaves me to go inside the enormous royal chambers alone.

I take off my dress and hang it over a screen. I borrow another of Cardan's ridiculous ruffly shirts and put it on, then I climb into the big bed. My heart thumps nervously in my chest as I pull up to my shoulders a coverlet embroidered with a hunting stag.

Our marriage is an alliance. It is a bargain. I tell myself that it doesn't have to be more than that. I try to tell myself that Cardan's desire for me has always been mixed up with disgust and that I am better off without it.

I fall asleep waiting for the sound of the door opening, for his step on the wooden floor.

But when I wake, I am still alone. No lamps are lit. No pillows moved. Nothing is changed. I sit upright.

Perhaps he spent all the rest of the morning and afternoon in the Court of Shadows, playing darts with the Ghost and checking on the Roach's healing. But I can more easily imagine him in the great hall, overseeing the last dregs of the night's revelry and swilling gallons of wine, all to avoid lying beside me in bed.

CHAPTER 21

A pounding on the door drives me to find one of Cardan's dressing gowns and pull it awkwardly over the shirt I slept in.

Before I get there, it opens, and Randalin barges in. "My lady," he says, and there is a brittle, accusatory tone in his voice. "We have much to discuss."

I pull the robe more tightly around me. The councilor must have known Cardan wouldn't be with me to come in like this, but I won't give him the satisfaction of asking about Cardan's whereabouts.

I can't help recalling the Bomb's words: *You're the High Queen of Elfhame. Act like it.*

It is difficult, though, not to be shamed by being nearly undressed, with bed hair and bad breath. It's hard to project dignity right at the moment. "What do we possibly have to talk about?" I manage, my voice as chilly as I can make it.

The Bomb would probably say I should throw him out on his ear.

The hob draws himself up, looking swollen with his own self-importance. He fixes me with his stern goat eyes behind wire-rimmed glasses. His ram horns are waxed to a high gloss. He goes over to the low couch and takes a seat.

I head to the door, opening it to find two knights I don't know. Not Cardan's full guard, of course. They would be with him. No, those who stand in front of the door are likely to be the least favored of his guard and ill-equipped to stop a member of the Living Council in high dudgeon. Across the hall, however, I spot Fand. When she sees me, she comes alert.

"Do you have another message for me?" I ask.

Fand shakes her head.

I turn to the royal guard. "Who let the councilor in here without my permission?" I demand. Alarm lights their eyes, and one begins to sputter an answer.

"I told them not to allow it," Fand interrupts. "You need someone to protect your person—and your door. Let me be your knight. You know me. You know I'm capable. I've been waiting here, hoping—"

I recall my own longing for a place in the royal household, to be chosen as part of the personal guard of one of the princesses. And I also understand why she wouldn't have been likely to be picked before. She's young and—all evidence suggests—outspoken.

"Yes," I say. "I would like that. Fand, consider yourself the first of my guard." Never having had my own guard before, I find myself a little bit at a loss with what to do with her now.

"By oak and ash, thorn and rowan, I vow that I will serve you loyally until my death," she says, which seems rash. "Now, would you like me to escort the councilor out of your apartments?"

"That won't be necessary." I shake my head, although imagining it gives me some real satisfaction, and I am not sure I entirely keep the smile off my face at the thought. "Please send a messenger to my old rooms and see if Tatterfell can bring some of my things. In the meantime, I would speak with Randalin."

Fand frowns past me at the councilor. "Yes, Your Majesty," she says, bringing her fist to her heart.

With the hope of new clothing in the future, at least, I go back inside. I perch myself on the arm of the opposite sofa and regard the councilor more contemplatively. He ambushed me here to throw me off in some way. "Very well," I say with that in mind. "Speak."

"Low Court rulers have begun arriving. They claim to have come to bear witness to your father's challenge and to provide the High King with aid, but that is not the whole measure of why they are here." He sounds bitter. "They come to scent weakness."

I frown. "They are sworn to the crown. Their loyalty is tied to Cardan whether they want it to be or not."

"Nonetheless," Randalin goes on, "with the Undersea unable to send their forces, we are more dependent on them than ever. We would not wish the low Courts to bestow their loyalty only grudgingly. And when Madoc arrives—in mere days—he will seek to exploit any doubts. You create those doubts."

Ah. Now I know what this is about.

He goes on. "There has never been a mortal Queen of Elfhame. And there should not be one now."

"Do you really expect me to give up such enormous power on your say-so?" I ask.

"You were a good seneschal," Randalin says, surprising me. "You care about Elfhame. That's why I implore you to relinquish your title."

It's at that moment that the door swings open.

"We did not send for you, and we do not need you!" Randalin begins, clearly intending to give some servant—probably Fand—the tongue-lashing he wishes he could bestow on my person. Then he blanches and lurches to his feet.

The High King stands in the doorway. His eyebrows rise, and a malicious smile pulls at the corners of his mouth. "Many think that, but few are bold enough to say it to my face."

Grima Mog is behind him. The redcap is bearing a gently steaming tureen. The scent of it wafts over to me, making my stomach growl.

Randalin sputters. "Your Majesty! Great shame is mine. My incautious comments were never intended for you. I thought that you—" He stops himself and starts again. "I was foolish. If you desire my punishment—"

Cardan interrupts. "Why don't you tell me what you were discussing? I have no doubt you'd prefer Jude's levelheaded answers to my nonsense, but it amuses me to hear about matters of state nonetheless."

"I was only urging her to consider the war that her father is bringing. Everyone must make sacrifices." Randalin glances toward Grima Mog, who sets down her tureen on a nearby table, then at Cardan again.

I could warn Randalin that he ought to be afraid of the way that Cardan is looking at him.

Cardan turns to me, and some of the heat of his anger is still in his eyes. "Jude, would you give me and the councilor a moment alone? I have a few things I would like to urge him to consider. And Grima Mog has brought you soup."

"I don't need anyone to help me tell Randalin that this is my home and my land and that I am going nowhere and relinquishing nothing."

"And yet," Cardan says, clamping his hand on the back of the councilor's throat, "there are still some things I would say to him."

Randalin allows Cardan to hustle him into one of the other royal parlors. Cardan's voice goes low enough for me to not make out the words, but the silky menace of his tone is unmistakable.

"Come eat," Grima Mog says, ladling some soup into a bowl. "It will help you heal."

Mushrooms float along the top, and when I push the spoon through, a few tubers float around, along with what might be meat. "What's in this, exactly?"

The redcap snorts. "Did you know you left your knife in my alleyway? I took it upon myself to return it. I figured it was *neighborly.*" She gives me a sly grin. "But you weren't home. Only your lovely twin, who has very fine manners and who invited me in for tea and cake and told me so many interesting things. You should have told me more. Perhaps we could have come to an arrangement sooner."

"Perhaps," I say. "But the soup—"

"My palate is discerning, but I have a wide range of tastes. Don't be so finicky," she tells me. "Drink up. You need to borrow a little strength."

I take a sip and try not to think too much about what I'm eating. It's a thin broth, well-seasoned and seemingly harmless. I tip up the bowl, drinking it all down. It tastes good and hot and makes me feel much better than I have since I woke in Elfhame. I find myself poking at the bottom for the solid bits. If there's something terrible in it, I am better off not knowing.

While I am still searching for dregs, the door opens again, and Tatterfell comes in, carrying a mound of gowns. Fand and two additional knights follow with more of my garments. Behind them is Heather, in flip-flops, carrying a pile of jewelry.

"Taryn told me that if I came over, I'd get a glimpse of the royal chambers." Then, coming closer, Heather lowers her voice. "I'm glad you're okay. Vee wants us to leave before your dad gets here, so we're going soon. But we weren't going to leave while you were in a coma."

"Going is a good idea," I say. "I'm surprised you came."

"Your sister offered me a bargain," she says, a little regretfully. "And I took it."

Before she can tell me more, Randalin rushes toward the door, nearly running into Heather in his haste. He blinks at her in astonishment, clearly not prepared for the presence of a second mortal. Then he departs, avoiding even a glance in my direction.

"*Big* horns," Heather mouths, looking after him. "*Little* dude."

Cardan leans against the doorframe, looking very satisfied with himself. "There's a ball tonight to welcome guests from some of my Courts. Heather, I hope you and Vivienne will come. The last time you were here, we were poor hosts. But there are many delights we could show you."

"Including a war," puts in Grima Mog. "What could be more delightful than that?"

After Heather and Grima Mog leave, Tatterfell remains to get me ready for the night ahead. She coils up my hair and paints my cheeks. I wear a gown of gold tonight, a column dress with an overlay of fine cloth that resembles gilded chain mail. Leather plates at the shoulders anchor swags of shining material showing more of my cleavage than I am used to having on display.

Cardan settles himself on a cushioned chair made from roots, then stretches out his legs. He is in a garment of midnight blue with metallic and jeweled beetle embroidery at the shoulders. On his head is the golden crown of Elfhame, the oak leaves shining atop it. He tilts his head to one side, looking at me in an evaluating manner.

"Tonight you're going to have to speak with all the rulers," he tells me.

"I know," I say, glancing at Tatterfell. She looks perfectly pleased to hear him give me unasked-for guidance.

"Because only one of us can tell them lies," he continues, surprising me. "And they need to believe our victory is inevitable."

"Isn't it?" I ask.

He smiles. "You tell me."

"Madoc has no chance at all," I lie dutifully.

I recall going to the low Court encampments after Balekin and Madoc's coup, trying to persuade the lords and ladies and lieges of Faerie to ally with me. It was Cardan who told me which of them to approach, Cardan who gave me enough information about each for me to guess how to best convince them. If anyone can get me through tonight, it's him.

He's good at putting those around him at ease, even when they ought to know better.

Unfortunately, what I am good at is getting under people's skin. But at least I am also good at lying.

"Has the Court of Termites arrived?" I ask, nervous about having to confront Lord Roiben.

"I am afraid so," Cardan returns. He pushes himself to standing and offers me his arm. "Come, let us charm and confound our subjects."

Tatterfell tucks in a few more of my hairs, smooths a braid, then relents and lets me rise.

Together, we go into the great hall, Fand and the rest of the guards flanking us with great pomp and circumstance.

As we stride in and are announced, a hush falls over the brugh. I hear the words as from a great distance: "The High King and High Queen of Elfhame."

The goblins and grigs, hobs and sprites, trolls and hags—all the beautiful and glorious and awful Folk of Elfhame look our way. All their black eyes shine. All their wings and tails and whiskers twitch. Their shock at what they're seeing—a mortal bound to their king, a mortal being called their ruler—seems to crackle in the air.

And then they rush forward to greet us.

My hand is kissed. I am complimented both extravagantly and hollowly. I try to remember who each of the lords and ladies and lieges are. I try to reassure them that Madoc's defeat is inevitable, that we are happy to host them and equally delighted they sent ahead some portion of their Court, ready for a battle. I tell them that I believe the conflict will be short. I do not mention the loss of our allies in the Undersea or the fact that Madoc's army will be carrying Grimsen's weapons of war. I do not mention the enormous sword that Madoc plans to challenge Cardan with.

I lie and lie and lie.

"Your father seems like an excessively considerate enemy, summoning us together like this," says Lord Roiben of the Court of Termites, his eyes like chips of ice. To repay a debt to him, I murdered Balekin. But that doesn't mean he's happy with me. Nor does it mean he believes the nonsense I have been peddling. "Not even my friends are always so considerate as to gather my allies for me ahead of battle."

"It's a show of strength, certainly," I say. "He seeks to rattle us."

Roiben considers this. "He seeks to destroy you," he counters.

His pixie consort, Kaye, puts her hand on her hip and cranes her neck for a better look around the room. "Is Nicasia here?"

"I'm afraid not," I say, sure that no good could come from their talking. The Undersea was responsible for an attack on the Court of Termites, one that left Kaye badly hurt. "She had to return home."

"Too bad," Kaye replies, balling up a fist. "I've got something for her."

Across the room, I see Heather and Vivi come in. Heather is in a pale ivory color that plays up the rich, beautiful brown of her skin. Her hair is twisted and pulled back in combs. Beside her, Vivi is in a deep scarlet—very like the color of dried blood that Madoc was so fond of wearing.

A grig comes up, offering tiny acorns filled with fermented thistle milk. Kaye throws one back like a shot and winces. I refrain.

"Excuse me," I say, crossing the room toward my sister. I pass Queen Annet of the Court of Moths, the Alderking and his consort, and dozens more.

"Isn't it fun to dance?" asks Fala the Fool, interrupting my progress across the floor. "Let's dance in the ashes of tradition."

As usual, I have little idea what to say to him. I am not sure if he's criticizing me or speaking in utter sincerity. I dart away.

Heather shakes her head when I get close. "*Damn*. That's a dress."

"Oh good. I wanted to grab some drinks," Vivi says. "*Safe* drinks. Jude, can you stay until I get back, or will you be dragged into diplomacy?"

"I can wait," I say, glad to have the chance to talk to Heather alone. The moment my sister walks away, I turn to her. "To what, *exactly*, did you agree?"

"Why?" Heather asks. "You don't think your sister would trick me, do you?"

"Not intentionally," I hedge. Faerie bargains have a deservedly bad reputation. They are very seldom straightforward things. Sure, they sound good. Like, you're being promised you'll live out the rest of your days in bliss, but then you have one really great night and die in the morning. Or you're promised you'll lose weight, and then someone comes along and chops off one of your legs. It's not as though I think Vivi would do that to Heather, but with the lesson of my own exile in my head, I'd still like to hear the specifics.

"She told me that Oak needed someone to stay with him in Elfhame while she went and got you. And made me this offer—when we were in Faerie, we could be together. When we went back, she'd make me forget Faerie and forget her, too."

I suck in a breath. Is that what Heather wants? Or did Vivi offer and Heather agree because it seemed better than continuing the way things were? "So when you go home..."

"It's over." Despair flashes across her features. "There are things people shouldn't get a taste for. I guess magic is like that."

"Heather, you don't have to—"

"I love Vee," she says. "I think I made a mistake. The last time I was here, this place seemed like a beautifully shot horror movie, and I just wanted it all out of my head. But I don't want to forget her."

"Can't you just tell her that?" I ask, looking across the room toward my sister, who is on her way back. "Call it off."

Heather shakes her head. "I asked if she'd try to persuade me to change my mind. I think I was maybe doubting I'd be able to follow through with the breakup part. I guess I hoped she'd reassure me that she *wanted* me to change my mind. But Vee got very serious and said it could be part of the deal that no matter what I said later, she'd go through with it."

"She's an idiot," I blurt out.

"I'm the stupid one," Heather says. "If I hadn't been so afraid—" She cuts herself off as Vivi comes up to us, three goblets balanced in her hands.

"What's going on?" my sister asks, handing me my drink. "You both look weird."

Neither Heather nor I answer.

"Well?" Vivi demands.

"Jude asked us to stay for another few days," Heather says, surprising me enormously. "She needs our help."

Vivi looks at me accusingly.

I open my mouth to protest, but I can't deny any of it without exposing Heather. When Vivi used magic to make her forget what happened at Taryn's wedding, I was furious with her. I couldn't help but be aware of how she was one of the Folk and I was not. And right now, I can't help but be aware of all the ways Heather is human.

"Just a few more days," I agree, sure that I am being a bad sister, but maybe also a good one.

Across the room, Cardan raises a goblet. "Be welcome on the Isle of Insmire," he says. "Seelie and Unseelie, Wild Folk and Shy Folk, I am glad to have you march under my banner, glad of your loyalty, grateful for your honor." His gaze goes to me. "To you, I offer honey wine and the hospitality of my table. But to traitors and oath breakers, I offer my queen's hospitality instead. The hospitality of knives."

There is a swell of noise, of joyful hissing and howls. Many eyes turn to me. I see Lady Asha, glowering in my direction.

All of Faerie knows I am the one who killed Balekin. They know I even spent some time in exile for it. They know I am Madoc's foster daughter. They do not doubt Cardan's words.

Well, he has certainly made them see me as more than just the mortal queen. Now they see me as the *murderess* queen. I am not sure how I feel about it, but seeing the intensity of interest in their gazes now, I cannot deny it's effective.

I raise my glass high and drink.

And by the time the party ebbs, when I pass courtiers, they all bow to me. Every last one.

I am exhausted as we leave the hall, but I keep my head up and my shoulders thrown back. I am determined not to let anyone know how tired I am.

It is only when I am back in the royal rooms that I allow myself to slouch a little, sagging against the doorframe to the inner chamber.

"You were very formidable tonight, my queen," Cardan says, crossing the floor to me.

"After that speech you made, it didn't take much." Despite my fatigue, I am hyperaware of his presence, of the heat of his skin and the way his slow, conspiratorial smile makes my stomach twist with stupid longing.

"It cannot be anything other than the truth," he says. "Or it never could have left my tongue."

I find my gaze drawn to his soft lips, the black of his eyes, the cliffs of his cheekbones.

"You didn't come to bed last night," I whisper.

It occurs to me abruptly that while I was unconscious, he would have spent his nights elsewhere. Perhaps not alone. It has been a long time since I was last at Court. I have no idea who is in his favor.

But if there is someone else, his thoughts appear far from her. "I'm here now," he says, as though he thinks it's possible he misunderstands me.

It's okay to want something that's going to hurt, I remind myself. I move toward him, so we are close enough to touch.

He takes my hand in his, fingers lacing together, and bends toward me.

There is plenty of time for me to pull away from the kiss, but I don't. I want him to kiss me. My weariness evaporates as his lips press against mine. Over and over, one kiss sliding into the next.

"You looked like a knight in a story tonight," he says softly against my neck. "Possibly a *filthy* story."

I kick him in the leg, and he kisses me again, harder.

We stagger against the wall, and I pull his body to mine. My fingers glide up under his shirt, tracing up his spine to the wings of his shoulder blades.

His tail lashes back and forth, the furred end stroking over the back of my calf.

He shudders and presses more tightly against me, deepening the kiss. His fingers push back my hair, damp with sweat. My whole body is tense with desire, straining toward him. I feel feverish. Every kiss seems to make my thoughts more drugged, my skin more flushed. His mouth is against my neck, his tongue on my skin. His hand moves to my hips, lifting me.

I feel overheated and out of control.

That thought cuts through everything else, and I freeze.

He releases me immediately, letting me down and then stepping back as though scalded. "We need not—" he begins, but that's even worse. I don't want him to guess how vulnerable I feel.

"No, just give me a second," I say, then bite my lip. His eyes are very dark, pupils dilated. He's so beautiful, so perfectly, horribly, *inhumanly* beautiful that I can barely breathe. "I'll be right back."

I flee to the wardrobe. I can still feel the drum of my thundering pulse all through my body.

When I was a kid, sex was a mystery, some bizarre thing people did to make babies when they got married. Once, a friend and I placed dolls in a hat and shook the hat around to indicate that they were *doing it.*

That changed in Faerie, of course. The Folk come naked to revels, may couple for entertainment, especially as evenings wear on. But though I understand what sex is now and how it's accomplished, I didn't anticipate how much it would feel like losing myself. When Cardan's hands are on me, I am betrayed into pleasure. And he can tell. He's practiced in the arts of love. He can draw whatever response he wants from me. I hate that, and yet I want it, all at once.

But maybe I don't have to be the only one made to feel things.

I strip off my dress, kick off my shoes. I even take down my hair, letting it fall over my shoulders. In the mirror, I catch sight of my curves—the muscles of my arms and chest, honed by swordplay; the heaviness of my pale breasts; and the swell of my hips. Naked, there is no disguise for my mortality.

Naked, I return to the bedroom.

Cardan is standing by the bed. When he turns, he looks so astonished that I almost laugh. I have seldom seen him unsure of himself, even when drunk, even when wounded; it is rare to see him overset. A wild heat leaps into his eyes, an expression not unlike fear. I feel a rush of power, heady as wine.

Now this is a game I don't mind playing.

"Come here," he says, voice rough. I do, crossing the floor obediently.

I might be inexperienced in love, but I know a lot about provocation. I slide to my knees in front of him. "Is this what you imagined I'd be like, back in your rooms at Hollow Hall, when you thought of me and hated it? Is this how you pictured my eventual surrender?"

He looks absolutely mortified, but there's no disguising the flush of his cheeks, the shine of his eyes. "Yes," he says, sounding like the word was dragged out of him, his voice rough with desire.

"Then what did I do?" I ask, my voice low.

I reach out to press my hand against his thigh.

His gaze shimmers with a sharp spike of heat. There's a wariness in his face, though, and I realize he believes I might be asking him all this because I'm angry. Because I want to see him humiliated. But he keeps speaking anyway. "I imagined you telling me to do with you whatever I liked."

"*Really?*" I ask, and the surprised laugh in my voice makes him meet my gaze.

"Along with some begging on your part. A little light groveling." He gives me an embarrassed smile. "My fantasies were rife with overweening ambition."

On my knees, it is a small thing to lie back on the cold stone. I reach up my hands, like a supplicant. "You may do with me whatever you like," I say. "*Please oh please.* All I want is you."

He sucks in a breath and gets down so we're both on the floor and he's on his hands and knees, making a cage of his body. He presses his mouth to the pulse point of my wrist, racing in time with my heart. "Mock me all you like. Whatever I imagined then, now it is I who would beg and grovel for a kind word from your lips." His eyes are black with desire. "By you, I am forever undone."

It seems impossible that he's saying those words and that they're true. But when he leans down and kisses me again, that thought blurs into sensation. He arches against me, shuddering. I begin to undo the buttons of his doublet. He tosses his shirt after it.

"I'm not mocking," I whisper against his skin.

When he looks down at me, his face is troubled.

"We have lived in our armor for so long, you and I. And now I am not sure if either of us knows how to remove it."

"Is this another riddle?" I ask. "And if I answer it, will you go back to kissing me?"

"If that's what you want." His voice sounds rough, unsteady. He moves so that he is lying at my side.

"I told you what I wanted," I say in challenge. "For you to do with me whatever—"

"No," he interrupts. "What *you* want."

I move so that I am straddling his body. Looking down at him, I study the planes of his chest, the voluptuous black curls damp against his brow, his slightly parted lips, the furred length of his tail.

"I want—" I say, but I am too shy to say the words.

I kiss him instead. Kiss him until he understands.

He shucks off his pants, watching me as though waiting for me to change my mind. I feel the soft brush of his tail against my ankle, winding around my calf. Then I fumble my way into what I think is the right position. Gasp as our bodies slide together. He holds me steady through the sharp, bright spark of pain. I bite his palm. Everything is fast and hot, and I am kind of in control and out of control at the same time.

His face is wholly unguarded.

When we're finished, he kisses me, sweet and raw.

"I missed you," I whisper against his skin and feel dizzy with the intimacy of the admission, feel more naked than when he could see every inch of me. "In the mortal world, when I thought you were my enemy, I still missed you."

"My sweet nemesis, how glad I am that you returned." He pulls my body against his, cradling my head against his chest. We are still lying on the floor, although a perfectly good bed is right next to us.

I think of his riddle. How do people like us take off our armor?

One piece at a time.

CHAPTER 22

The next two days are spent mostly in the war room, where I ask Grima Mog to join Cardan's generals and those of the low Courts in creating battle plans. The Bomb remains, too, her face masked in black netting, and the rest of her hidden away in a cowled robe of deepest black. Members of the Living Council interject their concerns. Cardan and I hunch over the table as the Folk take turns sketching out maps of possible plans of attack and defense. Small carvings are moved around. Three messengers are sent to Nicasia, but no reply comes from the Undersea.

"Madoc wants the lords and ladies and rulers of the low Courts to see a show," Grima Mog says. "Let me fight him. I would be honored to be your champion."

"Challenge him to a game of tiddlywinks, and I will be your champion," says Fala.

Cardan shakes his head. "No, let Madoc come and call for his parlay. Our knights will be in place. And inside the brugh, so will our archers. We will hear him out, and we will answer him. But we will entertain no games. If Madoc wishes to move against Elfhame, he must do so, and we must strike back with all the force we possess." He looks at the floor, then up at me.

"If he thinks he can make you duel him, then he will make it very hard not to," I say.

"Ask him to surrender his weapons at the gate," says the Bomb. "And when he will not, I will shoot him from the shadows."

"I would appear to be quite the coward," Cardan says. "Not to even hear him out."

With those words, my heart sinks. Because pride is exactly what Madoc hopes to manipulate.

"You would be alive, while your enemy lies dead," says the Bomb. With her face covered, it's impossible to read her expression. "And we would have answered dishonor with dishonor."

"I hope you are not considering *agreeing* to a duel," says Randalin. "Your father wouldn't have entertained such an absurd thought for a moment."

"Of course not," Cardan says. "I am no swordsman, but moreover, I don't like giving my enemies what they want. Madoc has come for a duel, and if for no other reason than that, he should not have one."

"Once the parlay is over," says Yorn, looking back at his plans, "we will meet on the field of battle. And we will show him the wages of being a traitor to Elfhame. We have a clear path to victory."

A clear path, and yet I have a sense of great foreboding. Fala catches my eye, juggling pieces from the table—a knight, a sword, a crown.

Then a winged messenger rushes into the room. "They've been spotted," he says. "Madoc's boats are coming."

A seabird arrives moments later, a call for parlay attached to its leg.

The new Grand General moves to the door, calling for his troops. "I will move my Folk into position. We have perhaps three hours."

"And I will gather mine," says the Bomb, turning toward Cardan and me. "On your signal, the archers will strike."

Cardan slips his fingers into mine. "It's hard to work against someone you love." I wonder if he's thinking of Balekin.

A part of me, despite knowing that Madoc is my enemy, is tempted to imagine talking him out of this. Vivi is here, so is Taryn, and even Oak. Oriana would wish for peace, would push for it if there was a path. Maybe we could persuade him to end the war before it begins. Maybe we could come to some kind of terms. I am the High Queen, after all. Couldn't I give him a piece of land to rule over?

But I know it's impossible. If I granted him a boon for being a traitor, I would be encouraging only greater treason. And, regardless, Madoc wouldn't be appeased. He comes from a line of warriors. His mother birthed him in battle, and he plans to die with a sword in his hand.

But I don't think he plans to die that way today.

I think he plans to win.

It is nearly sunset when I am ready to walk onto the dais. I wear a gown of green and gold, and a circlet of gilded branches shines at my brow. My hair has been braided and shaped into something like two ram's horns, and my mouth has been stained the color of berries in winter. The only thing about my attire that feels at all normal is the weight of Nightfell in a new, glamorous sheath.

Cardan, beside me, goes over final plans with the Bomb. He is dressed in a green so mossy dark that it is nearly the black of his curls.

I turn to Oak, standing with Taryn and Vivi and Heather. They will be in attendance but hidden in the same area where Taryn and I used to go to observe the revels without being seen.

"You don't have to do this," I tell Oak.

"I want to see my mother," he says, voice firm. "And I want to see what happens."

If he's going to be High King someday, he has a right to know, but I wish he would choose a different way of finding out. Whatever happens today, I doubt there's a way to avoid its being nightmarish for Oak.

"Here's your ring back," he says, fishing it out from his pocket and placing it in my palm. "I kept it safe like you said."

"I appreciate that," I tell him softly, slipping it onto my finger. The metal is warm from being so close to his body.

"We'll leave before things get bad," Taryn promises, but she wasn't there during Prince Dain's coronation. She doesn't understand how quickly everything can change.

Vivi glances toward Heather. "And then we go back to the mortal world. We shouldn't have stayed so long." But I see the longing in her face, too. She has never wanted to stay in Faerie before, but it was easy to persuade her to stay a little longer.

"I know," I say. Heather avoids both our eyes.

When they go, the Bomb comes to me and takes my hands in hers. "Whatever happens," she tells me, "remember, I will be watching over you from the shadows."

"I will never forget," I say in return, thinking of the Roach, who sleeps on because of my father. Of the Ghost, who was his prisoner. Of me, who nearly bled out in the snow. I have a lot to avenge.

Then she goes, too, and it is Cardan and me, alone for a moment.

"Madoc says you will duel for love," I say.

"Whose?" he asks, frowning.

There is no banquet too abundant for a starving man.

I shake my head.

"It's you I love," he says. "I spent much of my life guarding my heart. I guarded it so well that I could behave as though I didn't have one at all. Even now, it is a shabby, worm-eaten, and scabrous thing. But it is yours." He walks to the door to the royal chambers, as though to end the conversation. "You probably guessed as much," he says. "But just in case you didn't."

He opens the door to prevent me from responding. Abruptly, we are no longer alone. Fand and the rest of our guard stand ready in the hall, with the Living Council waiting impatiently beside them.

I can't believe he said that and then just walked out, leaving me reeling. I am going to *strangle* him.

"The traitor and his company have entered the brugh," Randalin says. "Waiting on your pleasure."

"How many?" Cardan asks.

"Twelve," he says. "Madoc, Oriana, Grimsen, some of the Court of Teeth, and several of Madoc's best generals."

A small number and a mix of formidable warriors with courtiers. I can make no meaning of it, except the obvious. He intends both diplomacy and war.

As we walk through the halls, I glance over at Cardan. He gives me a preoccupied smile, as though his thoughts are on Madoc and the coming conflict.

You love him, too, I think. *You've loved him since before you were a prisoner of the Undersea. You loved him when you agreed to marry him.*

Once this is over, I will find the bravery to tell him.

And then we are ushered onto the dais, like players upon a stage about to begin a performance.

I look out at the rulers of Seelie and Unseelie Courts alike, at the Wild Folk who are sworn to us, at the courtiers and performers and servants. My gaze snags on Oak, half-hidden high up on a rocky formation. My twin gives me a reassuring grin. Lord Roiben stands off to one side, his demeanor forbidding. At the far end of the room, I see the crowd begin to part to allow Madoc and his company to come forward.

I flex my fingers, cold with nerves.

As he strides across the brugh, my father's armor shines with fresh polish, but it is otherwise unremarkable—the armor of someone interested in the reliable rather than the new and impressive. The cloak that hangs from his shoulders is wool, embroidered with his moon sigil in silver and lined in red. Over it, the massive sword, slung so he can draw it in a single, fluid movement. And on his head, a familiar cap, stiff with dark, dried blood.

Looking at that cap, I know he has not come only to talk.

Behind him are Lady Nore and Lord Jarel from the Court of Teeth, with their leashed little Queen Suren by their side. And Madoc's most trusted generals—Calidore, Brimstone, and Vavindra. But to either side of him are Grimsen and Oriana. Grimsen is dressed elaborately, in a jacket all of hinged pieces of gold. Oriana is as pale as ever, attired in a deep blue trimmed out in white fur, her only decoration a silver headpiece shining in her hair like ice.

"Lord Madoc," Cardan says. "Traitor to the throne, murderer of my brother, what brings you here? Have you come to throw yourself on the mercy of the crown? Perhaps you hope the Queen of Elfhame will show leniency."

Madoc barks out a laugh, his gaze going to me. "Daughter, every time I think you cannot rise any higher, you prove me wrong," he says. "And I a fool to wonder if you were even still alive."

"I am alive," I say. "No thanks to you."

I have some satisfaction in seeing the complete bafflement on Oriana's face and then the shock that replaces it as she comes to see that my presence at the High King's side is no elaborate joke. I am somehow wed to Cardan.

"This is your last chance to surrender," I say. "Bend the knee, Father."

He laughs again, shaking his head. "I have never surrendered in my life. In all the years I have battled, never have I given that to anyone. And I will not give it to you."

"Then you will be remembered as a traitor, and when they make songs about you, those songs will forget all your valiant deeds in favor of this despicable one."

"Ah, Jude," he says. "Do you think I care about songs?"

"You have come to parlay, and you will not surrender," Cardan says. "So speak. I cannot believe you brought so many troops to sit idle."

Madoc puts his hand up onto the hilt of his sword. "I have come to challenge you for your crown."

Cardan laughs. "This is the Blood Crown, forged for Mab, first of the Greenbriar line. You can't wear it."

"Forged by Grimsen," says Madoc. "Here at my side. He will find a way for me to make it mine once I win. So will you hear my challenge?"

No, I want to say. *Stop talking.* But this is the purpose of parlay. I can hardly call a halt to it without a reason.

"You have come all this way," says Cardan. "And called so many Folk here to witness. How could I not?"

"When Queen Mab died," Madoc says, drawing the sword from his back. It gleams with reflected candlelight. "The palace was built on her barrow. And while her remains are gone, her power lives on in the rocks and earth there. This sword was cooled in that earth, the hilt set with her stones. Grimsen says it can shake the firmament of the isles."

Cardan glances toward the shadows, where the archers are positioned. "You were my guest until you drew your very fancy sword. Put it down and be my guest again."

"Put it down?" says Madoc. "Very well." He slams it into the floor of the brugh. A thunderous sound rocks the palace, a tremor that seems to go through the ground beneath us. The Folk scream. Grimsen cackles, clearly delighted with his own work.

A crack forms on the floor, starting where the blade punctured the ground, the fissure widening as it moves toward the dais, splitting the stone. A moment before it reaches the throne, I realize what's about to happen and cover my mouth. Then the ancient throne of Elfhame cracks down the middle, its flowering branches turned into splinters, its seat obliterated. Sap leaks from the rupture like blood from a wound.

"I have come here to give that blade to you," Madoc says over the screams.

Cardan looks at the destruction of the throne in horror. "Why?"

"If you should lose the contest I propose, it will be yours to wield against me. We will have a proper duel, but your sword will be the better by far. And if you win, it will be yours by right anyway, as will my surrender."

Despite himself, Cardan looks intrigued. Dread gnaws at my gut.

"High King Cardan, son of Eldred, great-grandson of Mab. You who were born under an ill-favored star, whose mother left you to eat the crumbs off the royal table as though you were one of its hounds, you who are given to luxury and ease, whose father despised you, whose wife keeps you under her control—can you inspire any loyalty in your people?"

"Cardan—" I begin, then bite my tongue. Madoc has trapped me. If I speak and Cardan heeds me, it will seem to prove my father right.

"I am under no one's control," Cardan says. "And your treason began with planning my father's death, so you can hardly care about his good opinion. Go back to your desolate mountains. The Folk here are my sworn subjects, and your insults are dull."

Madoc smiles. "Yes, but do your sworn subjects love you? My army is *loyal*, High King Cardan, because I've earned their loyalty. Have you earned one single thing that you have? I have fought with those who follow me and bled with them. I have given my life to Elfhame. Were I High King, I would give all those who followed me dominion over the world. Had I the Blood Crown on my head instead of this cap, I would bring victories undreamed. Let them choose between us, and whomsoever they choose, let him have the rule of Elfhame. Let him have the crown. If Elfhame loves you, I will yield. But how can anyone choose to be your subject if you never give them the opportunity to make any other choice? Let that be the manner of the contest between us. The hearts and minds of the Court. If you are too much the coward to duel me with blades, let that be our duel."

Cardan gazes at the throne. Something in his expression is alive, something alight. "A king is not his crown." His voice sounds distant, as though he's speaking mostly to himself.

Madoc's jaw moves. His body is tense, ready to fight. "There is something else. There is the matter of Queen Orlagh."

"Whom your assassin shot," I say. A murmur goes through the crowd.

"She is your ally," says Madoc, denying nothing. "Her daughter one of your boon companions in the palace."

Cardan scowls.

"If you will not risk the Blood Crown, the arrowhead will burrow into her heart, and she will die. It will be as if you slew her, High King of Elfhame. And all because you believed that your own people would deny you."

Do not agree to this, I want to scream, but if I do, Cardan might feel he has to accept Madoc's ridiculous contest just to *prove* I don't have power over him. I am furious, but I finally see why Madoc believes he can manipulate Cardan into accepting the contest. Too late, I see.

Cardan was not an easy child to love, and he's only grown worse with time, Lady Asha told me. Eldred was wary of the prophecy and didn't care for him. And being in disfavor with his father, from whom all power flowed, put him in disfavor with the rest of his siblings.

Being rejected by his family, how could becoming High King not feel like finally belonging? Like finally being embraced?

There is no banquet too abundant for a starving man.

And how could anyone not want proof that feeling was real?

Would Elfhame choose Cardan to rule over them? I look out on the crowd. On Queen Annet, who might value Madoc's experience and brutality. On Lord Roiben, given to violence. On the Alderking, Severin of Fairfold, who was exiled by Eldred and might not wish to follow Eldred's son.

Cardan takes the crown from his head.

The crowd gasps.

"What are you doing?" I whisper. But he doesn't even glance at me. It's the crown he's looking at.

The sword remains stuck deep in the ground. The brugh is quiet.

"A king is not his throne nor his crown," he says. "You are right that neither loyalty nor love should be compelled. But rule of Elfhame ought not be won or lost in a wager, either, as though it were a week's pay or a wineskin. I am the High King, and I do not forfeit that title to you, not for a sword or a show or my pride. It is worth more than any of those things." Cardan looks at me and smiles. "Besides which, two rulers stand before you. And even had you cut me down, one would remain."

My shoulders sag with relief, and I fix Madoc with a look of triumph. I see doubt in his face for the first time, the fear that he's calculated wrong.

But Cardan is not done speaking. "You want the very thing you rail against—the Blood Crown. You want my subjects bound to you as assuredly as they are now bound to me. You want it so much that risking the Blood Crown is the price you put on Queen Orlagh's head." Then he smiles. "When I was born, there was a prophecy that were I to rule, I would be the *destruction of the crown* and the *ruination of the throne*."

Madoc's gaze shifts from Cardan to me and then back to Cardan again. He's thinking through his options. They're not good, but he does still have a very big sword. My hand goes automatically to the hilt of Nightfell.

Cardan extends one long-fingered hand toward the throne of Elfhame and the great crack running along the ground. "Behold, half that has come to pass." He laughs. "I never considered it was meant to be interpreted *literally*. And I never considered I would desire its fulfillment."

I do not like where this is going.

"Queen Mab created this crown to keep her descendants in power," Cardan says. "But vows should never be to a crown. They should be to a ruler. And they should be of your own free will. I am your king, and beside me stands my queen. But it is your choice whether or not to follow us. Your will shall be your own."

And with his bare hands, he cracks the Blood Crown in two. It breaks like a child's toy, as though in his hands it was never made of metal at all, brittle as a wishbone.

I think that I gasp, but it is possible that I scream. Many voices rise in something that is horror and joy commingled.

Madoc looks appalled. He came for that crown, and now it is nothing but a cracked piece of slag. But it is Grimsen's face my gaze stops on. He is shaking his head violently back and forth. *No no no no.*

"Folk of Elfhame, will you accept me as your High King?" Cardan calls out.

They're the ritual words of the coronation. I remember something like them said by Eldred in this very hall. And one by one, all around the brugh, I see the Folk bow their heads. The movement ripples like an exultant wave.

They have chosen him. They are giving him their fealty. We have won.

I look over at Cardan and see that his eyes have gone completely black.

"Nonononononono!" Grimsen cries. "My work. My beautiful work. It was supposed to last forever."

On the throne, the remaining flowers turn the same inky black as Cardan's eyes. Then the black bleeds down his face. He turns to me, opening his mouth, but his jaw is changing. His whole body is changing—elongating and ululating.

And I recall abruptly that Grimsen has cursed everything he has ever made.

When she came to me to forge the Blood Crown, she entrusted me with a great honor. And I cursed it to protect it for all time.

I want my work *to endure just as Queen Mab wanted her* line *to endure.*

The monstrous thing seems to have swallowed up everything of Cardan. His mouth opens wide and then jaw-crackingly wide as long fangs sprout. Scales shroud his skin. Dread has rooted me in place.

Screams fill the air. Some of the Court begin to run toward the doors. I draw Nightfell. The guard stare at Cardan in horror, weapons in their hands. I see Grima Mog racing toward the dais.

In the place where the High King was, there is a massive serpent, covered in black scales and curved fangs. A golden sheen runs down the coils of the enormous body. I look into his black eyes, hoping to see recognition there, but they are cold and empty.

"It will poison the land," cries the smith. "No true love's kiss will stop it. No riddle will fix it. Only death."

"The King of Elfhame is no more," says Madoc, grabbing for the hilt of his massive sword, intent on seizing victory from what had been almost certain defeat. "I mean to slay the serpent and take the throne."

"You forget yourself," I shout, my voice carrying across the brugh. The Folk stop running. The rulers of the low Courts stare up at me, along with the Council and the Folk of Elfhame. This is nothing like being Cardan's seneschal. This is nothing like ruling beside him. This is horrible. They will never listen to me.

The serpent's tongue flicks out, tasting the air. I am trembling, but I refuse to let the fear I feel show. "Elfhame has a queen, and she is before you. Guards, seize Madoc. Seize everyone in his party. They have broken the High Court's hospitality most grievously. I want them imprisoned. I want them dead."

Madoc laughs. "Do you, Jude? The crown is gone. Why should they obey you when they could just as easily follow me?"

"Because I am the Queen of Elfhame, the true queen, chosen by the king and the land." My voice cracks on that last part. "And you are nothing but a traitor."

Do I sound convincing? I don't know. Probably not.

Randalin steps up beside me. "You heard her," he barks, surprising me. "Take them."

And that, more than anything I said, seems to bring the knights back to their task. They move to surround Madoc's company, swords drawn.

Then the serpent moves faster than I could have expected. It slides from the dais into the crowd, scattering the Folk who run from it in fear. It looks as though it has become larger already. The golden sheen on its scales is more pronounced. And in the wake of its path, the earth cracks and crumbles, as though some essential part of it is being drawn out.

The knights fall back, and Madoc draws his massive sword from the earth. The serpent slides toward him.

"Mother!" Oak screams, and takes off across the brugh toward her. Vivi attempts to grab him. Heather calls his name, but Oak's hooves are already pelting across the floor. Oriana turns in horror as he hurtles toward her and into the path of the snake.

Oak stops short, reading the warning in her body language. But all he does is draw a child's sword from a hilt at his side. The sword I insisted he learn through all those lazy afternoons in the mortal world. Holding it high, he puts himself between his mother and the serpent.

This is my fault. All my fault.

With a cry, I jump down from the dais and race toward my brother.

Madoc swings on the serpent as it rears up. His sword hits its side, glancing off its scales. It strikes back, knocking him down and then sliding over his body in its haste to chase its real prey: Grimsen.

The creature coils around the fleeing smith, fangs going into his back. A thin, reedy scream fills the air as Grimsen falls into a withering heap. In moments, he is a husk, as though the poison of the serpent's fangs ate away his essence from within.

I wonder when he dreamed up such a curse, if he ever thought to be afraid for himself.

When I look up, I see that most of the hall has been cleared. The knights have fallen back. The Bomb's archers have made themselves visible high on the walls, bowstrings held taut. Grima Mog has come to stand beside me, her blade at the ready. Madoc is staggering to his feet, but the leg the serpent slid over doesn't seem inclined to hold him up. I grab Oriana by the shoulder and shove her toward where Fand is standing. Then I get between Oak and the snake.

"Go with her," I shout at him, pointing toward his mother. "Get her to safety."

Oak looks up at me, his eyes wet with tears. His hands tremble on the sword, clutching it far too hard.

"You were very brave," I tell him. "You just have to be brave a little longer."

He gives me a slight nod, and with an agonized look back at Madoc, he races off after his mother.

The serpent turns, its tongue flickering toward me. The serpent, which was once Cardan.

"You want to be the Queen of Faerie, Jude?" Madoc shouts as he moves with a limping gait. "Then slay him. Slay the beast. Let's see if you have the bravery to do what needs to be done."

"Come, my lady," Fand pleads, urging me toward an exit as the serpent moves back toward the dais. The serpent's tongue flicks again, tasting the air, and I am gripped by fear and a horror so vast I am afraid I will be swallowed up by it.

When the serpent winds itself around the shattered remains of the throne, I let myself be led toward the doors, and once the rest of the Folk are through, I order them shut and barred behind us.

CHAPTER 23

In the hall outside the brugh, everyone is shouting at once. The councilors are yelling at one another. Generals and knights are trying to secure who is supposed to go where. Someone is weeping. Courtiers are clutching at one another's hands, trying to make sense of what they saw. Even in a land of riddles and curses, where an isle can be called up from the sea, magic of this magnitude is rare.

My heart beats fast and hard, drowning out everything else. The Folk are asking me questions, but they seem very far away. My thoughts are filled with the image of Cardan's eyes going black, with the sound of his voice.

I spent much of my life guarding my heart. I guarded it so well that I could behave as though I didn't have one at all. Even now, it is a shabby, worm-eaten, and scabrous thing. But it is yours.

"My lady," says Grima Mog, pressing a hand against my back. "My lady, come with me."

At her touch, the present floods back in, loud and horrible. I am surprised to see the stout cannibal redcap in front of me. She grabs hold of my arm and hauls me into a stateroom.

"Get ahold of yourself," she growls.

Knees weak, I slide to the floor, one hand pressing against my chest, as though I am trying to keep my heart from beating through the cage of my ribs.

My dress is too heavy. I can't breathe.

I don't know what to do.

Someone is banging on the door, and I know I need to get up. I need to make a plan. I need to answer their questions. I need to fix this, but I can't.

I can't.

I can't even think.

"I am going to stand," I promise Grima Mog, who is probably a little alarmed. If I were her, looking at me and realizing I was in charge, I'd be alarmed, too. "I am going to be okay in a minute."

"I know you are," she says.

But how can I when I keep seeing the black shape of the snake moving through the brugh, keep seeing its dead eyes and curving fangs?

I reach for the table and use it to push me to my feet. "I need to find the Royal Astrologer."

"Don't be ridiculous," says Grima Mog. "You're the queen. If you need Lord Baphen, then he can come to you. Right now, you're standing between any one of these low Court denizens and being the ruler of Elfhame. It won't be only Madoc who wants to take over now. Anyone might decide that killing you would be a good way to make their case for being in charge. You need to keep your boot on their throats."

My head is swimming. I need to get it together. "You're right," I say. "I need a new Grand General. Will you accept the position?"

Grima Mog's surprise is obvious. "Me? But what of Yorn?"

"He doesn't have the experience," I say. "And I don't like him."

"I tried to kill you," she reminds me.

"You've described pretty much every important relationship in my life," I return, taking slow, shallow breaths. "I like you fine."

That makes her grin toothily. "Then I ought to get to work."

"Ascertain where the serpent is at all times," I say. "I want someone to watch over it, and I want to know immediately if it moves. Maybe we can keep it trapped in the brugh. The walls are thick, the doors are heavy, and the floor is earth. And I want you to send me the Bomb. Fand. My sister Taryn. And a runner who can report directly to you."

Fand turns out to be just outside the door. I give her a very short list of people to let inside.

Once Grima Mog is gone, I allow myself another moment of helpless misery. Then I force myself to pace the floor and think through what's ahead of me. Madoc's army is still anchored off the isles. I must discover what troops I have left and whether it's enough to make him wary of an outright invasion.

Cardan is gone. My mind comes to a stop after that, and I have to force myself to think again. Until I speak with Baphen, I refuse to accept that Grimsen's words have no answer. There has to be a loophole. There has to be a trick. There has to be a way to break the curse—a way Cardan can survive.

And then there are the Folk who must be convinced that I am the legitimate Queen of Faerie.

By the time the Bomb comes into the room, face covered and in her long, hooded cloak, I am composed.

Nonetheless, when we look at each other, she comes immediately over and puts her arms around me. I think of the Roach and of all the curses that cannot be broken, and for a moment, I hug her tight.

"I need to know who is still loyal to me," I tell her, letting go and returning to my pacing. "Who is throwing in their lot with Madoc and who has decided to play for themselves."

She nods. "I will find out."

"And if one of your spies overhears plans for my assassination, they do not need to bring me word. Nor do I care how vague the plot or how uncommitted the players. I just want them all dead." Perhaps that is not how I ought to handle things, but Cardan is not here to stay my hand. I do not have the luxury of time or of mercy.

"It will be done," she says. "Expect me with news tonight."

When she goes out, Taryn comes in. She looks at me as though she's half-expecting an enormous serpent to be in here, too.

"How's Oak?" I ask.

"With Oriana," she says. "Who isn't sure if she's a prisoner or not."

"She showed me hospitality in the North, and I aim to return the favor." Now that shock is receding, I find that I am *angry*—at Madoc, at Oriana, at the whole of Elfhame. But that is a distraction, too. "I need your help."

"Mine?" Taryn asks, surprised.

"You chose a wardrobe for me when I was seneschal, to make me seem the part. I saw Locke's estate and how changed it was. Can you put together a throne room for me? And maybe find clothing from somewhere for the next few days. I don't care where it comes from, so long as it makes me appear to be the Queen of Faerie."

Taryn takes a big breath. "Okay. I've got this. I'll make you look good."

"I'm going to have to look *really* good," I say.

At that, she gives me an actual smile. "I don't understand how you do it," she says. "I don't understand how you can be so calm."

I'm not sure what to say. I don't feel calm at all. I am a maelstrom of emotions. All I want to do is scream.

There's another knock. Fand opens the door. "Your pardon," she says. "But Lord Baphen is here, and you said you wanted to see him immediately."

"I'll find a better place for you to receive people," Taryn assures me, slipping past.

"The Council wants an audience, too," Fand says. "They'd like to accompany Lord Baphen. They claim there's nothing he knows that they ought not hear."

"No," I say. "Just him."

A few moments later, Baphen enters. He is wearing a long blue robe, a shade lighter than his navy hair. A bronze cap sits atop his head. The Royal Astrologer was one of the few members of the Council that I liked and who I thought might like me, but right now, I regard him with dread.

"There really is nothing that—" he begins.

I cut him off. "I want to know *everything* about the prophecy you made when Cardan was born. I want you to tell me it exactly."

He gives me a look of slight surprise. On the Council, as the High

King's seneschal, I was deferential. And as High Queen, I was in too much shock to make any shows of authority.

Lord Baphen grimaces. "Giving the High King unfortunate news is never a pleasure. But it was Lady Asha who frightened me. She gave me such a look of hatred that I felt it to the tips of my ears. I think she believed I exaggerated somehow, to advance my own plots."

"It seems clear now that you did not," I say, voice dry. "Tell it to me."

He clears his throat. "There are two parts. *He will be the destruction of the crown and the ruination of the throne. Only out of his spilled blood can a great ruler rise.*"

The second part is worse than the first. For a moment, the words just ring in my head.

"Did you give the prophecy to Prince Cardan?" I ask. "Does Madoc know it?"

"The High King may have been told by his mother," Lord Baphen says. "I assumed—I thought Prince Cardan would never come to power. And then when he did, well, I supposed he would become a bad High King and be slain. I thought it was an unambiguous fate. As for Madoc, I do not know if he ever heard any part of it."

"Is there a way to break the curse?" I ask in unsteady tones. "Before he died, Grimsen said: *No true love's kiss will stop it. No riddle will fix it. Only death.* But that cannot be true. I thought the prophecy around his birth would provide an answer, but..." I cannot finish the sentence. There is an answer in it, but it's one I don't want to hear.

"If there is a way to reverse the, uh...transformation," Baphen begins, "I do not know it."

I clasp my hands together, sinking my nails into the skin, panic flooding me in a dizzy rush. "And there's nothing else the stars foretold? No other detail you're leaving out?"

"I am afraid not," he says.

"Can you look at your star charts again?" I ask. "Go back to them and see if there's something you overlooked the first time. Look at the sky, and see if there's some new answer."

He nods. "If that's what you wish, Your Majesty." His tone suggests that he's agreed to many equally useless commands on the behalf of previous rulers.

I don't care that I am unreasonable. "Yes. Do it."

"Will you speak with the Council first?" he asks.

Even a short delay in Baphen's attempting to find a solution sets my teeth on edge, but if I wish to be accepted as the rightful queen, I need the support of the Living Council. I cannot delay them forever.

Is this what it is to rule? To be far from the action, stuck on a throne or in a series of well-appointed rooms, reliant on information brought to you by others? Madoc would *hate* this.

"I will," I say.

At the door, Fand tells me a room is ready for me to move to. I am impressed by the swiftness with which Taryn has arranged things.

"Is there anything else?" I ask.

"A runner came from Grima Mog," she says. "The king—I mean, the serpent—is no longer in the throne room. It seems to have gotten out through the crack in the earth made by Madoc's blade. And—and I am not sure what to make of this, but it's snowing. *Inside* the brugh."

Cold dread races through me. My hand goes to the hilt of Nightfell. I want to ride out. I want to find it, but if I do—what then? The answer is more than I can bear. I close my eyes against it. When I open them, I feel as though I am spinning. Then I ask to be conducted to my new throne room.

Taryn stands at the entrance, waiting to escort me inside. She's chosen an enormous parlor and stripped it of its furniture. A large, carved wooden chair sits on a rug-covered platform in the echoing space. Candles glow from the floor, and I can see how the flickering shadows will help me appear intimidating—perhaps even play down my mortality.

Two of Cardan's old guard stand to either side of the wooden chair, and a small moth-winged page kneels on one of the rugs.

"Not bad," I tell my sister.

Taryn grins. "Get up there. I want to see the whole picture."

I sit in the chair, my back straight, and look out at the dancing flames. Taryn gives me a very mortal thumbs-up.

"Okay," I say. "Then I'm ready for the Living Council."

Fand nods and goes out to fetch them. As the door shuts, I see she and Taryn discussing something. But then I have to turn my attention to Randalin and the rest of the councilors, who are grim-faced as they enter the room.

You have only seen the least of what I can do, I think at them, trying to believe it myself.

"Your Majesty," Randalin says, but in such a way that it sounds a little like a question. He supported me in the brugh, but I am not sure how long that will last.

"I've appointed Grima Mog to be the Grand General," I tell them. "She cannot come and present herself at the moment, but we should have a report from her soon."

"Are you sure that's wise?" says Nihuar, pressing together her thin green lips, her mantis-like body shifting with obvious distress. "Perhaps we ought to wait for the High King to be restored before we come to any decision about such important matters."

"Yes," says Randalin eagerly, looking at me as though expecting some answer about how we'll do that.

"Slithery snake king," says Fala, dressed in lavender motley. "Rules over a Court of nice mice."

I remember the Bomb's words and do not flinch, nor do I attempt to argue. I wait, and my silence unnerves them into silence themselves. Even Fala goes quiet.

"Lord Baphen," I say quellingly, "does not yet have an answer to how the High King may be restored."

The others turn to him.

Only out of his spilled blood can a great ruler rise.

Baphen nods briefly in assent. "I do not, nor am I sure such a thing is possible."

Nihuar appears astonished. Even Mikkel seems taken aback by that news.

Randalin glares at me with accusation. As though everything is over and we've lost.

There is a way, I want to insist. *There is a way; I just don't know it yet.*

"I've come to make my report to the queen," comes a voice from the doorway. Grima Mog stands there.

She strides past the Council members with a brief nod. They eye her speculatively.

"We would all hear what you know," I say to murmurs of reluctant approval.

"Very well. We received intelligence that Madoc intends to attack at dawn the day after next. He hopes to catch us unprepared, especially since a few more Courts have flown to his banner. But our real problem is how many Folk plan to sit out the battle and see which way the wind blows."

"Are you sure this information is accurate?" Randalin asks suspiciously. "How did you obtain it?"

Grima Mog nods toward me. "With the help of her spies."

"*Her* spies?" Baphen repeats. I can see his putting together some of the information I had in the past and coming to new conclusions about how I got it. I feel a jolt of satisfaction at the thought that I no longer have to pretend to be entirely without my own resources.

"Do we have enough of our own army to push him back?" I ask Grima Mog.

"We are in no way assured of victory," she says diplomatically. "But he cannot yet overwhelm us."

That's a long way from where we were a day ago. But it's better than nothing.

"And there is a belief," Grima Mog says. "A belief that has grown swiftly—that the person to rule Elfhame is the one who will slay the serpent. That spilling Greenbriar blood is as good as having it in your veins."

"A very Unseelie belief," Mikkel says. I wonder if he agrees with it. I wonder if that's what he expects from me.

"The king had a pretty head," says Fala. "But can he do without it?"

"Where is he?" I ask. "Where is the High King?"

"The serpent was spotted on the shores of Insear. A knight from the

Court of Needles tried his luck against the creature. We found what was left of the knight's body an hour ago and tracked the creature's movements from there. It leaves marks where it goes, black lines scorching the earth. The difficulty is that those lines spread, blurring the trail and poisoning the land. Still, we followed the serpent back to the palace. It seems to have taken the brugh for its den."

"The king is tied to the land," says Baphen. "Cursing the king means cursing the land itself. My queen, there may be only one way to heal—"

"Enough," I say to Baphen and Randalin and the rest of the Council, startling the guards. I stand. "We are done with this discussion."

"But you must—" begins Randalin, then he seems to see something in my face and goes quiet.

"We're meant to advise you," says Nihuar in her syrupy voice. "We are thought to be very wise."

"Are you?" I ask, and the voice that comes out is honeyed malice, the exact tone Cardan would have used. It spills out of me as though I am no longer in control of my mouth. "Because wisdom ought to urge you not to court my displeasure. Perhaps a stay in the Tower of Forgetting will recall you to your place."

They all become very quiet.

I had imagined myself different from Madoc, but already, given the chance, I am becoming a tyrant, threatening in place of convincing. Unstable instead of steadying.

I am suited to the shadows, to the art of knives and bloodshed and coups, to poisoned words and poisoned cups. I never expected to rise so high as the throne. And I fear that I am utterly unsuited for the task.

It feels more like compulsion than choice as my fingers unlatch the heavy bolts of the brugh doors.

Beside me, Fand tries to dissuade me, not for the first time. "Let us at least—"

"Remain here," I tell her. "Do not follow me."

"My lady," she says, which is not exactly agreement but will have to do.

I slip inside the large chamber and let the cloak fall from my shoulders.

The serpent is there, coiled around the ruined throne. It has grown in size. The width of its body is such that it could swallow a horse whole with a mere stretch of its fanged jaws. There are yet some torches lit among the spilled food and turned-over tables, illuminating its black scales. Something of the golden sheen has dulled. I can't tell if it's illness or some further transformation. Fresh-looking scratches run along one side of its body, as though from a sword or spear. Out of the crack in the floor of the brugh, steam floats gently into the chamber, carrying the smell of hot stone.

"Cardan?" I ask, taking a few soft steps toward the dais.

The serpent's great head swings toward me. Its coils slide, unwinding itself to hunt. I stop, and it does not come for me, although its head moves sinuously back and forth, alert to both threat and opportunity.

I force myself to keep walking, one step after another. The serpent's golden eyes follow me, the only part of it—save for its temper—that seems like Cardan at all.

I might have grown into something else, a High King as monstrous as Dain. And if I did—if I fulfilled that prophecy—I ought *to be stopped. And I believe that you would stop me.*

I think of the stitches in my side and the white flowers pushing up through the snow. I concentrate on that memory and try to draw on the power of the land. He's a descendant of Mab and the rightful king. I am his wife. I healed myself. Surely I can heal him.

"Please," I say to the dirt floor of the brugh, to the earth itself. "I will do whatever you want. I will give up the crown. I will make any bargain. Just please fix him. Help me break the curse."

I concentrate and concentrate, but the magic doesn't come.

CHAPTER 24

The Bomb finds me there, stepping out of the shadows in a graceful movement. She isn't wearing her mask.

"Jude?" she says.

I realize how much closer to the serpent I have crept. I sit on the dais, perhaps three feet from him. He has grown so used to me that he's closed his golden eyes.

"Your sisters are worried," she says, coming as close to us as she dares. The serpent's head rises, tongue darting out to touch the air, and she goes very still.

"I'm fine," I say. "I just needed to think."

No true love's kiss will stop it. No riddle will fix it. Only death.

She gives the serpent an evaluating look. "Does he know you?"

"I can't tell," I say. "He seems not to mind my being here. I've been telling him how he can't hold me to my promises."

The hardest thing—the *impossible* thing—is to get past the memory of Cardan telling me he loved me. He said those words, and I didn't answer him. I thought there would be time. And I was happy—despite everything—I was *happy*, just before everything went so terribly wrong. We won. Everything was going to work out. And he loved me.

"There are a few things you need to know," the Bomb says. "I believe Grima Mog gave you a report about Madoc's movements."

"She did," I say.

"We caught a few courtiers speculating about assassinating the mortal queen. Their plans got blown up." A small smile crosses her face. "As did they."

I don't know if I should be happy about that or not. Right now it makes me feel tired.

"The Ghost has gathered information about the loyalties of the individual rulers," she says. "We can go over all those. But the most interesting thing is that you have a message from your father. Madoc wants a guarantee that he and Lady Nore and Lord Jarel may come to the palace and treat with you."

"They want to come here?" I climb down from the dais. The serpent's gaze follows me. "Why? Aren't they satisfied with the results of their last parlay?"

"I know not," she says, a brittleness in her voice that reminds me how much she hates the rulers of the Court of Teeth, and how deservedly. "But Madoc has asked to see you and your brother and sisters. As well as his wife."

"Very well," I say. "Let him come, along with Lady Nore and Lord Jarel. But let him know that he will bring no weapon into Elfhame. He does not come here as my guest. He has only my word that he will come to no harm, not the hospitality of my house."

"And what is your word worth?" the Bomb asks, sounding hopeful.

"I guess we'll find out." At the door, I look back toward the serpent. Beneath where it rests, the ground has blackened to almost the color of its scales.

After several messages back and forth, it is determined that Madoc and his company will arrive at dusk. I have agreed to receive them on the palace grounds, having no interest in letting them inside again. Grima Mog brings a semicircle of knights to watch over us, with archers in the trees. The Bomb brings spies, who hide themselves in higher and lower places. Among their number is the Ghost, his ears sealed with soft wax.

My carved chair has been brought outside and is set on a new, higher platform. Cushions rest below it, for my brother and sisters—and Oriana, if she will deign to sit with us.

There are no banquet tables and no wine. The only concession we have made to their comfort is a rug over the muddy ground. Torches blaze to either side of me, but that's for my own poor mortal eyesight, not for them.

Overhead, storm clouds sweep by, crackling with lightning. Earlier, hailstones as large as apples were reported raining down on Insweal. Weather like this is unknown in Elfhame. I can only assume that Cardan, in his cursed form, is cursing the weather as well.

I sit in the carved wooden chair and arrange my gown in what I hope is a regal way. I brush off dust from the hem.

"You missed a bit," the Bomb says, pointing. "Your Majesty."

She has taken up a place to the right of the platform. I shake off my skirts again, and she smothers a smile as my brother arrives with both of my sisters in tow. When the Bomb pulls on her face covering, she seems to recede entirely into the shadows.

The last time I saw Oak, his sword was drawn and terror was on his face. I am glad to replace that memory with this one: his rushing up to me, grinning.

"Jude!" he says, climbing up onto my lap, making short work of all the careful arranging of skirts. His horns butt against my shoulder. "I have been explaining skateboarding to Oriana, and she doesn't think I should do it."

I look out, expecting to see her, but there's only Vivi and Taryn. Vivi is dressed in jeans and a brocade vest over a floofy white shirt, a compromise between mortal and immortal style. Taryn is dressed in the gown I saw in her closet, the one patterned with forest animals looking out from behind leaves. Oak has on a little coat of midnight blue. On his brow someone has set a golden diadem to remind us all that he may be the very last of the Greenbriar line.

"I need your help," I tell Oak. "But it will be very hard and very annoying."

"What do I have to do?" he asks, looking highly suspicious.

"You have to look like you're paying attention, but stay quiet. No matter what I say. No matter what Dad says. No matter what happens."

"That's not helping," he protests.

"It would be a huge help," I insist.

With a dramatic sigh, he slides off me and takes his sulky place on the cushions.

"Where's Heather?" I ask Vivi.

"In the library," she says with a guilty look. I wonder if she thinks

Heather ought to be back in the human world and it's only Vivi's selfishness that's keeping her here, not realizing they are now both working toward the same goal. "She says that if this were a movie, someone would find a poem about cursed snakes and it would give us the clue we needed, so she's gone off to find one. The archivists don't know what to do with her."

"She's really adapting to Faerie," I say.

Vivi's only reply is a tight, sorrowful smile.

Then Oriana arrives, escorted in by Grima Mog, who takes a position parallel and opposite the Bomb. Like me, Oriana still wears the gown she had on in the brugh. Looking at the setting sun, I realize that an entire day must have passed since then. I am not sure how long I sat with the serpent, only that I seem to have lost time without noticing. It feels like forever and no time at all since Cardan was put under the curse.

"They're here," Fand says, hurrying up the path to stand beside the Bomb. And behind her is the thunder of hooves. Madoc comes mounted on a stag, dressed not in his customary armor but in a doublet of deep blue velvet. When he dismounts, I notice he has a pronounced limp where the serpent slid over him.

Behind him comes an ice coach pulled by faerie horses as crystalline as if they were conjured from frozen waves. As the rulers of the Court of Teeth climb out, the coach and the horses melt away.

Lady Nore and Lord Jarel are in white furs, despite the air not being particularly cold. Behind them are a single servant, bearing a small chest etched in silver, and Queen Suren. Though she is their ruler, she wears only a simple white shift. A gold crown has been stitched to her forehead, and a thin gold chain that penetrates the skin of her wrist functions as her new leash, with a bar on one side to keep the chain from slipping free.

Fresh scars cover her face in the shape of the bridle she wore when last I saw her.

I try to keep my face impassive, but the horror of it is hard to ignore.

Madoc steps ahead of the others, smiling at us as though we were sitting for a family portrait that he was about to join.

Oak looks up and pales, seeing Queen Suren's leash piercing her skin. Then he looks at Madoc, as though expecting an explanation.

None is forthcoming.

"Would you like cushions?" I ask Madoc's little group. "I can have some brought."

Lady Nore and Lord Jarel take in the gardens, the knights, the Bomb with her covered face, Grima Mog, and my family. Oak goes back to sulking, lying facedown on a pillow instead of sitting. I want to give him a shove with my foot for rudeness, but maybe it's a good moment for him to be rude. I can't let the Court of Teeth think they are of too great importance to us. As for Madoc, he knows us too well to be impressed.

"We will stand," Lady Nore says, lip curling.

It's hard to sit in a dignified way on a cushion, and it would require her lowering herself very far beneath me. Of course she refused my offer.

I think of Cardan and the way he wore his crown askew, the way he lounged on the throne. It gave him an air of unpredictability and reminded everyone that he was powerful enough to make the rules. I have resolved to try to emulate his example where I can, including with annoying seating.

"You are bold to come here," I say.

"Of all people, you should appreciate a little boldness." Madoc's gaze goes to Vivi and Taryn and then back to me. "I mourned you. I truly believed you died."

"I'm surprised you didn't wet your cap in my blood," I say. At my side, Grima Mog's eyebrows rise.

"I cannot blame you for being angry," he says. "But we have been angry at each other for too long, Jude. You're not the fool I took you for, and for my part, I don't want to hurt you. You're the High Queen of Faerie. Whatever you did to get there, I can only applaud it."

He might not want to hurt me, but that doesn't mean he won't.

"She *is* the queen," Taryn says. "The only reason she didn't die out in the snow is that the land healed her."

A murmur moves through the Folk around us. Lady Nore looks at me with open disgust. I note that neither she nor her husband has made a proper bow, nor used my title. How it must gall her to see me on even this approximation of a throne. How she must hate the very idea that I have a claim to the real one.

"It is the nature of the child to achieve what a parent can only dream," says Madoc. Now he looks at Oriana, eyes narrowing. "But let us remember that much of this family disagreement came from my attempt to put Oak on the throne. I have always been as happy to rule through my children as to wear the crown myself."

Anger flares up inside me, hot and bright. "And woe to those children if they will not be ruled by you."

He makes a gesture of dismissal. "Let us think through your next moves, High Queen Jude. You and your army, led by your formidable new general, clash with mine. There is a great battle. Perhaps you win, and I retreat to the North to make new plans. Or perhaps I am dead.

"Then what? There is still a serpent king to contend with, one whose scales are harder than the hardest armor, whose poison seeps into the land. And you are still mortal. There is no more Blood Crown to keep the Folk of Elfhame tied to your rule, and even if there were, you could not wear it. Already Lady Asha is gathering a circle of courtiers and knights around herself, all of them telling her that as Cardan's mother, she should be regent until his return. No, you will be fending off assassins and pretenders for your entire reign."

I glance over at the Bomb, who did not mention Lady Asha in her list of things I needed to know. The Bomb gives a slight nod of acknowledgment.

It's a bleak picture, and no part of it is untrue.

"So maybe Jude quits," Vivi says, sitting upright on the cushions by sheer force of will. "Abdicates. Whatever."

"She won't," Madoc says. "You've only ever half-understood anything Jude was up to, perhaps because if you did, you couldn't continue to act as though there are easy answers. She's made herself a target to keep the target from being on her brother's back."

"Don't lecture me," Vivi returns. "This is all your fault. Oak's being in danger. Cardan's being cursed. Jude's nearly dying."

"I am here," says Madoc. "To make it right."

I study his face, recalling the way he told the person he thought was Taryn that if it pained her that she murdered her husband, then she could put the weight on him. Perhaps he sees what he's doing now as something in the same line, but I cannot agree.

Lord Jarel takes a step forward. "That child at your feet, that's the rightful heir of the Greenbriar line, isn't it?"

"Yes," I say. "Oak will be High King one day."

Thankfully, this once, my brother doesn't contradict me.

Lady Nore nods. "You are mortal. You will not last long."

I decide not to even argue. Here, in Faerie, mortals can remain young, but those years will come on us the moment we set foot in the human world. Even if I could avoid that fate, Madoc's argument was persuasive. I will not have an easy time on the throne without Cardan.

"That's what *mortal* means," I say with a sigh that I don't have to fake. "We die. Think of us like shooting stars, brief but bright."

"Poetic," she says. "And fatalistic. Very well. You seem as though you can be reasonable. Madoc wishes us to make you an offer. We have the means to control your serpent husband."

I feel the blood rush behind my ears. "Control him?"

"As you would any animal." Lord Jarel gives me a smile that's full of menace. "We have a magical bridle in our possession. Created by Grimsen himself to leash anything. In fact, it will fit itself to the creature being restrained. Now that Grimsen is no more, such an item is more valuable than ever."

My gaze goes to Suren and her scars. Is that what she was wearing? Did they cut it off her to give to me?

Lady Nore speaks, taking up her husband's theme. "The straps will slowly sink into his skin, and Cardan will be forever yours."

I am not sure what she quite means by that. "*Mine?* He's under a curse."

"And unlikely to ever be otherwise, if Grimsen's words are to be believed," she goes on. "But were he somehow to be returned to his former state, he would still remain eternally in your power. Isn't that delicious?"

I bite down on my tongue to avoid reacting. "That's an extraordinary offer," I say, turning from her to Madoc. "By which I mean it sounds like a trick."

"Yes," he says. "I can see that. But we will each get what we want. Jude, you will be the High Queen for as long as you like. With the serpent bound, you can rule unopposed. Taryn, you will be the sister to the queen and back in the good graces of the Court. No one can keep you from claiming Locke's land and estates for yourself. Perhaps your sister will even throw in a title."

"You never know," I say, which is dangerously close to being drawn in to the picture he's painting.

"Vivienne, you shall be able to return to the mortal world and have all the fun you can conjure, without the intrusion of family. And Oak can live with his mother again." He looks at me with the intensity of battle in his eyes. "We will do away with the Living Council, and I will take their place. I will guide your hand, Jude."

I look over at the Court of Teeth. "And what will they get?"

Lord Jarel smiles. "Madoc has agreed to marry your brother, Oak, to our little queen, so that when he ascends the throne, his bride will ascend with him."

"Jude...?" Oak asks nervously. Oriana takes his hand and squeezes it tightly.

"You can't be serious," Vivi says. "Oak shouldn't have anything to do with these people or their creepy daughter."

Lord Jarel fixes her with a look of furious contempt. "You, Madoc's only trueborn child, are the person of least consequence here. What a disappointment you must be."

Vivi rolls her eyes.

My gaze goes to the little queen, studying her pale face and her oddly blank eyes. Although it is her fate we are discussing, she does not look very interested. Nor does she look as though she has been well treated. I can't imagine tying her to my brother.

"Put the question of Oak's marriage aside for a moment," Madoc says. "Do you want the bridle, Jude?"

It is a monstrous thing, the idea of tying Cardan to me in eternal obedience. What I *want* is him back, him standing beside me, him laughing at all this. I would settle for even his worst self, his cruelest trickster self, if only he could be here.

I think of Cardan's words in the brugh, before he destroyed the crown: *neither loyalty nor love should be compelled.*

He was right. Of course he was right. And yet, I want the bridle. I want it desperately. I can imagine myself on a rebuilt throne with the serpent torpid beside me, a symbol of my power and a reminder of my love. He would never be entirely lost to me.

It is a horrific image and just as horrifically compelling.

I would have hope, at least. And what is the alternative? Fighting a battle and sacrificing the lives of my people? Hunting down the serpent and giving up any chance of having Cardan back? For what? I am tired of fighting.

Let Madoc rule through me. Let him try, at least.

"Swear to me that the bridle does nothing else," I say.

"Nothing," says Lady Nore. "Only allows you to control the creature it's used on—if you say the words of command. And once you've agreed to our terms, we will tell them to you."

Lord Jarel waves forward his servant, who removes the bridle from the chest, throwing it down in a heap in front of me. It shines, golden. A bunch of straps, finely wrought, and a possible future that doesn't involve losing what I have left.

"I wonder," I say, considering it, "with such a powerful object in your possession, why you didn't use it yourselves."

He doesn't answer for a moment that drags on just a little too long. "Ah," I say, recalling the fresh scratches along the serpent's scales. If I inspect that bridle, I bet there's still drying blood on it from knights of the Court of Teeth—perhaps volunteers from Madoc's army as well. "You *couldn't* bridle him, could you? How many did you lose?"

Lord Jarel looks ill-pleased with me.

Madoc answers. "A battalion—and part of the Crooked Forest caught on fire. The creature wouldn't allow us to approach it. He's fast and deadly, and his poison seems inexhaustible."

"But in the hall," says Lady Nore, "he knew Grimsen was his enemy. We believe you can lure him. Like maidens with unicorns of old. You can bridle him. And if you die trying, Oak comes to his throne early with our queen beside him."

"Pragmatic," I say.

"Consider taking the deal," Grima Mog says. I turn to her, and she shrugs. "Madoc's right. It will be hard to hold the throne otherwise. I have no doubt you'll be able to bridle the serpent, nor that it will make for a weapon the likes of which no army in all of Faerie has seen before. That's power, girl."

"Or we could murder them right now. Take the bridle as our spoils," the Bomb says, removing the netting that covers her face. "They're already traitors. They're unarmed. And knowing them, they intend to trick you. You admitted as much yourself, Jude."

"Liliver?" says Lady Nore. It's odd to hear her called by something other than her code name, but the Bomb was held in the Court of Teeth before she became a spy. They would only know to call her by what she went by then.

"You remember me," the Bomb says. "Know that I also remember you."

"You may have the bridle, but you do not yet know how to work it," Lord Jarel says. "You cannot bind the serpent without us."

"I think I could get it out of her," the Bomb says. "I'd enjoy trying."

"Are you going to allow her to speak to us that way?" Lady Nore demands of Madoc, as though he can do anything.

"Liliver wasn't speaking to you at all," I say, mild-voiced. "She was speaking to me. And since she's my advisor, I would be foolish not to give her words careful consideration."

Madoc barks out a laugh. "Oh, come now, if you've met Lord Jarel and Lady Nore, you know they are spiteful enough to deny you, no matter what torment your spy invented. And you want that bridle, daughter."

The Court of Teeth backed Madoc to get closer to the throne. Now they see a path to ruling Elfhame themselves, through Oak. As soon as Oak and Suren are married, I will have a target on my back. And so will Madoc.

But I will also have the serpent, bound to me.

A serpent who is a corruption on the land itself.

"Show me you are acting in good faith," I say. "Cardan fulfilled what you asked of him in the matter of Orlagh of the Undersea. Release her from whatever doom you hold over her. She and her daughter hate me, so you cannot worry about their rushing to my aid."

"I imagined you hated them as well," says Madoc, frowning.

"I want to see Cardan's sacrifice mean what he wanted it to mean," I say. "And I want to know that you aren't weaseling out of every bargain you can."

He nods. "Very well. It is done."

I take a deep breath. "I will not commit Oak to anything, but if you want to call a halt to the war, tell me how the bridle works, and let us work toward peace."

Lord Jarel steps up onto the platform, causing the guards to move in front of him, weapons keeping him from me.

"Would you prefer I say it aloud, in front of everyone?" he asks, annoyed.

I wave away the guards, and he leans down to whisper the answer in my ear. "Take three hairs from your own head and knot them around the bridle. You will be bound together." Then he steps back. "Now, do you agree to our compact?"

I look at the three of them. "When the High King is bridled and tame, then I will give you everything you asked for, everything that's within my power to give. But you will have nothing before that."

"Then this is what you must do, Jude," Madoc tells me. "Tomorrow, hold a feast for the low Courts and invite us. Explain that we have put aside our differences in the face of a larger threat and that we gave you the means to capture the serpent king.

"Our armies will gather on the rocks of Insweal, but not to fight. You will take the bridle and lure the serpent to you. Once you put it on him, issue the first command. He will show himself tame, and everyone will cheer for you. It will cement your power and give you an excuse to reward us. And reward us you shall."

Already, he seeks to rule through me. "It will be nice to have a queen who can tell all the lies you cannot, won't it?" I say.

Madoc smiles at me with no malice in it. "It will be good to be a family again."

Nothing about this feels right, except for the smooth leather of the bridle in my hands.

On my way out of the palace, I pass by the throne room, but when I let myself inside, there is no sign of the serpent except for papery folds of torn golden skin.

I walk through the night to the rocky beach. There, I kneel on the stone and toss a wadded-up scrap of paper into the waves.

If you ever loved him, I wrote, *help me.*

CHAPTER 25

I lie on my back on the rug before the fire in my old rooms. Taryn sits next to me, picking at a roasted chicken she got from the palace kitchen. A whole tray of food is spread out on the floor—cheese and bread, currants and gooseberries, pomegranates and damson plums, along with a pitcher of thick cream. Vivi and Heather rest on the other side, their legs tangled together and hands clasped. Oak is lining up berries and then bowling them over with plums, something I would have once objected to but am not about to now.

"It's better than fighting, right?" Taryn says, taking a steaming kettle off the hob and pouring water into a pot. She adds leaves, and the scent of mint and elderflower fills the air. "A truce. An unlikely truce."

None of us answers, mulling over the question. I promised Madoc nothing concrete, but I have no doubt that at the banquet tonight, he intends to begin pulling authority toward himself. A trickle that swiftly becomes a flood, until I am only a figurehead with no real power. The temptation of this line of attack is that one can always convince oneself that that fate is avoidable, that one can reverse any losses, that one can outmaneuver him.

"What was wrong with that girl?" Oak asks. "Queen Suren."

"They're not particularly nice, the Court of Teeth," I tell him, sitting up to accept a cup from Taryn. Despite going so long without sleep, I am not tired. Nor am I hungry, though I have made myself eat. I do not know what I am.

Vivi snorts. "I guess you could say that. You could also call a volcano 'warm.'"

Oak frowns. "Are we going to help her?"

"If you decide to marry her, we could demand that the girl live here until you're older," I say. "And if she did, we'd keep her unfettered. I guess that would be a boon to her. But I still don't think you should do it."

"I don't want to marry her—or anyone," Oak says. "And I don't want to be High King. Why can't we just *help* her?"

The tea is too hot. The first sip burns my tongue.

"It's not easy to help a queen," Taryn says. "They're not supposed to need helping."

We lapse into silence.

"So will you take over Locke's estate?" Vivi asks, turning toward my twin. "You don't have to. You don't have to have his baby, either."

Taryn takes a gooseberry and rolls the pale citrine fruit between her fingers. "What do you mean?"

"I know that in Faerie, children are rare and precious and all that, but in the mortal world, there's such a thing as abortion," Vivi says. "And even here, there are changelings."

"And adoption," Heather puts in. "It's your decision. No one would judge you."

"If they did, I could cut off their hands," I volunteer.

"I want the child," Taryn says. "Not that I am not scared, but I'm also kind of excited. Oak, you're not going to be the youngest kid anymore."

"Good," he says, rolling his bruised plum toward the cream jar.

Vivi intercepts it and takes a bite.

"Hey!" he says, but she only giggles mischievously.

"Did you find anything in the library?" I ask Heather, and try to pretend that my voice doesn't quaver a little. I know she didn't. If she had, she would have told me. And yet I ask anyway.

She yawns. "There were some wild stories. Not helpful, but wild. One was about a king of serpents who commands all the snakes in the world. Another about a serpent who puts two faerie princesses under a curse so they're snakes—but only sometimes.

"And then there was this one about wanting a baby," she says with a glance at Taryn. "A gardener's wife couldn't get pregnant. One day, she spots a cute green snake in her garden and gets all weird about how even snakes have kids but she doesn't. The snake hears her and offers to be her son."

I raise my eyebrows. Oak laughs.

"He's an okay son, though," Heather says. "They make him a hole in the corner of their house, and he lives there. They feed him the same dinners they eat. It's all good until he gets big and decides he wants to marry a princess. And not like a viper princess or an anaconda princess, either. The snake wants to marry the human princess of the place where they live."

"How's that going to work?" Taryn asks.

Heather grins. "Dad goes to the king and makes the proposal on behalf of his snake kiddo. The king isn't into it, and so, in the manner of all fairy-tale people, instead of just refusing, he asks the snake to do three impossible things: first, turn all the fruit in the orchard to gems, then turn the floors of the palace to silver, and last, turn the walls of the palace to gold. Each time the dad reports back with one of these quests, the snake tells him what to do. First, Dad has to plant pits, which make jasper and jade fruit bloom overnight. Then he has to rub the floors of the palace with a discarded snakeskin to make them silver. Last, he has to rub the walls of the palace with venom, which turns them to gold."

"The dad is the one putting in all the effort," I murmur. It's so warm by the fire.

"He's kind of a helicopter parent." Heather's voice seems to come from very far away. "Anyway, finally, in despair, the king admits to his daughter that he basically sold her to a snake and that she has to go through with the marriage. So she does, but when they're alone, the snake takes off its skin and reveals itself as a banging hot guy. The princess is thrilled, but the king bursts into their bedroom and burns the skin, believing he's saving her life.

"The snake guy gives a great howl of despair and turns into a dove, flying away. The princess freaks out and weeps like crazy, then decides she's going to find him. Along the way, because this is a fairy tale and literally nothing makes sense, the princess meets a gossipy fox, who tells her that the birds are talking smack about a prince who was under the curse of an ogress and could not be cured without the blood of a bunch of birds—and also the blood of a fox. So you can pretty much figure out the rest. Poor fox, right?"

"Cold," Vivi says. "That fox was helping."

And that's the last I hear before I fall asleep to the sound of friendly voices talking over one another.

I wake to the dying embers of the fire, with a blanket over me.

Sleep has worked its strange magic, making the horror of the last two days recede enough for me to think a little better.

I see Taryn on the couch, wrapped in a blanket. I walk through the silent rooms and find Heather and Vivi in my bed. Oak isn't there, and I suspect that he's with Oriana.

I leave, finding a knight waiting for me. I recognize him as a member of Cardan's royal guard.

"Your Majesty," he says, hand to his heart. "Fand is resting. She asked me to watch over you until she returned."

I feel guilty not to have thought of whether Fand was working too long or too hard. Of course I need more than a single knight. "What shall I call you?"

"Artegowl, Your Majesty."

"Where are the rest of the High King's guard?" I ask.

He sighs. "Grima Mog has put us in charge of tracking the serpent's movements."

What a strange and sorrowful change from their previous mission, to keep Cardan safe. But I do not know if Artegowl would welcome my thoughts, nor if it is appropriate for me to give them. I leave him outside the doors to the royal chambers.

Inside, I am startled to find the Bomb sitting on the couch, turning a snow globe over in her hands. It has a cat inside and the words CONGRATULATIONS ON YOUR PROMOTION—the gift Vivi brought for Cardan after his coronation. I didn't realize he kept it. As I watch the glittering white crystals swirl, I recall the report of snow falling inside the brugh.

The Bomb looks up at me, her shoulders slumped. The despair in her face mirrors my own.

"Probably I shouldn't have come," she says, which isn't like her at all.

"What's wrong?" I ask, coming fully inside the room.

"When Madoc came to make you his offer, I heard what Taryn said about you." She waits for me to understand, but I don't.

I shake my head.

"That the *land* healed you." She looks as though she half-expects me to deny it. I wonder if she's thinking about the stitches she removed in this room or how I survived a fall from the rafters. "I thought that maybe...you could use that power to wake the Roach."

When I joined the Court of Shadows, I knew nothing of spying. The Bomb has seen me fail before. Still, this failure is hard to admit. "I tried to break the curse on Cardan, but I couldn't. Whatever I did, I don't know how I did it or if I can do it again."

"When I saw Lord Jarel and Lady Nore again, I couldn't help remembering how much I owe the Roach," the Bomb says. "If it wasn't for him, I wouldn't have survived them. Even aside from how much I love him, I owe him. I have to make him better. If there's anything you can do—"

I think about the flowers blooming up out of the snow. In that moment, I was magic.

I think about hope.

"I'll try," I say, stopping her. "If I can help the Roach, of course I want to. Of course I'll try. Let's go. Let's go now."

"Now?" the Bomb says, rising. "No, you came back to your chambers to sleep."

"Even if the truce with Madoc and the Court of Teeth goes a lot better than I suspect it will, it's possible that the serpent won't allow me to bridle him," I say. "I might not survive much longer. Better to do it as soon as possible."

The Bomb puts her hand lightly on my arm. "Thank you," she says, the human words awkward in her mouth.

"Don't thank me yet," I say.

"Perhaps a gift instead?" From her pocket, she pulls out a mask of black netting to match her own.

I change into black clothes and throw a heavy cloak over my shoulders. Then I don the mask, and we go together out the secret passage. I am surprised to find it has been modified since the last time I went through it, connected to the rest of the passageways through the walls of the palace. We go down through the wine cellar and into the new Court of Shadows. It's much larger than the old rooms and much better appointed. It's clear that Cardan financed this—or that they robbed the treasury behind his back. There is a kitchen area, full of crockery and with a fireplace large enough to cook a smallish pony in. We pass training rooms and costume rooms and a strategy room to rival the one belonging to the Grand General. I spot a few spies, some I know and some I do not.

The Ghost looks up from a table where he's sitting, laying out cards in one of the back rooms, sandy hair hanging over his eyes. He looks at me with suspicion. I roll up my mask.

"Jude," he says with relief. "You came."

I don't want to give either of them false hope. "I don't know if I can do anything, but I'd like to see him."

"This way," the Ghost says, rising and leading me to a little room hung with glowing glass orbs. The Roach lies on a bed. I am alarmed by the change in him.

His skin looks sallow, no longer the rich deep green of ponds, and there's a disturbing waxiness to it. He moves in sleep, then cries out and opens his eyes. They are unfocused, bloodshot.

I catch my breath, but a moment later, he has succumbed to dreams again.

"I thought he was sleeping," I say, horrified. I imagined the fairy-tale sleep of Snow White, imagined him still in a glass case, preserved exactly as he was.

"Help me find something to secure him with," the Bomb says, pressing his body down with hers. "The poison takes him like this sometimes, and I have to restrain him until the fit passes."

I can see why she came to me, why she feels as though something has to be done. I look around the room. Above a chest, there's a pile of spare sheets. The Ghost starts tearing them into strips. "Go ahead and start," he says.

With no idea what to do, I move to stand by the Roach's feet and close my eyes. I imagine the earth under me, imagine the power of it seeping up through the soles of my feet. I picture it filling my body.

Then I feel self-conscious and stupid and stop.

I can't do this. I am a mortal girl. I am the furthest thing from magic. I can't save Cardan. I can't heal anyone. This isn't going to work.

I open my eyes and shake my head.

The Ghost puts his hand on my shoulder, steps as close as he did when instructing me in the art of murder. His voice is soft. "Jude, stop trying to force it. Let it come."

With a sigh, I close my eyes again. And again I try to feel the earth beneath me. The land of Faerie. I think of Val Moren's words: *Do you think a seed planted in goblin soil grows to be the same plant it would have in the mortal world?* Whatever I am, I have been nurtured here. This is my home and my land.

I feel once again that strange sensation of being stung all over with nettles.

Wake, I think, putting my hand on his ankle. *I am your queen, and I command you to wake.*

A spasm racks the Roach's body. A vicious kick catches me in the stomach, knocking me against the wall.

I sag to the floor. The pain is intense enough that I am reminded how recently I received a gut wound.

"Jude!" the Bomb says, moving to secure his legs.

The Ghost kneels down by my side. "How hurt are you?"

I give a thumbs-up to indicate I'm okay, but I can't speak yet.

The Roach cries again, but this time, it dwindles to something else. "Lil—" he says, voice sounding soft and scratchy, but speaking.

He's conscious. Awake.

Healed.

He grabs hold of the Bomb's hand. "I'm dying," he says. "The poison—I was foolish. I don't have long."

"You're not dying," she says.

"There's something I could never tell you while I lived," he says, pulling her closer to him. "I love you, Liliver. I've loved you from the first hour of our meeting. I loved you and despaired. Before I die, I want you to know that."

The Ghost's eyebrows rise, and he glances at me. I grin. With both of us on the floor, I doubt the Roach has any idea we're there.

Besides, he's too busy looking at the Bomb's shocked face.

"I never wanted—" he begins, then bites off the words, clearly reading her expression as horror. "You don't have to say anything in return. But before I die—"

"*You're not dying*," she says again, and this time he seems to actually hear her.

"I see." His face suffuses with shame. "I shouldn't have spoken."

I creep toward the kitchen, the Ghost behind me. As we head toward the door, I hear the Bomb's soft voice.

"If you hadn't," she says, "then I couldn't tell you that your feelings are returned."

Outside, the Ghost and I walk back toward the palace, looking up at the stars. I think about how much cleverer the Bomb is than I am, because when she had her chance, she took it. She told him how she felt. I failed to tell Cardan. And now I never can.

I veer toward the pavilions of the low Courts.

The Ghost looks a question at me.

"There's one more thing I need to do before I sleep," I tell him.

He asks me nothing more, only matches his steps to mine.

We visit Mother Marrow and Severin, son of the Alderking who had Grimsen so long in his employ. They are my last hope. And though they meet me under the stars and hear me out politely, they have no answers.

"There must be a way," I insist. "There must be *something*."

"The difficulty," says Mother Marrow, "is that you already know how to end the curse. *Only death*, Grimsen said. You want another answer, but magic is seldom so convenient as to conform to our preferences."

The Ghost glowers nearby. I am grateful for his being with me, particularly right at the moment, when I am not sure I can bear to hear this alone.

"Grimsen would not have intended for the curse to be broken," says Severin. His curved horns make him look fearsome, but his voice is gentle.

"All right." I slump onto a nearby log. It wasn't as though I was expecting good news, but I feel the fog of sorrow closing over me again.

Mother Marrow narrows her eyes at me. "So you're going to use this bridle from the Court of Teeth? I'd like to see it. Grimsen made such interestingly awful things."

"You're welcome to have a look," I say. "I'm supposed to tie my own hair to it."

She snorts. "Well, don't do that. If you do that, you'll be bound along with the serpent."

You will be bound together.

The rage I feel is so great that for a moment, everything goes white, like a strike of lightning where the thunder is just behind it.

"So how ought it work?" I ask, my voice shaking with fury.

"There is probably a word of command," she tells me with a shrug. "Hard to know what that would be, though, and the thing is useless without it."

Severin shakes his head. "There's only one thing the smith ever wanted anyone to remember."

"His name," I say.

It is not long after I arrive back at the palace that Tatterfell comes with the dress that Taryn found for me to wear to the banquet. Servants bring food and set about drawing me a bath. When I emerge, they perfume me and comb my hair as though I were a doll.

The gown is of silver, with stiff metal leaves stitched over it. I hide three knives in straps on my leg and one in a sheath between my breasts. Tatterfell looks askance at the fresh bruises coming up where I was kicked. But I say nothing of my misadventure, and she does not ask.

Growing up in Madoc's household, I have gotten used to the presence of servants. There were cooks in the kitchens and grooms to care for the stables and a few household servants to make sure the beds were made and that things were decently tidy. But I came and went mostly as I pleased, free to set my own schedule and do what I liked.

Now, between the royal guard, Tatterfell, and the other palace servants, my every move is accounted for. I am barely ever alone and then not for long. In all the time I gazed at Eldred, high upon his throne, or at Cardan, tipping back yet another goblet of wine at a revel with a forced laugh, I didn't understand the horror of being so powerful and so utterly powerless all at the same time.

"You may go," I say to them when my hair is braided and my ears hung in shining silver in the shapes of arrowheads.

I cannot trick a curse and do not know how to fight one. I must somehow set that aside and focus on what I can do: evade the trap set for me by the Court of Teeth and avoid Madoc's bid to restrict my power. I believe he intends to keep me High Queen, with my monstrous High King forever by my side. And imagining that, I cannot help thinking how terrible it would be for Cardan to be trapped forever as a serpent.

I wonder if he's in pain now. I wonder what it feels like to have corruption spread from your skin. I wonder if he has enough consciousness to feel humiliation being bridled before a Court that once loved him. Whether hate will grow in his heart. Hate for them. Hate for me.

I might have grown into something else, a High King as monstrous as Dain. And if I did—if I fulfilled that prophecy—I ought *to be stopped. And I believe that you would stop me.*

Madoc, Lord Jarel, and Lady Nore plan to accompany me to the banquet, where I am to announce our alliance. I will have to establish my authority and hold it through the evening, a tricky proposition. The Court of Teeth are both presumptuous and sneering. I will look weak if I allow that to be directed at me—yet it would be unwise to risk our alliance by returning it. As for Madoc, I don't doubt he will be full of fatherly advice, pushing me into the role of sullen daughter if I reject it too vociferously. But if I cannot stop them from getting the upper hand with me, then everything I've done, everything I've planned, will be for nothing.

With all that in mind, I throw back my shoulders and head to where our banquet will be held.

I keep my head high as I walk across the mossy grass. My dress flows behind me. The strands of silver woven through my hair shine under the stars. Following me comes the moth-winged page, holding up my train. The royal guard flank me at a respectful distance.

I spot Lord Roiben standing near an apple tree, his half-moon sword gleaming in a polished sheath. His companion, Kaye, is in a green dress very close to the color of her skin. Queen Annet is speaking with Lord Severin. Randalin is drinking cup after cup of wine. All of them seem subdued. They have seen a curse unfold, and if they are still here, it is because they intend to fight on the morrow.

Only one of us can tell them lies. I recall Cardan's words to me the last time we spoke to the rulers of the low Courts.

But tonight it is not lies that I need. And it is not precisely the truth, either.

At the sight of me with Madoc and the rulers of the Court of Teeth, a hush goes over the gathered company. All those inkdrop eyes look in my direction. All those hungry, beautiful faces, turning to me as though I were a wounded lamb in a world of lions.

"Lords and ladies and denizens of Elfhame," I speak into the silence. Then I hesitate. I am as unused to giving speeches as anyone could be. "As a child in the High Court, I grew up with wild, impossible wonder tales—of curses and monsters. Tales that even here, in Faerie, were too incredible to be believed. But now our High King is a serpent, and we are all plunged into a wonder tale.

"Cardan destroyed the crown because he wanted to be a different kind of ruler and to have a different kind of reign. At least in one way, that has already been accomplished. Madoc and Queen Suren of the Court of Teeth laid down their arms. We met and hammered out the terms of a truce."

A low murmur goes through the crowd.

I do not look to my side. Madoc must not like that I am characterizing this alliance as *my* triumph, and Lord Jarel and Lady Nore must hate my treating their daughter as though she is the member of the Court of Teeth owed deference.

I go on. "I have invited them here tonight to feast with us, and tomorrow we will all meet on the field, not to battle, but to tame the serpent and end the threat to Elfhame. Together."

There is scattered, uncertain applause.

With my whole heart, I wish Cardan was here. I can almost imagine him lounging on a chair, giving me pointers on speechmaking. It would have annoyed me so much, and now, thinking of it, there's a cold pit of longing in my stomach.

I miss him, and the pain of it is a yawning chasm, one into which I yearn to let myself fall.

I lift my goblet, and all around, goblets and glasses and horns are raised. "Let us drink to Cardan, our High King, who sacrificed himself for his people. Who broke the hold of the Blood Crown. Let us drink to those alliances that have proved to be as firm as the bedrock of the isles of Elfhame. And let us drink to the promise of peace."

When I tip back my goblet, everyone drinks with me. It seems as though something has shifted in the air. I hope it's enough.

"A fine speech, daughter," Madoc says. "But nowhere in it was my promised reward."

"To make you first among my councilors? And yet already you lecture me." I fix him with a steady look. "Until we have the serpent bridled, our deal is not yet struck."

He frowns. I do not wait for him to argue the point but step away and go to a small knot of the Folk from the Court of Teeth.

"Lady Nore." She looks surprised that I've addressed her, as though it ought to be presumption on my part. "You have not perhaps met Lady Asha, mother to the High King."

"I suppose not," she agrees. "Although—"

I take her arm and steer her to where Lady Asha stands, surrounded by her favorite courtiers. Lady Asha looks alarmed by my approach and even more alarmed when I begin speaking.

"I have heard that you wish for a new role in the Court," I say to her. "I am thinking of making you an ambassador to the Court of Teeth, so it seemed useful for you to meet Lady Nore."

There is absolutely no truth to what I'm saying. But I want Lady Asha to know that I have heard of her plotting and that if she crosses me, I am capable of sending her away from the comforts she prizes most. And it seems like a fitting punishment for both of them to be afflicted with each other.

"Would you really force me so far from my son?" she asks.

"If you'd prefer to remain here and have a hand in caring for the serpent," I say, "you have only to say so."

Lady Asha looks as though what she'd *really* prefer is to stab me in the throat. I turn away from her and Lady Nore. "Enjoy your conversation." Maybe they will. They both hate me. That gives them at least one thing in common.

A blur of dishes is brought out by servants. Tender stalks of fern, walnuts wrapped in rose petals, wine bottles choked with herbal infusions, tiny birds roasted whole with honey. As I stare out at the Folk, it seems as though the gardens are spinning around me. A strange sense of unreality intrudes. Dizzily, I look around for one of my sisters, for someone from the Court of Shadows. Even Fand.

"Your Majesty," comes a voice. It is Lord Roiben at my elbow. My chest constricts. I am not sure I am able to project authority to him, of all people, right now.

"It was good of you to stay," I say. "After Cardan broke the crown, I wasn't sure you would."

He nods. "I never cared much for him," he says, staring down at me with his gray eyes, pale as river water. "It was you who persuaded me to pledge to the crown in the first place, and you who brokered peace after the Undersea broke their treaty."

By killing Balekin. I can hardly forget.

"And I might have fought for you regardless if for no other reason than a mortal Queen of Faerie cannot help but delight many people I hold dear and annoy many people I dislike. But after what Cardan did in the great hall, I understand why you were willing to take mad gamble after mad gamble to put him on the throne, and I would have fought until the breath left my body."

I never expected such a speech from him. It grounds me to the spot.

Roiben touches a bracelet at his wrist, with woven green threads running through it. No, not thread. Hair. "He was willing to break the Blood Crown and trust in the loyalty of his subjects instead of compel it. He's the true High King of Faerie."

I open my mouth to reply when, across the expanse of grass, I see Nicasia in a shimmering gown the silver of fish scales weaving between courtiers and rulers.

And I notice Roiben's consort, Kaye, moving toward her.

"Um," I say. "Your, um, girlfriend is about to—"

He turns to look just in time for both of us to see Kaye punch

Nicasia right in the face. She stumbles into another courtier and then hits the ground. The pixie shakes her hand as though she hurt her knuckles.

Nicasia's selkie guards run toward her. Roiben immediately begins moving through the crowd, which parts for him. I try to follow, but Madoc blocks my way.

"A queen does not race toward a fight like a schoolgirl," he says, grabbing hold of my shoulder. I am not so distracted by annoyance not to see the opportunity before me. I pull out of his grip, taking three strands of his hair with me.

A redheaded knight shoves her way between Kaye and Nicasia's selkie guards. I don't know her, but by the time Roiben gets there, it seems clear that everyone is threatening to duel everyone else.

"Get out of my way," I growl at Madoc, then take off at a run. I ignore anyone who tries to speak with me. Maybe I look ridiculous, holding up my gown to my knees, but I don't care. I certainly look ridiculous when I tuck something into my cleavage.

Nicasia's jaw is red, and her throat is flushed. I have to choke down a wholly inappropriate laugh.

"You best not defend a pixie," she tells me grandly.

The redheaded knight is mortal, wearing the livery of the Alderking's Court. She's got a bloody nose, which I assume means that she and the selkies already got into it. Lord Roiben looks ready to draw the blade at his hip. Since he was just talking about fighting until the breath left his body, that's something I'd rather avoid.

Kaye is wearing a more revealing gown than she did the last time I saw her. It shows a scar that starts at her throat and runs down over her chest. It looks half like a cut, half like a burn, and definitely something it makes sense for her to be angry about. "I don't need any defending," she says. "I can handle my own business."

"You're lucky all she did was hit you," I tell Nicasia. Her presence makes my pulse thrum with nerves. I can't help remembering what it was to be her captive in the Undersea. I turn to Kaye. "But this is over now. Understood?"

Roiben puts his hand on her shoulder.

"I guess," Kaye says, and then stomps off in her big boots. Roiben waits a moment, but I shake my head. Then he follows his consort.

Nicasia touches fingers to her jaw, regarding me carefully.

"I see you got my note," I say.

"And I see you are consorting with the enemy," she returns with a glance in Madoc's direction. "Come with me."

"Where?" I ask.

"Anywhere no one can hear us."

We walk off together through the gardens, leaving both our guard behind. She grabs hold of my hand. "Is it true? Cardan is under a curse? He is transformed into a monster whose scales have broken the spears of your Folk."

I give a tight nod.

To my astonishment, she sinks down to her knees.

"What are you doing?" I say, aghast.

"Please," she says, her head bent. "Please. You must try to break the curse. I know that you are the queen by right and that you may not want him back, but—"

If anything could have increased my astonishment, it was that. "You think that I'd—"

"I didn't know you, before," she says, the anguish clear in her voice.

There is a hitch in her breath that comes with weeping. "I thought you were just some mortal."

I have to bite my tongue at that, but I don't interrupt her.

"When you became his seneschal, I told myself that he wanted you for your lying tongue. Or because you'd become biddable, although you never were before. I should have believed you when you told him he didn't know the least of what you could do.

"While you were in exile, I got more of the story out of him. I know you don't believe this, but Cardan and I were friends before we were lovers, before Locke. He was my first friend when I came here from the Undersea. And we *were* friends, even after everything. I hate that he loves you."

"He hated it, too," I say with a laugh that sounds more brittle than I'd like.

Nicasia fixes me with a long look. "No, he didn't."

To that, I can only be silent.

"He frightens the Folk, but he's not what you think he is," Nicasia says. "Do you remember the servants that Balekin had? The human servants?"

I nod mutely. Of course I remember. I will never forget Sophie and her pockets full of stones.

"They'd go missing sometimes, and there were rumors that Cardan hurt them, but it wasn't true. He'd return them to the mortal world."

I admit, I'm surprised. "Why?"

She throws up a hand. "I don't know! Perhaps to annoy his brother. But you're human, so I thought you'd like that he did it. And he sent you a gown. For the coronation."

I remember it—the ball gown in the colors of night, with the stark outlines of trees stitched on it and the crystals for stars. A thousand times more beautiful than the dress I commissioned. I had thought perhaps it came from Prince Dain, since it was his coronation and I'd sworn to be his creature when I joined the Court of Shadows.

"He never told you, did he?" Nicasia says. "So see? Those are two nice things about him you didn't know. And I saw the way you used to look at him when you didn't think anyone was watching you."

I bite the inside of my cheek, embarrassed despite the fact that we were lovers, and wed, and it should hardly be a secret that we like each other.

"So promise me," she says. "Promise me you'll help him."

I think of the golden bridle, about the future the stars predicted. "I don't know *how* to break the curse," I say, all the tears I haven't shed welling up in my eyes. "If I could, do you think I would be at this stupid banquet? Tell me what I must slay, what I must steal, tell me the riddle I must solve or the hag I must trick. Only tell me the way, and I will do it, no matter the danger, no matter the hardship, no matter the cost." My voice breaks.

She gives me a steady look. Whatever else I might think of her, she really does care for Cardan.

And as tears roll over my cheeks, to her astonishment, I think she realizes I do, too.

Much good it does him.

When we finish talking, I go back to the banquet and find the new Alderking. He looks surprised to see me. Beside him is the mortal knight with the bloody nose. A red-haired human I recognize as Severin's consort is stuffing her nose with cotton. The consort and the knight are twins, I realize. Not identical, like Taryn and me, but twins all the same. Twin humans in Faerie. And neither of them looking particularly discomfited by it.

"I need something from you," I tell Severin.

He makes his bow. "Of course, my queen. Whatever is mine is yours."

That night, I lie on Cardan's enormous bed in his enormous bedchambers. I spread out, kick at the covers.

I look at the golden bridle sitting on a chair beside me, glowing in the low lamplight.

If I got it on the serpent, I would have him with me always. Once bridled, I could bring him here. He could curl up on the rug in this very room, and though it might make me as much a monster as he is, at least I wouldn't be alone.

Eventually I sleep.

In my dreams, Cardan the snake looms over me, his black scales gleaming.

"I love you," I say, and then he devours me.

CHAPTER 26

"You're not healed enough," Tatterfell gripes, poking my scar with her sharp fingers. The imp has been seeing to me since I got out of bed, getting me ready to face the serpent as though I was going to another banquet, and complaining the whole way. "Madoc nearly cut you in half not so long ago."

"Does it bother you that you were sworn to him, but you're still here with me?" I ask as she finishes the tight braid on top of my head. The sides are pulled back, and the rest of it is pinned into a bun. No ornamentation in my ears or around my throat, of course, nothing that can be grabbed.

"This is where he sent me," Tatterfell says, taking a brush from the table where she has laid out her tools and touching it to a pot of black ash. "Maybe he regrets it. After all, I could be scolding him right now, instead of you."

That makes me smile.

Tatterfell paints my face, shadowing my eyes and reddening my lips.

There's a knock on the door, and then Taryn and Vivi come in. "You won't believe what we found in the treasury," Vivi says.

"I thought treasuries were just full of gems and gold and stuff." I recall, ages back, Cardan's promise that he would give the contents of Balekin's treasury to the Court of Shadows if they would only betray me and release him. It's an odd feeling, remembering how panicked I felt then, how charming he was, and how I hated it.

Tatterfell snorts as the Roach comes in, pulling a chest behind him. "There's no keeping your sisters out of trouble."

His skin has returned to its normal deep green, and he looks thin, but well. It's an immense relief to see him up and moving so quickly. I wonder how he was recruited to help my sisters, but I wonder more what the Bomb said to him. There is a new kind of joy in his face. It lives in the corners of his mouth, where a smile hovers, and in the brightness of his eyes.

It hurts to look at.

Taryn grins. "We found armor. Glorious armor. For you."

"For a queen," Vivi says. "Which, you may recall, there hasn't been in a little while."

"It may well have belonged to Mab herself," Taryn goes on.

"You're really building this up," I tell them.

Vivi leans down to unlock the chest. She draws out armor of a fine scale mail, worked so that it appears like a fall of miniature metal ivy leaves. I gasp at the sight of it. It truly is the most beautiful armor I've ever seen. It appears ancient, and the workmanship is distinct, nothing like Grimsen's. It's a relief to know that other great smiths came before him and that others will follow.

"I knew you'd like it," Taryn says, grinning.

"And I have something you'll like almost as well," the Roach says. Reaching into his bag, he takes out three strands of what looks like silver thread.

I tuck it into my pocket, beside the hair I plucked from Madoc's head.

Vivi is too busy taking out more items from the chest to notice. Boots covered in curved plates of metal. Bracers in a pattern of briars. Shoulder plates of more leaves, curled up at the edges. And a helm that resembles a crown of golden branches with berries gathered on either side.

"Well, even if the serpent bites off your head," says Tatterfell, "the rest of you will still look good."

"That's the spirit," I tell her.

The army of Elfhame assembles and readies itself to march. Whippet-thin faerie steeds, swampy water horses, reindeer with jutting antlers, and massive toads are all being saddled. Some will even be armored.

Archers line up with their elf-shot, with sleep-poisoned arrows and enormous bows. Knights ready themselves. I see Grima Mog across the grass, standing in a small knot of redcaps. They are passing around a carafe of blood, taking swigs and dotting their caps. Swarms of pixies with small poisoned darts fly through the air.

"We'll be prepared," Grima Mog explains, walking over, "in the event that the bridle doesn't work the way they claim. Or in case they don't like what happens next." Taking in my armor and the borrowed sword strapped to my back, she smiles, showing me her blood-reddened teeth. Then she places a hand over her heart. "High Queen."

I try to give her a grin, but I know it is a sickly one. Anxiety chews at my gut.

Two paths are before me, but only one leads to victory.

I have been Madoc's protégé and Dain's creature. I don't know how to win any other way but theirs. It is no recipe for being a hero, but it is a recipe for success. I know how to drive a knife through my own hand. I know how to hate and be hated. And I know how to win the day, provided I am willing to sacrifice everything good in me for it.

I said that if I couldn't be better than my enemies, then I would become worse. Much, much worse.

Take three hairs from your own head and knot them around the bridle. You will be bound together.

Lord Jarel thought to trick me. He thought to keep the word of power to himself, to use it only after I bridled the serpent, and then to control us both. I am sure Madoc doesn't know Lord Jarel's scheme, which suggests that part of it will involve murdering Madoc.

But it is a scheme that can be turned on its head. I have tied their hair to the golden bridle, and it will not be me who is bound with the serpent. Once the serpent is bridled, Madoc and Lord Jarel will become my creatures, as surely as Cardan was once mine. As surely as Cardan will be mine again with golden straps digging into his scales.

And if the serpent grows in monstrousness and corruption, if it poisons the land of Elfhame itself, then let me be the queen of monsters.

Let me rule over that blackened land with my redcap father as a puppet by my side. Let me be feared and never again afraid.

Only out of his spilled blood can a great ruler rise.

Let me have everything I ever wanted, everything I ever dreamed, and eternal misery along with it. Let me live on with an ice shard through my heart.

"I have looked at the stars," says Baphen. For a moment, my mind is still too lost in my own wild imaginings to focus. His deep blue robes fly behind him in the early-afternoon breeze. "But they will not speak to me. When the future is obscured, it means an event will permanently reshape the future for good or ill. Nothing can be seen until the event is concluded."

"No pressure, then," I mutter.

The Bomb emerges from the shadows. "The serpent has been spotted," she says. "Near the shoreline by the Crooked Forest. We must go quickly before we lose it again."

"Remember the formation," Grima Mog calls to her troops. "We drive from the north. Madoc's people will hold the south, and the Court of Teeth, the west. Keep your distance. Our goal is to herd the creature into our queen's loving arms."

The scales of my new armor chime together, making a musical sound. I am handed up onto a high black steed. Grima Mog is seated on an enormous armored buck.

"Is this your first battle?" she asks me.

I nod.

"If fighting breaks out, focus on what's in front of you. Fight *your* fight," she tells me. "Let someone else worry about theirs."

I nod again, watching Madoc's army set off to take up its position. First come his own soldiers, handpicked and stolen away from the standing army of Elfhame. Then there are those low Courts that took up his banner. And, of course, the Court of Teeth, carrying icy weapons. Many of them seem to have frost-tipped skin, some as blue as the dead. I do not relish the idea of fighting them, today or any other day.

The Court of Termites rides behind Grima Mog. It's easy to pick out Roiben's salt-white hair. He is on the back of a kelpie, and when I look over, he salutes me. Beside him are the Alderking's troops. Severin's mortal consort isn't with him; instead, he's riding beside the red-haired mortal knight whose nose was bloodied by Nicasia's selkie guards. She looks disturbingly chipper.

Back at the palace, Vivi, Oriana, Heather, and Oak wait for us with a retainer of guards, the better part of the Council, and many courtiers from Courts both low and high. They will watch from the parapets.

My grip tightens on the golden bridle.

"Cheer up," Grima Mog says, seeing my face. She adjusts her hat, stiffened with layers of blood. "We go to glory."

Through the trees we ride, and I cannot help thinking that when I pictured knighthood, I pictured something like this. Facing down magical monsters, clad in armor, sword at my side. But like so many imaginings, it was absent all the horror.

A screech carries through the air from a denser patch of woods up ahead. Grima Mog gives a sign, and the armies of Elfhame stop marching and spread out. Only I ride on, weaving around dead tree after dead tree until I see the black coils of the serpent's body perhaps thirty feet from where I stand. My horse shies back, chuffing.

Holding the bridle, I swing down from its back and move closer to the monstrous creature that was once Cardan. It has grown in size, longer now than one of Madoc's ships, head large enough that were it to open its mouth, a single fang would be half the size of the sword on my back.

It's absolutely terrifying.

I force my feet to move across the wilted and blackened grass. Beyond the serpent, I see the banners with Madoc's crest fluttering in the breeze.

"Cardan," I say in a whisper. The golden net of the bridle shines in my hands.

As if in answer, the serpent draws back, neck curving in a swinging movement as though evaluating how best to strike.

"It's Jude," I say, and my voice cracks. "Jude. You like me, remember? You trust me."

The serpent explodes into motion, sliding fast over the grass in my direction, closing the distance between us. Soldiers scatter. Horses rear up. Toads hop into the shelter of the forest, ignoring their riders. Kelpies run for the sea.

I lift the bridle, having nothing else in my hands to defend myself with. I prepare to throw. But the serpent pauses perhaps ten feet from where I am standing, winding around itself.

Looking at me with those gold-tipped eyes.

I tremble all over. My palms sweat.

I know what I must do if I want to vanquish my enemies, but I no longer want to do it.

This close to the serpent, I can think only of the bridle sinking into Cardan's skin, of his being trapped forever. Having him under my control was once such a compelling thought. It gave me such a raw rush of power when he was sworn to me, when he had to obey me for a year and a day. I felt that if I could control everything and everyone, then nothing could hurt me.

I take another step toward the serpent. And then another. This close, I am stunned all over again by the creature's sheer size. I raise a wary hand and place it against the black scales. They feel dry and cool against my skin.

Its golden eyes have no answer, but I think of Cardan lying beside me on the floor of the royal rooms.

I think of his quicksilver smile.

I think of how he would hate to be trapped like this. How unfair it would be for me to keep him this way and call it love.

You already know how to end the curse.

"I do love you," I whisper. "I will always love you."

I tuck the golden bridle into my belt.

Two paths are before me, but only one leads to victory.

But I don't want to win like this. Perhaps I will never live without fear, perhaps power will slip from my grasp, perhaps the pain of losing him will hurt more than I can bear.

And yet, if I love him, there's only one choice.

I draw the borrowed sword at my back. Heartsworn, which can cut through anything. I asked Severin for the blade and carried it into battle, because no matter how I denied it, some part of me knew what I would choose.

The golden eyes of the serpent are steady, but there are surprised sounds from the assembled Folk. I hear Madoc's roar.

This wasn't supposed to be how things ended.

I close my eyes, but I cannot keep them that way. In one movement,

I swing Heartsworn in a shining arc at the serpent's head. The blade falls, cutting through scales, through flesh and bone. Then the serpent's head is at my feet, golden eyes dulling.

Blood is everywhere. The body of the serpent gives a terrible coiling shudder, then goes limp. I sheath Heartsworn with trembling hands. I am shaking all over, shaking so hard that I fall to my knees in the blackened grass, in the carpet of blood.

I hear Lord Jarel shout something at me, but I can't hear it.

I think I might be screaming.

The Folk are running toward me. I hear the clang of steel and the hiss of arrows soaring through the air. It seems to come from very far away.

All that is loud in my ears is the curse Valerian spoke before he died. *May your hands always be stained with blood. May death be your only companion.*

"You ought to have taken what we offered," Lord Jarel says, swinging his spear down toward me. "Your reign will be very short, mortal queen."

Then Grima Mog is there on her stag, taking the weight of his blade. Their weapons slam together, ringing with the force of the impact. "First I am going to kill you," she tells him. "And then I am going to eat you."

Two black arrows fly out of the trees, embedding themselves in Lord Jarel's throat. He slides off his horse as a cry goes up from the Court of Teeth. I catch a flash of the Bomb's white hair.

Grima Mog whirls away, battling three knights from the Court of Teeth. She must have known them once, must have commanded them, but she fights them just the same.

There are more cries all around me. And the sounds of battle ebbing.

From the shoreline, I hear a horn.

Out past the black rocks, the water is frothing. From the depths, merfolk and selkies rise, their shining scales catching the sunlight. Nicasia is rising with them, seated on the back of a shark.

"The Undersea honors its treaty with the land and with the queen," she calls, her voice carrying across the field. "Lay down your arms."

A moment later, the armies of the Undersea are rushing the shore.

Then Madoc is standing in front of me. His cheek and part of his forehead are painted in gore. There is a glee in his face, a terrible joy. Redcaps are born for this, for bloodshed and violence and murder. I think some part of him delights in being able to share this with me, even now. "Stand up."

I have spent most of my life answering to his orders. I push myself to my feet, my hand going to the golden bridle at my belt, the one tied with his hair, the one I could have used to bind him and the one I can bind him with still. "I am not going to fight you." My voice sounds so distant. "Though I would not delight to see the straps sink into your skin, neither would I mourn."

"Enough blustering," he says. "You've already won. Look."

He takes me by the shoulders and turns me so that I can see where the great body of the serpent lies. A jolt of horror goes through me, and I try to wrench out of his grip. And then I notice the fighting has ebbed, the Folk are staring. From within the body of the creature emanates a glow.

And then, through that, Cardan steps out. Cardan, naked and covered in blood.

Alive.

Only out of his spilled blood can a great ruler rise.

And all around, people go to their knees. Grima Mog kneels. Lord Roiben kneels. Even those who moments before were intent on murder seem overcome. Nicasia looks on from the sea as all of Elfhame bows to the High King, restored and reborn.

"I will bend my head to you," Madoc says to me under his breath. "And only you."

Cardan takes a step forward, and little cracks appear from his footfalls. Fissures in the very earth. He speaks with a boom that echoes through everyone gathered there. "The curse is broken. The king is returned."

He's every bit as terrifying as any serpent.

I don't care. I run into his arms.

CHAPTER 27

Cardan's fingers dig into my back. He's trembling, and whether it is from ebbing magic or horror, I am not sure. But he holds me as though I am the only solid thing in the world.

Soldiers approach, and Cardan lets go abruptly. His jaw sets. He waves away a knight who proffers his cloak, despite being clad only in blood.

"I haven't worn anything in days," the High King drawls, and if there is something brittle in his eyes, nearly everyone is too awed to notice. "I don't see why I ought to start now."

"Modesty?" I force out, playing along, surprised he can joke about the curse, or anything.

He gives me a dazzling, insouciant smile. The kind of smile you can hide behind. "Every part of me is a delight."

My chest hurts, looking at him. I feel like I can't breathe. Though he is in front of me, the pain of losing him hasn't faded.

"Your Majesty," Grima Mog says, addressing me. "Do I have leave to chain your father?"

I hesitate, thinking of the moment when I confronted him with the golden bridle. *You've already won.*

"Yes," Cardan says. "Chain him."

A carriage is brought, wheels wobbling over the rocks. Grima Mog shouts orders. Two generals clasp manacles around Madoc's wrists and ankles, the heavy chains clanking with even the slightest movement. Archers keep arrows trained on him as they lead him away.

His army is surrendering, taking oaths of submission. I hear the whir of wings, the clank of armor, and cries from the wounded. Redcaps freshen the pigment of their hats. A few Folk feast on the dead. There's smoke in the air, mingling with the scents of the sea and of blood and moss. The aftermath of even a brief battle is all dwindling adrenaline, bandages, and feting the victors.

The revel will have already begun back at the palace and will last far longer than the fighting.

Inside the carriage, Cardan slumps. I stare at him, at the blood drying in tide lines over his body and crusting in his curls like tiny garnets. I force myself to look out the window instead.

"How long have I—" He hesitates.

"Not even three days," I tell him. "Barely any time at all." I do not mention how long it has seemed.

Nor do I say how he might have been trapped as a serpent for all time, bridled and bound. Or dead.

He could be dead.

Then the carriage draws up, and we are chivied out. Servants have brought an enormous velvet cloak for Cardan, and this time he accepts it, wrapping it around his shoulders as we make our way through the chilly underground halls.

"You will want to bathe perhaps," Randalin says, an understandable sentiment.

"I want to see the throne," says Cardan.

No one is inclined to gainsay him.

The brugh is full of turned-over tables and rotting fruit. A crack runs through the ground to the split throne, with its wilted flowers. Cardan spreads his hands, and the earth heals along the seam, rock and stone bubbling up to fill it back in. Then he twists his fingers, and the divided throne grows anew, blooming with briars, sprouting into two separate thrones where there was once only one.

"Do you like it?" he asks me, which seems a little like asking if someone enjoys the crown of stars they conjured from the sky.

"Impressive," I choke out.

Seemingly satisfied, he finally allows Randalin to guide us to the royal chambers, which are full of servants, generals, and most of the Living Council. A bath is drawn for the High King. A carafe of wine is brought, along with an ornate goblet studded with cabochons. Fala sings a song about the king of snakes, and Cardan seems both charmed and horrified by all of it.

Unwilling to strip off my armor in front of all these Folk and sticky with blood, I slip out and go to my old rooms.

But when I get there, I find Heather. She stands up from the couch, holding an enormous tome. The pink of her hair is faded, but everything else about her looks vibrant. "Congratulations, if that's not too weird of a thing to say. I don't know how to talk about fights, but I hear you won."

"We won," I confirm, and smile.

She tugs at a double strand of very poorly strung rowan berries around her neck. "Vee made me this. For the after-party." Heather seems to notice what I am wearing for the first time. "That's not your blood—"

"No," I say. "I'm fine. Just gross."

She nods slowly.

"And Cardan," I say. "He's fine, too."

The tome tumbles out of her hand and onto the couch. "He's not a big snake anymore?"

"No," I say. "But I think I might be hyperventilating. That's what you call it, right? Breathing too fast. Dizzy."

"Nobody in this place knows anything about human medicine, do they?" She walks over and starts working on my armor. "Let's get this off you, and see if that helps."

"Talk to me," I say. "Tell me another fairy tale. Tell me something."

"Okay," she says, trying to figure out how to undo the armor. "I took your advice and talked to Vee. Finally. I told her that I didn't want my memories to be taken away and that I was sorry I let her make the promise."

"Was she glad?" I help Heather with one of the clasps.

"We had a huge fight. Screaming fight," she says. "With a lot of crying, too."

"Oh," I say.

"Do you remember the fairy tale with the snake who has the helicopter parents and marries the princess?"

"Helicopter?" I echo. I did fall asleep at the end, so maybe I missed that part.

"When the boy's snakeskin is burned, the princess had to earn him back by going on a quest. Well, I told Vee she has to go on a quest. She has to meet me all over again and do it right this time. Tell me the truth from the start. And convince me to love her."

"Damn." The last of my armor comes off, clanking to the floor, and I realize that her talking has distracted me enough for my breathing to return to normal. "That is some serious fairy-tale business. A *quest*."

Heather reaches out her hand to take mine. "If she succeeds, all my memories come back. But if not, then tonight's the last time I am going to see you."

"I hope you drink the cellars dry at the revel," I say to her, pulling her into a tight embrace. "But more than that, I hope Vee is good enough to win your hand again."

The door opens, and Oriana comes in. Upon seeing me, she looks panicked. Immediately, she bows low, pressing her forehead nearly to the floor.

"You don't have to do that," I say, and she fixes me with a sharp look. I can see she has *a lot* of thoughts about my behavior as High Queen, and there's a moment of sharp satisfaction that she can't tell me any of them without breaking her own rules of what's appropriate.

She rises from her bow. "I hope that you will grant mercy to your father. For your brother's sake, if not for your own."

"I've already been merciful," I say, and lifting my armor, I flee into the hallway.

I should not have left the royal chambers. It was an old impulse, to leave Cardan to rule while I operated from the shadows. And it was a relief to be away from all those staring eyes. But far from Cardan, everything has taken on a tinge of unreality, and I worry that somehow the curse was never broken, that all this is the fantasy of a feverish mind. I hurriedly retrace my steps through the hall, clad in only the padded gambeson and leg coverings under my armor.

When I get back, I find Cardan gone, along with all the dignitaries. The bathwater is still warm, and there are candles still burning, but the rooms are empty.

"I refilled it," says Tatterfell, coming out of I-don't-know-where and startling me. "Get in. You're a mess."

"Where's Cardan?" I ask, starting to strip off the last of my clothes.

"The brugh. Where else?" she says. "You're the one who's late. But as the hero of the hour, that's all to the good. I am going to make you into a vision."

"Sounds like a lot of work on your part," I tell her, but climb obediently into the tub, disturbing primrose petals floating there. The hot water feels good on my sore muscles. I let myself sink under it. The problem with coming through something terrible and big is that afterward, you're left feeling all the feelings that you shoved down and pushed away. For many long days, I have been terrified, and now, when I ought to be feeling great, what I want to do is hide under a table in the brugh with Cardan until I can finally convince myself he's all right.

And maybe make out with his face, if he's feeling up to that.

I surface from the water and wipe my hair back from my eyes. Tatterfell hands me a cloth. "Scrub the blood off your knuckles," she instructs.

Once more, she braids my hair into horns, this time threaded with gold. She has a bronze velvet tunic for me. Over it, she puts a bronze leather coat with a high curled collar and a cape-like train that blows in even the slightest wind. And last, bronze gloves with wide cuffs.

Dressed in such finery, it would have been difficult to slip into the brugh unnoticed, even if horns didn't blare at my entrance.

"The High Queen of Elfhame, Jude Duarte," announces a page in a carrying voice.

I spot Cardan, sitting at the head of the high table. Even from across the room, I can feel the intensity of his gaze.

Long tables have been set up for a proper feast. Each platter is heavy with food: great globes of fruit, hazelnuts, bread stuffed with dates. Honey wine perfumes the air.

I can hear performers competing to get the lyrics right on their new compositions, many of them in honor of the serpent king. At least one is in my honor, however:

Our queen sheathed her sword and closed her eyes,

And said, "I thought the snake would be of larger size."

A fresh batch of servants come from the kitchens, carrying trays heaped with pale meat in different preparations—grilled and poached in oil, roasted and stewed. It takes me a moment to recognize what I am looking at. It's serpent meat. Meat cut from the body of the enormous serpent that had been their High King and might give them a measure of his magic. I look at it and feel the overwhelming disorientation of being mortal. Some faerie ways will never not horrify me.

I hope that Cardan is undisturbed. Certainly, he appears blithesome, laughing as courtiers heap their plates.

"I always supposed I would be delicious," I hear him say, although I note that he does not take any of the meat for himself.

Again, I imagine ducking underneath the table and hiding there, as I did when I was a child. As I did after the bloody coronation, with him.

But I go to the high table instead and find my place, which is, of course, at the head of the opposite end. We stare at each other across the expanse of silver and cloth and candles.

Then he rises, and all across the brugh, the Folk fall silent. "Tomorrow we must deal with all that has befallen us," he says, lifting a goblet high. "But tonight let us remember our triumph, our trickery, and our delight in one another."

We all toast to that.

There are songs—a seemingly endless array of songs—and dishes enough that even a mortal like myself can eat my fill. I watch Heather and Vivi weave through the tables to dance. I spot the Roach and the Bomb, sitting in the shadows of the re-formed thrones. He is tossing grapes into her mouth and never missing, not once. Grima Mog is discussing something with Lord Roiben, half her plate heaped with snake and half her plate heaped with another meat that I do not recognize. Nicasia sits in a place of honor, not far from the high table, her subjects around her. I spot Taryn near the musicians, telling a story with great sweeps of her hands. I see the Ghost, too, watching her.

"Your pardon," someone says, and I see the Minister of Keys, Randalin, at Cardan's shoulder.

"Councilor," Cardan says, leaning back against the table, his posture the easy languor of someone who's already in his cups. "Were you hoping for one of these little honey cakes? I could have passed them down the table."

"There's the matter of the prisoners—Madoc, his army, what remains of the Court of Teeth," Randalin says. "And many other matters we were hoping to take up with you."

"Tomorrow," Cardan insists. "Or the next day. Or perhaps next week." And with that, he rises, takes a long drink from his goblet, sets it down on the table, and walks to where I sit.

"Will you dance?" he asks, presenting his hand.

"You may remember that I am not particularly accomplished at it," I say, rising. The last time we danced was the night of Prince Dain's coronation, just before everything went sideways. He had been very, very drunk.

You really hate me, don't you? he'd asked.

Almost as much as you hate me, I'd returned.

He draws me down to where fiddle players are exhorting everyone to dance faster and faster, to whirl and spin and jump. His hands cover mine.

"I don't know what to apologize for first," I say. "Cutting off your head or hesitating so long to do it. I didn't want to lose what little there was left of you. And I can't quite think past how wonderous it is that you're alive."

"You don't know how long I've waited to hear those words," he says. "You don't want me dead."

"If you joke about this, I am going to—"

"Kill me?" he asks, raising both black brows.

I think I might hate him after all.

Then Cardan takes my hands in his and pulls me away from the other dancers, toward the secret chamber he showed me before, behind the dais. It is as I remember it, its walls thick with moss, a low couch resting beneath gently glowing mushrooms.

"I only know how to be cruel or to laugh when I am discomposed," he says, and sits down on the couch.

I let go of him and remain standing. I promised myself I would do this, if I ever had the chance again. I promised I would do this the first moment I could.

"I love you," I say, the words coming out in an unintelligible rush.

Cardan looks taken aback. Or possibly I spoke so fast he's not even sure what I said. "You need not say it out of pity," he says finally, with great deliberateness. "Or because I was under a curse. I have asked you to lie to me in the past, in this very room, but I would beg you not to lie now."

My cheeks heat at the memory of those lies.

"I have not made myself easy to love," he says, and I hear the echo of his mother's words in his.

When I imagined telling him, I thought I would say the words, and it would be like pulling off a bandage—painful and swift. But I didn't think he would doubt me. "I first started liking you when we went to talk to the rulers of the low Courts," I say. "You were *funny*, which was weird. And when we went to Hollow Hall, you were *clever*. I kept remembering how you'd been the one to get us out of the brugh after Dain's coronation, right before I put that knife to your throat."

He doesn't try to interrupt, so I have no choice but to barrel on.

"After I tricked you into being the High King," I say. "I thought once you hated me, I could go back to hating you. But I didn't. And I felt so stupid. I thought I would get my heart broken. I thought it was a weakness that you would use against me. But then you saved me from the Undersea when it would have been much more convenient to just leave me to rot. After that, I started to hope my feelings were returned. But then there was the exile—" I take a ragged breath. "I hid a lot, I guess. I thought if I didn't, if I let myself love you, I would burn up like a match. Like the whole matchbook."

"But now you've explained it," he says. "And you do love me."

"I love you," I confirm.

"Because I am *clever* and *funny*," he says, smiling. "You didn't mention my handsomeness."

"Or your deliciousness," I say. "Although those are both good qualities."

He pulls me to him, so that we're both lying down on the couch. I look down at the blackness of his eyes and the softness of his mouth. I wipe a fleck of dried blood from the top of one pointed ear. "What was it like?" I ask. "Being a serpent."

He hesitates. "It was like being trapped in the dark," he says. "I was alone, and my instinct was to lash out. I was perhaps not entirely an animal, but neither was I myself. I could not reason. There were only feelings—hatred and terror and the desire to destroy."

I start to speak, but he stops me with a gesture. "And you." He looks at me, his lips curving in something that's not quite a smile; it's more and less than that. "I knew little else, but I always knew you."

And when he kisses me, I feel as though I can finally breathe again.

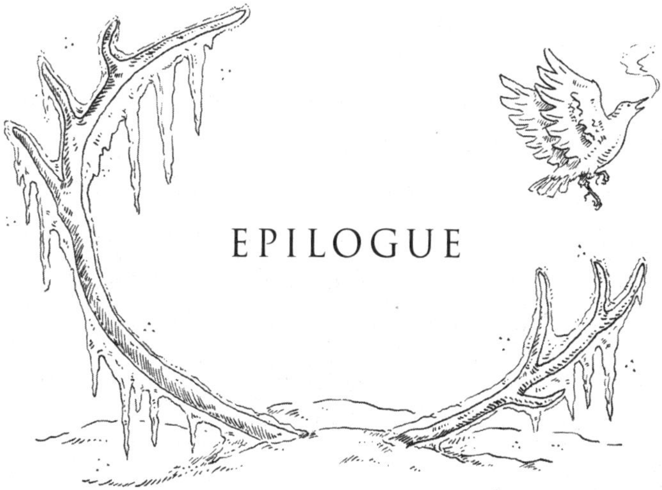

EPILOGUE

My coronation comes a week later, and I am stunned at how many of the low Court rulers, along with subjects of the realms, travel to witness it. Interestingly, many take great pains to bring mortals as their guests, changeling children and human artists and lovers. It's utterly surreal to see this attempt to curry favor, and it's gratifying all the same.

Cardan chose three faerie makers to be given places in the household of Elfhame. One is Mother Marrow. The second is an ancient-looking hob who seems to hide behind an enormous and heavily braided beard. I am surprised to find that the third, a mortal smith, corresponded with my human father. When I meet him, Robert of Jersey spends some time admiring Nightfell and tells me a funny story about a conference they both attended a decade before.

Since the makers have settled in, they've been busy.

The ceremony begins at nightfall, and we have it under the stars on the new Isle of Insear. Braziers blaze, and the sky is thick with sea spray and incense. The ground beneath us is moon-blooming phlox.

I am in a gown of deep forest green with crow feathers covering the shoulders and sleeves, while Cardan wears a doublet ornamented with bright beetle wings. Baphen, in one of his long blue robes—with many celestial ornaments in his beard—will conduct the ceremony.

Oak is outfitted in white with gold buttons. Taryn kisses him on the forehead, for courage, since he will have to put the crowns on both of our heads.

"Long has the Greenbriar tradition been held in the High Court," Baphen begins. "Blood crowns blood. And while the crown is gone and vows of obedience with it, we will yet follow tradition. And so, High King, accept your new crown from Oak, your blood and your heir."

Oak looks unhappy about being called the heir, but he takes the crown from the pillow, a circlet of rich gold with nine points in the shape of leaves around the band. Being High King, Cardan isn't supposed to kneel to anyone, so Vivienne lifts Oak. With a laugh, my brother places a new crown on Cardan's head to the delight of the crowd.

"Folk of Elfhame," Baphen says, using the ritual words that Cardan never received before, rushed as our last ceremony was. "Will you accept Cardan of the Greenbriar line as your High King?"

The chorus goes up. "We will."

Then it's my turn. "It is uncommon for any Court to have two rulers. Yet you, Jude Duarte, High Queen, have shown us why it can be a strength instead of a weakness. When the High Court was threatened, you stood against our enemies and broke the spell that might have destroyed us. Come forward and accept your crown from Oak, your brother and your heir."

I walk forward, standing as Vivienne swoops my brother back into her arms. He plops the crown on my head. It is a twin to Cardan's, and I am surprised by the weight of it.

"Folk of Elfhame," he says. "Will you accept Jude Duarte as your High Queen?"

For a moment, in the silence, I believe that they will renounce me, but the ritual words come from their many mouths. "We will."

I grin irrepressibly at Cardan. He smiles back, with a little surprise. It's possible I don't smile like that very often.

Cardan turns to the crowd before us. "Now we have boons to distribute and betrayals to reward. First the boons."

He signals toward a servant, who brings forth Madoc's sword, the one that split the throne of Elfhame.

"To Grima Mog, our Grand General," he says. "You shall have Grimsen's final work and wear it for so long as you should remain in our service."

She receives it with a bow and a clasped hand to her heart.

He continues. "Taryn Duarte, our tribunal was never formally concluded. But consider it concluded now, in your favor. The Court of Elfhame has no quarrel with you. We grant all of Locke's estates and land to you and your child."

There are murmurs at that. Taryn comes forward to make a low curtsy.

"Last," he says. "We would like our three friends from the Court of Shadows to step forward."

The Ghost, the Bomb, and the Roach walk onto the carpet of white flowers. They are shrouded in cloaks that cover them from head to toe, even covering their faces with thin black netting.

Cardan beckons, and pages come forward, carrying pillows. On each is a silver mask, denoting nothing of gender, just a gently blank metal face with something slightly impish about the curve of the mouth.

"You who dwell in shadows, I wish for you to stand with us sometimes in the light," says Cardan. "To each, I give a mask. When you wear it, no one will be able to recall your height or the timbre of your voice. And in that mask, let no one in Elfhame turn you away. Every hearth will be open to you, including mine."

They bow and lift the masks to their faces. When they do, there's a sort of distortion around them.

"You are kind, my king," says one, and even I, who know them, cannot tell which is speaking. But what no mask can hide is how, once they give their bows and depart, one masked figure takes another's gloved hand.

Or how the third turns his shiny metal face toward Taryn.

Then it's my turn to step forward. My stomach flutters with nerves. Cardan insisted that I be the one to pass judgment on the prisoners. *You won the day*, he told me, *and the lion's share of the hard work along with it. You choose their fate.*

Whatever punishment I see fit, from execution to exile to a curse, will be considered just—the more so if it's witty.

"We will see the petitioners now," I say. Oak has moved to one side and stands between Taryn and Oriana.

Two knights come forward and kneel. One speaks first. "I have been tasked to plead for all those whose story is as mine. Once we were part of the army of Elfhame, but we knowingly went with General Madoc to the North when our vows were lifted. We betrayed the High King and—" Here he stumbles. "We sought to end his reign. We were wrong.

We wish to atone and to prove we can and will be loyal from this day forward."

Then the second speaks. "I have been tasked to plead for all those whose story is as mine. Once we were part of the army of Elfhame and we knowingly went with General Madoc to the North when our vows were lifted. We betrayed the High King and sought to end his reign. We have no wish to atone. We followed our commander faithfully, and though we will be punished, still we would not have chosen otherwise."

I glance again at the crowd, at the denizens of Elfhame who fought and bled, at those who sorrowed for lost lives—lives that might have stretched on through centuries if they hadn't been cut down. I take a breath.

"It is the parlance of the High Court that the soldiers are called falcons," I say, and am surprised by the steadiness of my voice. "For those who do not wish to atone, become falcons in earnest. Fly through the skies and hunt to your heart's content. But you will not have your own true form back until such time as you hurt no living thing for the space of a full year and a day."

"But how will we eat if we can hurt nothing?" asks the knight.

"The kindness of others will have to sustain you," I say, my voice as cold as I can make it. "To those who would atone, we will accept your vow of loyalty and love. You will be once again part of the High Court. But you will be marked by your betrayal. Let your hands always be red, as though stained with the blood you hoped to shed."

Cardan gives me an encouraging smile. Randalin looks annoyed that only I am making pronouncements. He clears his throat, but he dares not actually interrupt me.

The next petitioner is Lady Nore from the Court of Teeth. Queen

Suren trails behind her. Suren's crown is still sewn to her head, and while no leash binds her, the hole in her wrist is still there, the skin around it still raw.

I call for a servant to come forward with the bridle, still unused.

"We would have followed you," says Lady Nore, going down on one knee. "We made you an offer, and it was you who rejected it. Let us return to the North. Have we not been punished enough?"

"Lord Jarel tried to trick me into bondage. Did you know of it?" I ask, indicating the bridle.

Since she cannot lie, she does not speak.

"And you?" I ask Suren.

The girl gives a frightening, savage little laugh. "I know all the secrets they think they hide away." Her voice is thin and rough, as from disuse.

There's a tug on my sleeve, and I am surprised to find Oak beside me. He signals for me to bend down and let him whisper in my ear. Randalin's frown deepens when I do.

"Remember when you said we couldn't help her," he reminds me. "We can help her now."

I pull back, looking at him eye to eye. "So you want to intercede for Queen Suren?"

"I do," he says.

I send him back to Oriana, slightly more optimistic that he will one day want to sit on the throne of Faerie. "My brother has asked for leniency. Queen Suren, will you swear your loyalty to the crown?"

She glances at Lady Nore as if looking for permission. Lady Nore nods.

"I am yours, High Queen," the girl says. Her gaze shifts. "And High King."

I turn to Lady Nore. "I would like to hear you make a vow of loyalty to your queen."

Lady Nore looks startled. "Of course I give you my fealty—"

I shake my head. "No, I want you to give it to *her*. Your queen. The Queen of the Court of Teeth."

"Suren?" Her eyes dart around as though looking for an escape. For the first time since coming before me, Lady Nore appears afraid.

"Yes," I say. "Swear to her. She is your queen, is she not? You can either make your vow or you can wear the golden bridle yourself."

Lady Nore grits her teeth, then mutters the words. Still, she gets them out. Queen Suren's expression becomes strange, remote.

"Good," I say. "The High Court will keep the bridle and hope it never needs to be used. Queen Suren, because my brother interceded for you, I send you on your way with no punishment but this—the Court of Teeth will be no more."

Lady Nore gasps.

I go on. "Your lands belong to the High Court, your titles are abolished, and your strongholds will be seized. And should you, Nore, attempt to defy this command, remember that it will be Suren, to whom you swore, that punishes you in whatever way she sees fit. Now go forth and be grateful for Oak's intercession."

Suren, no longer a queen, smiles in a way that's not friendly at all, and I notice that her teeth have been filed into small points. Their tips are stained a disturbing red. I consider for the first time that perhaps Suren was being restrained for fear of what she might do if she were not.

The last penitent brought forth is Madoc. His wrists and ankles are bound in a heavy metal that, from the pain in his face, I worry has iron in it.

He does not kneel. Nor does he beg. He only looks from one of us to the other, and then his gaze moves to Oak and Oriana. I see a muscle in his jaw move, but no more than that.

I try to speak, but I feel as though my throat has closed up.

"Have you nothing to say?" Cardan asks him. "You had so much before."

Madoc tilts his head toward me. "I surrendered on the battlefield. What more is there? The war is over, and I have lost."

"Would you go to your execution so stoically?" I ask. From nearby, I hear Oriana's gasp.

But Madoc remains grim. Resigned. "I raised you to be uncompromising. I ask only for a good death. Quick, out of the love that we had for each other. And know that I bear you no grudge."

Since the battle ended, I have known I would be called upon to pass judgment on him. I have turned over the question of punishment in my mind, thinking not just of his army and his challenge, not just of our duel in the snow, but of the old crime, the one that has forever been between us. Do I owe him revenge for the murder of my parents? Is that a debt that must be paid? Madoc would understand that, would understand that love could not stand before duty.

But I wonder if what I owe to my parents is a more flexible view of love and duty, one that they themselves might have embraced. "I told you once that I am what you made me, but I am not only that. You raised me to be uncompromising, yet I learned mercy. And I will give you something like mercy if you can show me that you deserve it."

His gaze comes to mine in surprise and a little wariness.

"Sire," puts in Randalin, clearly exasperated by my handing down every final decision. "Surely you have something to say about all—"

"Silence," says Cardan, his manner utterly changed, his tongue a lash. He looks at Randalin as though the next sentence might be passed on the Minister of Keys. Then he nods to me. "Jude was just getting to the interesting bit."

I don't take my gaze off Madoc. "First, you will swear to forget the name that you know. You will put it from your mind, and it will never again fall from your lips or fingers."

"Would you like to hear it first?" he asks, the faintest smile at the edges of his lips.

"I would not." This doesn't seem the place to tell him I know it already. "Second, you must give us your vow of loyalty and obedience," I say. "And third, you must do both of those things without hearing the sentence for your crimes, which I will nonetheless bestow on you."

I can see him wrestling with his dignity. A part of him wants to be like the soldiers who denied the desire for atonement. A part of him would like to go to his grave with his back straight and his jaw set. Then there's a part of him that doesn't want to go to a grave at all.

"I want mercy," he says finally. "Or, as you said, something like it."

I take a deep breath. "I sentence you to live out the rest of your days in the mortal world and to never put your hand on a weapon again."

He presses his mouth into a thin line. Then he bows his head. "Yes, my queen."

"Good-bye, Father," I whisper as he is led away. I say it softly, and I do not think he hears me.

After the coronation, Taryn and I decide to accompany Vivi and Oak, who are heading back to the mortal world. Now that the war is over, Oak could return to Faerie and go to the palace school just as Taryn and I did. But he wants to live a little longer among humans, not just because he's been there for the better part of the last year, but because Oriana has decided to move with Madoc—and Oak misses his parents.

Vivi has been back and forth for the last week, going on dates with Heather, to whom she's just reintroduced herself. But now that she's leaving for good, she gathers up rose hip jams, spider-silk jackets, and other things she wishes to take back from Faerie. As she does, she speculates about all the aspects of the mortal world she's going to have to explain to Dad. "Like cell phones," she says. "Or self-checkout in the grocery store. Oh, this is going to be amazing. Seriously, his exile is the best present you ever got me."

"You know that he's going to be so bored that he's going to try to micromanage your life," Taryn says. "Or plan your invasion of a neighboring apartment building."

At that, Vivi stops smiling.

It makes Oak giggle, though.

Taryn and I help Vivi pack four saddlebags of stuff, even though Vivi has planted plenty of ragwort in the woods near her apartment building and can return for more supplies anytime she wants. Grima Mog gives Vivi a list of things she'd like sent back to Elfhame, which appears to be mostly instant coffee and hot sauce.

What I don't expect is that Cardan offers to journey with us.

"You should absolutely come," says Taryn. "We can throw a party. You two got married, and no one did anything to celebrate."

I am incredulous. "Oh, we're fine. We don't need any—"

"It's settled, then," Vivi says, forever my older sister. "I bet Cardan has never even tried pizza."

Oak looks scandalized by this pronouncement and starts explaining about different toppings, from pineapple to sausage to anchovies. We're not even in the mortal world and already I am filled with dread. Most likely, Cardan will hate it, and the only question is whether he's going to be awful about it.

Before I can think of a way to dissuade him, we're loading the saddlebags onto ragwort steeds. Then we're flying over the water. Before long, we touch down in a patch of grass near the complex, but not so close to the apartment that Vivi's neighbors are likely to recognize her.

I climb off and take note of the dullness of the grass and the scent of car exhaust in the air. I look over at Cardan warily, worried he will be wrinkling his nose, but he appears merely curious, his gaze going to the lit windows and then toward the roar of the nearby highway.

"It's early," says Vivi. "And the pizza place is close enough to walk." She looks us over. "We should go to the apartment and change first, though."

I guess I can see what she means. Cardan looks as though he just stepped off the stage at a playhouse, and while he can glamour himself, I am not at all sure he knows what it is he's supposed to wear in the illusion.

Vivi lets us into the apartment and puts on a pot of coffee, adding cinnamon to the grounds. Oak goes in the back and gets some kind of electronic game, immediately immersing himself in it on the couch while we sort out clothes.

Cardan's tight pants and boots are passable, and he finds a T-shirt a human friend left there that fits him well enough to wear instead of his fancy doublet. I borrow a dress from Vivi that's loose on her. It's a lot less loose on me.

"I told Heather about you guys," Vivi says. "I am going to call her and see if she can come over and bring some supplies. You can meet her—*again*. And Oak will show you the way to the pizza place."

Taking my hand with a laugh, my little brother starts pulling Cardan and me down the stairs. Vivi chases after us to give me some money. "This is your cash. From Bryern."

"What did you do?" Cardan asks.

"Beat Grima Mog in a duel," I say.

He looks at me incredulously. "He ought to have paid you in gold."

That makes me grin as we walk along the sidewalk. Cardan doesn't appear to be at all discomfited, whistling a tune and goggling a bit at the humans we pass. I hold my breath, but he doesn't curse them with a tail to match his own or tempt them with everapple or do anything else that a wicked faerie king might.

We go into the pizza place, where Oak orders three extremely large pies covered with a bizarre array of toppings that I am almost entirely sure no one has ever let him order before: half meatball and half prawn, garlic and tomatoes, goat cheese and black olives, and mushroom and bacon.

When we return to the apartment with our stack of steaming cardboard boxes, Heather and Vivi have tied up a silvery banner that reads

CONGRATULATIONS, NEWLYWEDS! in bright colors. Under it, on the kitchen table, is an ice-cream cake with scattered gummy snakes on it and several bottles of wine.

"It's so nice to meet you," I say, going over to Heather and giving her a hug. "I just know I'm going to love you."

"She's told me some wild things about you all," Heather says.

Vivi blows a noisemaker. "Here," she says, passing out paper crowns for us to wear.

"This is ridiculous," I complain, but put mine on.

Cardan looks at his reflection in the door of the microwave and adjusts his crown so it's at an angle.

I roll my eyes, and he gives me a quick grin. And my heart hurts a little because we are all together and safe, and it wasn't something I'd known how to want. And Cardan looks a little shy in the face of all this happiness, as unused to it as I am. There will be struggles to come, I am certain, but right now I am equally sure we will find our way through them.

Vivi opens pizza boxes and uncorks a bottle of wine. Oak takes out a slice of the prawn pizza and digs in.

I raise a plastic glass. "To family."

"And Faerieland," says Taryn, raising hers.

"And pizza," says Oak.

"And stories," says Heather.

"And new beginnings," says Vivi.

Cardan smiles, his gaze on me. "And scheming great schemes."

To family and Faerieland and pizza and stories and new beginnings and scheming great schemes. I can toast to that.

ACKNOWLEDGMENTS

Finishing this book would have been immensely difficult without the support, help, criticism, and thematic derring-do of Sarah Rees Brennan, Leigh Bardugo, Steve Berman, Cassandra Clare, Maureen Johnson, Joshua Lewis, Kelly Link, and Robin Wasserman. Thank you, my roguish crew!

Thank you to all the readers who came out to see me on the road, wrote messages, drew Folk of the Air art, and/or dressed up as the characters. Every bit of it meant more to me than I can say.

A massive thank-you to everyone at Little, Brown Books for Young Readers for supporting my weird vision. Thanks especially to my amazing editor, Alvina Ling, and to Ruqayyah Daud, Siena Koncsol, Victoria Stapleton, Bill Grace, Emilie Polster, Natali Cavanagh, and Valerie Wong, among others. And in the UK, thank you to Hot Key Books, particularly Jane Harris, Emma Matthewson, Roisin O'Shea, and Tina Mories.

Thank you to Joanna Volpe, Hilary Pecheone, Pouya Shahbazian, Jordan Hill, Abigail Donoghue, and everyone at New Leaf Literary for making hard things easier.

Thank you to Kathleen Jennings for her wonderful and evocative illustrations.

And thanks most of all to my husband, Theo, for helping me figure out the stories I want to tell, and to our son, Sebastian, for reminding me that sometimes the most important thing to do is play.

Turn the page for a sneak preview of

AVAILABLE NOW

CHAPTER 1

The slant of the moon tells me that it's half past ten when my unsister comes out the back door. She's in her second year of college and keeps odd hours. As I watch from the shadows, she sets down an empty cereal bowl on the top step of the splintery and sagging deck. Then she glugs milk into it from a carton. Spills a little. Squatting, she frowns out toward the tree line.

For an impossible moment, it's as though she's looking at me.

I draw deeper into the dark.

The scent of pine needles is heavy in the air, mingling with leaf mold and the moss I crush between my bare toes. The breeze carries the smell of the sticky, rotten, sugary dregs still clinging to bottles in the recycling bin; the putrid something at the bottom of the empty garbage can; the chemical sweetness of the perfume my unsister is wearing.

I watch her hungrily.

Bex leaves the milk for a neighborhood cat, but I like to pretend it's me she's leaving it for. Her forgotten sister.

She stands there for a few minutes while moths flit above her head and mosquitoes buzz. Only when she goes back inside do I slink closer to the house, peering through the window to watch my unmother knit in front of the television. Watching my unfather in the breakfast nook with his laptop, answering email. He puts a hand to his eyes, as though tired.

In the Court of Teeth, I was punished if I called the humans who raised me my mother and father. *Humans are animals*, Lord Jarel would say, the admonishment coming with a breathtakingly hard blow. *Filthy animals. You share no blood with them.*

I taught myself to call them unmother and unfather, hoping to avoid Lord Jarel's wrath. I keep the habit to remind myself of what they were to me, and what they will never be again. Remind myself that there is nowhere that I belong and no one to whom I belong.

The hair on the back of my neck prickles. When I look around, I note an owl on a high branch, observing me with a swivel of its head. No, not an owl.

I pick up a rock, hurling it at the creature.

It shifts into the shape of a hob and takes off into the sky with a screech, beating feathered wings. It circles twice and then glides off toward the moon.

The local Folk are no friends to me. I've seen to that.

Another reason I am no one, of nowhere.

Resisting the temptation to linger longer near the backyard where I once played, I head for the branches of a hawthorn at the edge of town. I stick to the dimness of shadowed woodland, my bare feet finding their way through the night. At the entrance to the graveyard, I stop.

Huge and covered in the white blooms of early spring, the hawthorn towers over headstones and other grave markers. Desperate locals, teenagers especially, come here and tie wishes to the branches.

I heard the stories as a kid. It's called the Devil's Tree. Come back three times, make three wishes, and the devil was supposed to appear. He'd give you what you asked for and take what he wanted in return.

It's not a devil, though. Now that I have lived among the Folk, I know the creature that fulfills those bargains is a glaistig, a faerie with goat feet and a taste for human blood.

I climb into a cradle of branches and wait, petals falling around me with the sway of the tree limbs. I lean my cheek against the rough bark, listening to the susurration of leaves. In the cemetery that surrounds the hawthorn, the nearby graves are more than a hundred years old. These stones have weathered thin and bone pale. No one visits them anymore, making this a perfect spot for desperate people to come and not be seen.

A few stars wink down at me through the canopy of flowers. In the Court of Teeth, there was a nisse who made charts of the sky, looking for the most propitious dates for torture and murder and betrayal.

I stare up, but whatever riddle is in the stars, I can't read it. My education in Faerie was poor, my human education, inconsistent.

The glaistig arrives a little after midnight, clopping along. She is dressed in a long burgundy coat that stops at the knees, designed to highlight her goat feet. Her bark-brown hair is pulled up and back into a tight braid.

Beside her flies a sprite with grasshopper-green skin and wings to match. It's only a bit larger than a hummingbird, buzzing through the air restlessly.

The glaistig turns to the winged faerie. "The Prince of Elfhame? How interesting to have royalty so close by..."

My heart thuds dully at *prince*.

"Spoiled, they say," the sprite chirps. "And wild. Far too irresponsible for a throne."

That doesn't sound like the boy I knew, but in the four years since I saw him last, he would have been inducted into all the pleasures of the High Court, would have been served up a surfeit of every imaginable debauched delight. Sycophants and toadies would be so busy vying for his attention that, these days, I wouldn't be allowed close enough to kiss the hem of his cloak.

The sprite departs, darting up and away, thankfully not weaving through the branches of the tree where I crouch. I settle in to observe.

Three people come that night to make wishes. One, a sandy-haired young man I went to fourth grade with, the year before I was taken. His fingers tremble as he ties his scrap of paper to the branch with a bit of twine. The second, an elderly woman with a stooped back. She keeps wiping at her wet eyes, and her note is tearstained by the time she affixes it with a twist tie. The third is a freckled man, broad-shouldered, a baseball cap pulled low enough to hide most of his face.

This is the freckled man's third trip, and at his arrival, the glaistig steps out of the shadows. The man gives a moan of fear. He didn't expect this to be real. They seldom do. They embarrass themselves with their reactions, their terror, the sounds they make.

The glaistig makes him tell her what he wants, even though he's written it three separate times on three separate notes. I don't think she ever bothers to read the wishes.

I do. This man needs money because of some bad business deal. If he doesn't get it, he will lose his house, and then his wife will leave him. He whispers this to the glaistig, fidgeting with his wedding ring as he does so. In return, she gives him her terms—every night for seven months and seven days, he must bring her a cube of fresh human flesh. He may cut it from himself, or from another, whichever he prefers.

He agrees eagerly, desperately, foolishly, and lets her tie an ensorcelled piece of leather around his wrist.

"This was crafted from my own skin," she tells him. "It will let me find you, no matter how you try to hide from me. No mortal-made knife can cut it, and should you fail to do as you have promised, it will tighten until it slices through the veins of your arm."

For the first time, I see panic on his face, the sort that he ought to have felt all along. Too late, and part of him knows it. But he denies it a moment later, the knowledge surfacing and being shoved back down.

Some things seem too terrible to seem possible. Soon he may learn that the worst thing he can imagine is only the beginning of what they are willing to do to him. I recall that realization and hope I can spare him it.

Then the glaistig tells the freckled man to gather leaves. For each one in his pile, he'll get a crisp twenty-dollar bill in its place. He'll have three days to spend the money before it disappears.

In the note he attached to the tree, he wrote that he needed $40,000. That's *two thousand* leaves. The man scrambles to get together a big enough pile, searching desperately through the well-manicured graveyard. He collects some from the stretch of woods along the border and rips handfuls from a few trees with low-hanging branches. Staring at what he assembles, I think of the game they have at fairs, where you guess the number of jelly beans in a jar.

I wasn't good at that game, and I worry he isn't, either.

The glaistig glamours the leaves into money with a bored wave of her hand. Then he's busy stuffing the bills into his pockets. He races after a few the wind takes and whips toward the road.

This seems to amuse the glaistig, but she's wise enough not to hang around to laugh. Better he not realize how thoroughly he's been had. She disappears into the night, drawing her magic to shroud her.

When the man has filled his pockets, he shoves more bills into his shirt, where they settle against his stomach, forming an artificial paunch. As he walks out of the graveyard, I let myself drop silently out of the tree.

I follow him for several blocks, until I see my chance to speed up and grab hold of his wrist. At the sight of me, he screams.

Screams, just like my unmother and unfather.

I flinch at the sound, but the reaction shouldn't surprise me. I know what I look like.

My skin, the pale blue of a corpse. My dress, streaked with moss and mud. My teeth, built for ease of ripping flesh from bone. My ears are pointed, too, hidden beneath matted, dirty blue hair, only slightly darker than my skin. I am no pixie with pretty moth wings. No member of the Gentry, whose beauty makes mortals foolish with desire. Not even a glaistig, who barely needed a glamour if her skirts were long enough.

He tries to pull away, but I am very strong. My sharp teeth make short work of the glaistig's string and her spell. I've never learned to glamour myself well, but in the Court of Teeth I grew skilled at breaking curses. I'd had enough put on me for it to be necessary.

I press a note into the freckled man's hands. The paper is his own, with his wish written on one side. *Take your family and run*, I wrote with one of Bex's Sharpies. *Before you hurt them. And you will.*

He stares after me as I race off, as though I am the monster.

I have seen this particular bargain play out before. Everyone starts out telling themselves that they will pay with their own skin. But seven months and seven days is a long time, and a cube of flesh is a lot to cut from your own body every night. The pain is intense, worse with each new injury. Soon it's easy to justify slicing a bit from those around you. After all, didn't you do this for their sake? From there, things go downhill fast.

I shudder, remembering my own unfamily looking at me in horror and disgust. People who I believed would always love me. It took me the better part of a year to discover that Lord Jarel had *enchanted* their love away, that his spells were the reason he was so certain they wouldn't want me.

Even now, I do not know if the enchantment is still on them.

Nor do I know whether Lord Jarel amplified and exploited their actual horror at the sight of me or created that feeling entirely out of magic.

It is my revenge on Faerie to unravel the glaistig's spells, to undo every curse I discover. Free anyone who is ensnared. It doesn't matter if the man appreciates what I've done. My satisfaction comes at the glaistig's frustration at another human slipping from her net.

I cannot help them all. I cannot prevent them from taking what she offers and paying her price. And the glaistig is hardly the only faerie offering bargains. But I try.

By the time I return to my childhood home, my unfamily has all gone to bed.

I lift the latch and creep through the house. My eyes see well enough in the dark for me to move through the unlit rooms. I go to the couch and press my unmother's half-finished sweater to my cheek, feeling the softness of the wool, breathing in the familiar scent of her. Think of her voice, singing to me as she sat at the end of my bed.

Twinkle, twinkle, little star.

I open the garbage and pick out the remains of their dinner. Bits of gristly steak and gobs of mashed potatoes clump together with scattered pieces of what must have been a salad. It's all mixed in with crumpled-up tissues, plastic wrap, and vegetable peels. I make a dessert of a plum that's mushy on one end and the little bit of jam at the bottom of a jar in the recycling bin.

I gobble the food, trying to imagine that I am sitting at the table with them. Trying to imagine myself as their daughter again, and not what's left of her.

A cuckoo trying to fit back into the egg.

Other humans sensed the wrongness in me as soon as I set foot in the mortal world. That was right after the Battle of the Serpent, when the Court of Teeth had been disbanded and Lady Nore fled. With nowhere else to go, I came here. That first night back, I was discovered by a handful of children in a park who picked up sticks to drive me off. When one of the bigger ones jabbed me, I ran at him, sinking my sharp teeth into the meat of his arm. I opened up his flesh as though he were a tin can.

Sharona Jacobs

HOLLY BLACK

is the #1 *New York Times* bestselling author of more than thirty fantasy novels for kids and teens. She was a finalist for an Eisner Award and the Lodestar Award and the recipient of the Mythopoeic Award, a Nebula Award, and a Newbery Honor. Her books have been translated into thirty-two languages worldwide and adapted for film. She currently lives in New England with her husband and son in a house with a secret library. Her website is blackholly.com.

RETURN TO FAERIE

in the complete critically acclaimed Modern Faerie Tales trilogy from #1 *New York Times* bestselling author Holly Black.

"Dark, edgy, beautifully written, and compulsively readable."—*Booklist*

PRINT AND EBOOK EDITIONS AVAILABLE
From Margaret K. McElderry Books
simonandschuster.com/teen

MORE FROM HOLLY BLACK

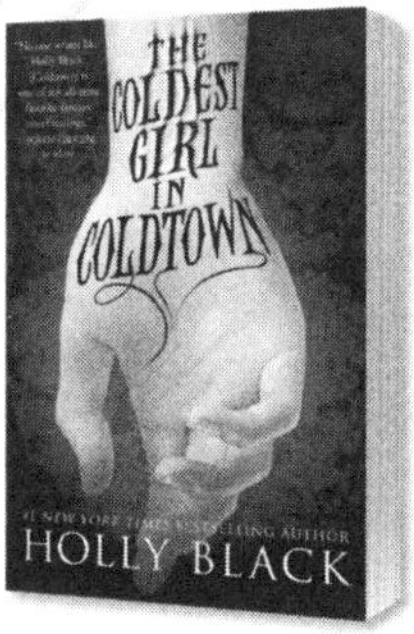

THE NOVELS OF ELFHAME

DIGITAL NOVELLA

theNOVL.com

NOVL

BOB1134